DOUBLE CROSS

JAMES PATTERSON

DOUBLE CROSS

headline

First published in Great Britain in 2007
by HEADLINE PUBLISHING GROUP

1

Cataloguing in Publication Data is available from British Library

ISBN 978 0 7553 3031 7 (Hardback)
ISBN 978 0 7553 3032 4 (Trade paperback)

Typeset in Palatino Light by
Palimpsest Book Production Limited, Grangemouth, Stirlingshire

Printed and bound in Great Britain by
Clays Ltd, St Ives plc

HEADLINE PUBLISHING GROUP
An Hachette Livre UK Company
338 Euston Road
London NW1 3BH

www.headline.co.uk
www.hodderheadline.com

DOUBLE CROSS

For Kyle Craig, the *real* Kyle, one of the straightest
shooters around and a good friend

PROLOGUE

IN YOUR HONOR

One

At the time of his formal sentencing in Alexandria, Virginia, for eleven known murders, the former FBI agent and pattern killer Kyle Craig, known as the Mastermind, was lectured and condescended to by US District Judge Nina Wolff. At least that's the way he took the judicial scolding, and he definitely took it personally, and very much to heart.

'Mr Craig, you are, by any criteria I know, the most evil human being who has ever come before me in this courtroom, and some despicable characters have come—'

Craig interrupted, 'Thank you so very much, Judge Wolff. I'm honored by your kind and, I'm quite sure, thoughtful words. Who wouldn't be pleased to be the best? Do continue. This is music to my ears.'

Judge Wolff nodded calmly, then went on as if Craig hadn't spoken a word.

'In reparation for these unspeakable murders and repeated acts of torture, you are hereby sentenced to death. Until such sentence is carried out, you will spend the remainder of your life in a supermaximum-security prison. Once there, you will be cut off from human contact as most of us know it. You will never see the sun again. Take him out of my sight!'

'Very dramatic,' Kyle Craig called to Judge Wolff as he was escorted from the courtroom, 'but it's not going to happen that way. You've just given yourself a death sentence.

'I will see the sun again, and I'll see you, Judge Wolff. You can bet on it. I'll see Alex Cross again. For sure, I will see Alex Cross. And his charming family. You have my word on it, my solemn promise before all these witnesses, this pathetic audience of thrill seekers and press hyenas, and all the rest of you who honor me with your presence today. *You haven't seen the last of Kyle Craig.'*

In the audience, among the 'thrill seekers and press hyenas,' was Alex Cross. He listened to his former friend's empty threats. And yet he couldn't help hoping that ADX Florence was as secure as it was supposed to be.

Two

Four years to the day later, Kyle Craig was still being held, or perhaps *smothered* was the more apt description, in the maximum-security prison in Florence, Colorado, about a hundred miles from Denver. He hadn't seen the sun in all that time. He was cut off from most human contact. His anger was growing, blossoming, and that was a terrifying thing to consider.

His fellow inmates included the Unabomber – Ted Kaczynski; Oklahoma City conspirator Terry Nichols; and Al Qaeda terrorists Richard Reid and Zacarias Moussaoui. None of them had required much sunblock lately either. The prisoners were kept locked away in soundproof seven-by-twelve concrete cells for twenty-three hours every day, completely isolated from anyone other than their lawyers and high-security guards. The solitary experience at ADX Florence had been compared to 'dying every single day.'

Even Kyle admitted that escaping from Florence was a daunting challenge, maybe impossible. In fact, none of the prisoners inside had ever succeeded, or even come close. Still, one could only hope, one could dream, one could plot and exercise the old imagination. One could most definitely *plan* a little revenge.

His case was currently on appeal, and his lawyer from Denver, Mason Wainwright, visited once a week. This day, he arrived as he always did, promptly at four p.m.

Mason Wainwright sported a long silver-gray ponytail, scuffed black cowboy boots, and a cowboy hat worn jauntily back on his head. He had on a buckskin jacket, a snakeskin belt, and large horn-rimmed glasses that gave him the appearance of a rather studious country-and-western singer, or a country-and-western-loving college professor, take your pick. He seemed a curious choice as an attorney, but Kyle Craig had a reputation for brilliance, so the selection of Wainwright wasn't seriously questioned.

Craig and the lawyer hugged when Wainwright arrived. As he usually did, Kyle whispered near the lawyer's ear, 'There's no videotaping permitted in this room? That rule is still in force? You're sure of it, Mr Wainwright?'

'There's no videotape,' answered Wainwright. 'You have attorney–client privilege, even in this pathetic hellhole. I'm sorry that I can't do more for you. I sincerely apologize for that. You know how I feel about you.'

'I don't question your loyalty, Mason.'

Following the hug, Craig and the lawyer sat on opposite sides of a gray metal conference table, which was bolted securely to the concrete floor. So were the chairs.

Kyle now asked the lawyer eight specific questions, always the same questions, in session after session. He asked them rapidly, leaving no time for any answers by his attorney, who just sat there in respectful silence.

'That great consoler of mass-murdering prisoners, Truman Capote, once said that he was afraid of two things, and two things only. So which of these is worse, betrayal or abandonment?' Kyle Craig began, then went right to the next question.

'What was the very first thing you forced yourself not to cry over, and how old were you when it occurred?'

And then, 'Tell me this, Counselor: what is the average length of time it takes a drowning person to lose consciousness?

'Here's something I'm curious about – do most murders take place indoors or out?

'Why is laughing at a funeral considered unacceptable, while crying at a wedding is not?

'Can you hear the sound of one hand clapping if all the flesh is removed from the hand?

'How many ways are there to skin a cat, if you wish it to remain alive through the entire process?

'And, oh yes, how are my Boston Red Sox doing?'

Then there was silence between Kyle and the lawyer. Occasionally, the convicted murderer would ask a few more specifics – perhaps additional detail about the Red Sox or about the Yankees, whom he despised, or about some interesting killer working on the outside whom the lawyer had informed him about.

Then came another hug as Mason Wainwright was about to leave the room.

The lawyer whispered against Kyle's cheek. 'They're ready to go. The preparations are complete. There will be important doings in Washington, DC, soon. There will be payback. We expect a large audience. *All in your honor.*'

Kyle Craig didn't say anything to this news, but he put his index fingers together and pressed them hard against the lawyer's skull. Very hard indeed, and he made an unmistakable impression that traveled instantly to Mason Wainwright's brain.

The fingers were in the shape of a cross.

PART ONE

ALL THE WORLD'S A STAGE

Chapter One

*W*ashington, DC.
  The first story, a thriller, involved an Iraqi soldier and a crime writer. This soldier was observing a twelve-story luxury apartment building, and he was thinking, *So this is how the rich and famous live. Stupidly at best, and very dangerously for sure.*

He began his checklist of possibilities for a break-in.

The service entrance at the back of the superluxury Riverwalk apartment building was rarely, if ever, used by the residents, or even by their sullen lackeys. More secluded than the main entry or the underground parking garage, it was also more vulnerable.

A single reinforced door showed off no external hardware. The frame was wired on all sides.

Any attempt at forced entry would trigger simultaneous alarms at the Riverwalk's main office and with dispatch at a private security firm based just a few blocks away.

Static overhead cameras monitored all deliveries and other foot traffic during the day.

Use of the entrance was forbidden after seven p.m., when motion detectors were also engaged.

None of this was a serious problem, the soldier believed. Actually, it was an advantage for him.

Yousef Qasim had been a captain for twelve years with the Mukhabarat under Saddam. He had a sixth sense about such things, anything to do with the illusion of security. Qasim could see what the Americans could not – that their love of technology made them complacent and blind to danger. His best way into the Riverwalk was also the easiest.

Garbage was the answer. Qasim knew it was carried out every Monday, Wednesday, and Friday afternoon, without fail. American efficiency, so valued here, was another of the luxury building's vulnerabilities.

Efficiency was predictability.
Predictability was weakness.

Chapter Two

Sure enough, at 4:34 p.m. the door to the service entrance opened from inside. A tall black lackey in stained green coveralls and a silver Afro latched a chain from inside the door to a hook on the outside wall. His flatbed dolly, loaded with bulging plastic garbage bags, was too wide to negotiate the opening.

The man moved slowly, lazily, carrying two bags at a time to a pair of commercial Dumpsters at the far end of a covered loading dock.

This man is still a slave to the whites, Qasim thought to himself. *And look at him – the pathetic shuffle, the downcast eyes. He knows it too. He hates his job and the terrible people in the Riverwalk building.*

Qasim watched closely, and he counted. Twelve paces away from the door, nine seconds to throw the garbage bags in, then back again.

On the man's third trip, Qasim slipped by him unnoticed. And if his own cap and green coveralls weren't enough to fool the camera, it was no crucial matter. He'd be long gone by the time anyone came to investigate the security breach.

He found the poorly lit service stairs easily enough. Qasim took the first flight cautiously, then ran up the next three. Actually, the running released pent-up adrenaline, which was useful to get under control.

On the fourth-floor landing was an unused utility closet, where he stashed the garment bag he had carried in, then continued up to twelve.

Less than three and a half minutes after entering the luxury building, he stood at the front door to apartment 12F. He gauged his position relative to the peephole in the door. His finger hovered over the buzzer, a recessed white button in the painted brick.

But he went no further than that. He didn't actually push the buzzer today.

Without making a sound, he turned on his heels and left the way he had come. Minutes later, he was back out on the street, busy Connecticut Avenue.

The drill, the rehearsal, had gone fairly well. There were no major issues, no surprises either. And now Qasim jostled along with the rush-hour pedestrian traffic. He was invisible here, just as unseen in this herd as he needed to be.

He felt no impatience for the execution up on the twelfth floor. Patience and impatience were irrelevant to him. Preparation, timing, completion, success: those were the things that mattered.

When the time came, Yousef Qasim would be ready to do his part. And he would.

One American at a time.

Chapter Three

I was out of police work, and had been for a while now. So far, that was okay with me.

I was standing with my back against the kitchen door, sipping a mug of Nana's coffee, thinking that maybe it was something in the water, but all I knew was this: my three kids were growing up too fast. Blink-of-an-eye stuff. And here's the thing – either you can't stand to even think of your kids leaving home or you can't wait, and I was definitely, firmly, in the former camp.

My youngest, Alex Jr – Ali – was going to be a kindergartner now. He was a sharp little guy too, who rarely, if ever, shut up except when *he* knew *you* wanted to know something from him. His passions at the moment included Animal Planet's *Most Extreme*, the Washington Nationals baseball team, the Michael Jordan biography *Salt in His Shoes*, and anything to do with outer space, including a very strange TV show called *Gigantor*, with even stranger theme music that I couldn't get out of my head.

Preteen Jannie had begun trading in that twiggy body of hers for a set of starter curves. She was our resident artist and actress, and was taking painting classes through the Corcoran ArtReach Program.

And Damon, who had just passed the six-foot-one mark, was looking forward to high school. So far, he didn't whoop and shout or trash-talk, and seemed more generally aware of his surroundings than his peers were. Damon was even being recruited by a couple of prep schools, including a persistent one in Massachusetts.

Things were changing for me too. My private-therapy practice was going pretty well. For the first time in years, my life had nothing 'official' to do with law enforcement. I was out of the loop.

Well, *almost*, anyway. I did have a certain senior homicide detective in my life: Brianna Stone, also known as The Rock, if you asked some of the detectives who worked with her. I'd met Bree at a retirement party for a cop we both knew. We spent the first half hour that night talking about The Job and the next few hours talking about ourselves – kind of crazy things like her 'race-hand release' as a paddler on the Dragon Boat Racing Team. By the end of the night, I barely had to ask her out. In fact, as I think about it now, she might have asked me. But then one thing led to another, and another, and I went home with Bree that night and we never looked back. And yes, I think Bree asked me to come home with her that night too.

Bree was fully in control of herself – intense, in all the good ways and none of the bad. And it didn't hurt that she seemed to have a natural chemistry with the kids. They dug her. She was, in fact, right now chasing Ali at Olympic speed through the first floor of the house on Fifth Street, roaring like the child-eating alien she had apparently become, while Ali used a *Star Wars* lightsaber to keep her at bay. 'That sword can't hurt me!' she shouted. 'Prepare to eat carpet!'

Bree and I didn't stick around on Fifth Street too long on that particular morning, though. To be honest, if we had stayed there, I probably would have been forced to sneak her upstairs to show her my nonexistent etchings, or maybe my lightsaber.

For the first time since we'd been going out, we had managed to synchronize our schedules for a few days away. I went out the front door loudly singing the end of Stevie Wonder's very first hit, 'Fingertips Part 2': '*Good-bye, good-bye. Good-bye, good-bye. Good-bye, good-bye, good-bye.*' I knew the words by heart, one of my gifts.

I winked at Bree and pecked her cheek. 'Always leave them laughing,' I said.

'Or at least confused,' she said, and winked back.

Our destination, Catoctin Mountain Park in Maryland, was on the eastern rampart of the Appalachian Mountains, not too far from Washington – and not too close either. The mountains were perhaps best known as the site of Camp David, but Bree knew about a campground open to mere mortals like us. I couldn't wait to get there and be alone with her.

I could almost feel the thrum of DC move out of my head as we headed north. The windows of my R350 were down, and as always I was loving the ride of this marvelous vehicle. Best buy I'd made in a long time. The late, great Jimmy Cliff wailed on the stereo. Life was pretty good right at the moment. Hard to beat.

As we zipped along, Bree had a question: 'Why the Mercedes?'

'It's comfortable, yes?'

'Very comfortable.'

I touched the gas. 'Responsive, quick.'

'Okay, I get the point.'

'But most important, it's *safe*. I've had enough danger in my life. I don't need it on the road.'

At the park entrance, as we were paying for the site, Bree leaned across me to speak to the ranger on duty. 'Thanks a lot. We'll be respectful to your park.'

'What was that about?' I asked Bree as we pulled away.

'What can I say, I'm an environmentalist.'

The campsite was definitely spectacular, and worthy of our respect. It sat on its own little point of land, with shimmering blue water on three sides and nothing but dense forest greenness looming behind. In the far distance, I could see something called Chimney Rock, which we planned on hiking the next day. What I couldn't see was a single other person.

Just the one that mattered, Bree, who happened to be the sexiest woman I'd ever known. Just the sight of her got me going, especially out here on our own.

She took hold of me around the waist. 'What could be more perfect than this?'

I couldn't think of anything that would spoil our weekend up here in the woods.

Chapter Four

The story, the thriller, continued. Forty-eight hours after his rehearsal, his flawless walk-through, Yousef Qasim returned to the Riverwalk apartment building, with its wealthy and careless American tenants.

This wasn't practice, though; it was the real thing, and his stomach was queasy. This was a truly big day for him, and for his cause.

Sure enough, at 4:34 p.m. the door to the service entryway opened and the same tall black porter lethargically lugged his garbage bags to the street. *Old Black Joe,* Qasim thought. *Still in chains. Nothing really changes in America, does it? Not in hundreds of years.*

Less than five minutes later, Qasim was upstairs on the twelfth floor, standing outside the apartment of a woman named Tess Olsen.

This time he rang the bell. Twice. He had been waiting for this moment for such a long time – months, maybe all his life, if he was honest with himself.

'Yes?' Tess Olsen's eye flickered behind the peephole of 12F. 'Who is it?'

Yousef Qasim made sure she saw his coveralls and the cap that said MO. No doubt he would look like any other brown-skinned maintenance worker to this woman – someone who was *supposed* to notice details in her profession. She was a well-known crime writer after all, and that was important for the story. A crucial detail.

'Mrs Olsen? There is gas leak in your apartment. Someone call you from office?'

'What? Say again.'

His accent was impossibly thick, and English seemed to be torture for him. He spoke slowly, like some kind of idiot. 'Gas leak. Please, missus? I can fix leak? Someone call? Tell you I come?'

'I just got home. No one called,' she said. 'I don't know anything about it. I don't think there was a message. I suppose I can check.'

'You like me come back later? Fix gas leak then? You smelling gas?'

The woman sighed with the unconcealed exasperation of a person with too many trivial duties and not enough hired help. 'Oh, for God's sake,' she said. 'Come in, then. Hurry it up. Your timing is just *exquisite*. I have to finish getting dressed and be out of here in twenty minutes.'

At the click of the dead bolt, Yousef Qasim readied himself. The moment the woman cracked the door and he saw both her eyes, he charged forward.

Extreme force was unnecessary in this case, physically speaking, but it had great utility. Tess Olsen fell back several steps and then thumped down hard on her behind. She came right out of her high-heeled pumps, exposing bright-red toenails and long, bony feet.

Before her shock and surprise gave way to a scream, Qasim was on top of her, pressing against her chest with his full body weight. The rectangle of silver duct tape he'd stuck to his pants leg was transferred quickly to the woman's mouth. He put the tape on *hard*, to show that he meant business and that she would be foolish to resist.

'I mean you no harm,' he said, the first of many lies.

Then he flipped her onto her stomach and pulled a red dog leash from his pocket, securing it around her neck. The leash was a key part of the plan. It was inexpensive nylon mesh but more than strong enough.

The leash was a *clue*, and just the first that he would leave here for the police and for whoever else became interested.

The woman was maybe forty, hair dyed blond, not physically strong, in spite of the fact that she seemed to work out to keep herself thin.

He showed her something now – a box cutter! Very nasty-looking tool. Convincing.

Her eyes widened.

'Get up, you weak coward,' he said close to her ear. 'Or I will cut your face in ribbons.' He knew that the softness of his voice was more threatening than any shouting could be. Also, the fact that his English had suddenly improved would confuse and frighten her.

When she tried to rise, he startled her with a sharp grab at the back of her scrawny neck. He stopped her right there – still on all fours.

'That's quite far enough, Mrs Olsen. Don't move, not another inch. Be very still, *very still*. I'm using the box cutter now.'

Her expensive black dress fell away as he cut it down the back. Now she trembled uncontrollably and tried to scream from behind her gag. She was prettier without her clothes – firm, somewhat appealing, though not to him.

'Don't worry. I am no dog-style fucker. Now go forward on your knees. Do as I say! This won't take much of your busy day.'

She only moaned in response. It took the heel of Yousef's shoe at her backside to get the idea across.

Then finally she began to crawl.

'How do you like it?' he asked. '*Suspense.* Isn't that what you write about? That's why I'm here, you know. Because you write about crime in your books. Can you solve this one?'

They moved slowly through the kitchen and the dining room, and then into a spacious living room. One entire wall was books, many of them her own. Glass sliding doors at the far end led to a terrace filled with fancy garden furniture and a shiny black grill.

'Look at all your books! I'm very impressed. You wrote all of these? Foreign editions too! You do any translations yourself? Of course you don't! Americans speak only English.'

Qasim pulled up sharply on the leash, and Mrs Olsen fell over onto her side.

'Don't move from there. Stay! I have work to do. Clues to plant. Even you are a clue, Mrs Tess Olsen. Have you figured it out yet? Solved the mystery?'

He quickly set up the living room just the way he wanted it. Then he returned to the woman, who hadn't moved and who seemed to be getting her part down now.

'Is that *you?* In this picture?' he asked suddenly, with surprise in his voice. 'It *is* you.'

Qasim prodded her chin with his foot to get her to look. A large oil portrait hung above the ornately scrolled sofa. It showed Tess Olsen in a long silver gown, her hand resting on a polished round table with an elaborate floral arrangement. The face was austere, full of unearned pride.

'It doesn't look like you. You're prettier in real life. Sexier without any clothes,' he said. 'Now, *outside*! Onto the terrace. You're going to be a very famous lady. I promise. Your fans are waiting.'

Chapter Five

After Qasim gave another strong pull on the leash, Tess Olsen struggled to her feet, then put her arms out, finally gaining some balance so that she could walk, at least.

Everything about this felt so unreal. Trembling, she backed her way onto the terrace – until the iron railing caught the small of her back.

Her whole body shivered. Twelve stories below, rush-hour traffic was crawling along Connecticut Avenue. Pedestrians, hundreds of them, navigated the sidewalks, most of them with their heads down, unaware of what was happening up in the Riverwalk tower. It was perfect symbolism for life in Washington, DC.

Yousef Qasim reached out and tore the tape off the woman's mouth.

'Now, scream,' he said. 'Scream like you mean it! Scream like you are terrified out of your mind! I want them to hear you *in Virginia.* In Ohio! In California!'

But the woman spoke to him instead, spoke in a barely intelligible rush. 'Please. You don't have to do this. I can help you. I have a lot of money. You can take anything you want from the apartment. I have a safe inside, in the second bedroom. Please, just tell me—'

'What I want, Mrs Tess Olsen,' Qasim said, and held the barrel of a gun up to one of the diamond studs in her ears, 'is for you to *scream.* Very, very loud. Right now! On cue, as it were. Do you follow me? It's a simple instruction – *scream!*'

But her scream came out as little more than a sob, a pitiful whimper that was swallowed up in the wind.

'*Fine,*' Qasim said, and grabbed the woman's bare legs. 'We'll do it your way!' With one powerful hoist, he had her over the railing, hanging upside down.

Now the screams came, high and clear as a security alarm going off. And Tess Olsen clawed at the air for a handhold that simply didn't exist.

The red leash at her neck blew free in the wind like a stream of blood from her jugular. *A nice effect, cinematic,* Qasim thought. Just what he was looking for. All part of the plan.

Immediately, a crowd began to gather below. People stopped and pointed upward. Some began making cell-phone calls. Others used the phones to snap pictures – pornographic ones, if they stopped to think about it.

Finally Qasim reeled Tess Olsen back in and set her down on the terrace.

'You did very well,' he told her, his voice softening. 'Beautiful work, and I mean that. Can you believe those people with their cameras? Some world we live in.'

Her next words came out in a torrent. 'Oh, dear God, please, I don't want to die like this. There has to be something you want. I've never hurt anyone in my life. I don't understand any of this! *Please . . . stop.*'

'We'll see. Don't lose hope. Do exactly as you are told. That's the best thing.'

'I will. I promise. I'll do what you say.'

He leaned over to better see Connecticut Avenue, and all the people.

Even in the last few seconds, the crowd down below had grown, and grown again. He wondered if those on their cell phones were calling the police – or maybe just someone they wanted to impress or titillate. *You won't believe what I'm seeing right now. Here, look for yourself!*

The audience wouldn't believe what they were about to see either. No one would, which was why millions would watch these images on television, again and again.

Until he topped this murder with his next.

'In your honor,' he whispered. '*All in your honor.*'

Chapter Six

'You start the fire,' Bree suggested. 'I'll gussy up the suite.'

I shrugged, then I winked at her. 'I think the, um, *fire's ready,*' I said. 'I know it is.'

'Patience,' Bree said. 'It'll be worth it. *I'm* worth it, Alex. For the moment, though, let's remember the scoutmaster's motto – if you fail to plan, then you plan to fail.'

'I was never a scout,' I said. 'I'm too horny to be a scout.'

'Patience. If you must know, I'm horny too.'

While I went and looked for kindling, Bree unpacked the rest of the back of the car. The equipment I'd pulled from the attic at home looked like relics next to her gear. She quickly put up an ultralight tent and proceeded to fill it with an air mattress, a thermal blanket, and a couple of Coleman lanterns. She even had a water-filtration system, just in case we wanted to drink from a stream. Finally she hung a little wind chime in the flap. *Nice touch.*

For my part, I had a pair of lobster tails and two nicely marbled Delmonico steaks marinating in the cooler, ready for grilling. Black bears could be a fear factor here, but dehydrated food wasn't an option for us.

'You need a hand there?' I asked once the fire was going pretty good, blowing sparks skyward. Bree had just pulled a sailcloth out of the backseat, presumably to use as a shade of some kind.

'Yeah, open that cabernet. Please, Alex. We're almost there.'

By the time the wine was breathing, Bree had strung the tarp up onto three branches overhead, with looping knots she could use to raise or lower the corners from right there on the ground.

'We have to be careful with the food,' she said. 'Bobcats and bears, you know. There *are* bears in these parts.'

'So I've heard.' I handed her a glass. 'You know, you're pretty handy around the house.'

'And you're a good little cook, I'll bet.'

Sometimes I missed what Bree said because I was too busy with those enchanting hazel eyes of hers. They were the first thing I had ever noticed about her. Some people just have great eyes. Of course, it wasn't just the eyes that were distracting me. Not right now, anyway. She'd already shucked her shoes and was unbuttoning her cutoffs. And her blouse. Then she was standing there in pale-blue bra and panties. I had forgotten about her eyes for the moment, glorious as they might be.

She handed her glass back to me. 'You know the very best thing about this spot?'

'Not really sure, but I think I'm going to find out. Am I?'

'Yes, you most definitely are.'

Chapter Seven

I have always felt that life was on the borderline of being absurd and meaningless, but it can still be pretty, if you look at it in the right light.

And so the rest of the early evening was perfect for us. Bree and I hurried, hand in hand, down to the very inviting Big Hunting Creek. We took off the rest of our clothes and waded in. After an uncomfortable minute or so, the water felt like a second skin on our bodies.

At that point, I didn't know if I could ever get out again. And I didn't want to. We kissed and held each other, then swam and splashed around like a couple of kids on vacation. Somewhere nearby, bullfrogs were attempting to serenade us with a steady *glunk, glunk, glunk*.

'You think this is funny?' Bree called to the frogs. 'Well, actually, I guess it is. *Glunk! Glunk!*'

We kissed some more, and one very good thing led to another, which is where the old-time movies used to cut to the scene of the speeding, steaming train racing through the tunnel. Except that Bree and I weren't in any kind of hurry to get in and out of that tunnel. She whispered to me that I had the gentlest hands and asked for light tickling all over, and *don't stop*. I liked what I was doing, and I told her she had the softest body, which was strange considering how buff she was. That kind of sensual exploration had to lead to trouble, and it did.

We took a few steps back until we were in water up to our chests. Then Bree floated upward and wrapped her legs around me as I went inside of her. Being in the water like that made everything last longer, but all good things must come to an end. Bree screamed, so did I, and even the damn bullfrogs shut up for a minute.

Afterward, we lay on a blanket on the grassy beach, where the late-day sun dried us off, and we did things that maybe could have gotten us into trouble again. Eventually we took our sweet time getting dressed and then fixed some dinner. 'I could get used to this,' I told Bree. 'In fact, I'm already used to it.'

After the steak and lobster, and my semifamous tossed salad, there was a batch of killer brownies for dessert, compliments of Nana, who highly approved of Bree. At this point I was about ready to try out the tent with my companion.

By the time it was dark, we were feeling pretty relaxed and happy. Work was just a memory. The bears and bobcats were only mild concerns.

I looked down at her, nestled in the curve of my body by the fire. She seemed as soft and vulnerable now as she was strong and unflappable at her job.

'You're amazing,' I whispered. 'This whole day has been like a dream. Don't wake me, okay?'

'I love you,' she said. Then she quickly added, 'Whoops.'

Chapter Eight

Bree's words hung in the air for the next few seconds, which was a first – the first time I'd ever been at a loss for words with her.

'It just kind of slipped out. *Who* said that, anyway? Sorry. *Sorry,*' she said.

'Bree, I . . . why *sorry?*' I asked.

'Alex, you don't need to say anything more. Neither of us does. *Wow.* Would you look at those stars!'

I reached and took Bree's hand. 'It's okay. This is just happening a little faster than probably both of us are used to. That isn't necessarily a bad thing.'

Bree answered me with kisses, and then laughter, and more laughter. The whole thing could have been uncomfortable, but somehow it was just the opposite. I hugged her close, and we started to kiss again. I stared into her eyes. '*Wow* back at you,' I said.

And so the fact that her pager went off at that moment was . . . what? Poetic justice, I guess. Classic irony? The not-so-funny part was that I'd always been the one getting the cell-phone call at just the wrong time.

The pager inside the tent buzzed again. Bree looked over at me without moving.

'Go ahead,' I told her. 'It's yours. You have to answer it. I know the drill.'

'Let me just see who it is.'

'It's okay,' I said. 'See who it is.'

Somebody's dead. We have to go back to DC.

She ducked inside. A few seconds later, I heard her talking on the phone. 'This is Bree Stone. What's going on?'

I was kind of glad for Bree that she was so much in demand. Kind of glad. I'd heard from my friend Detective John Sampson that her future with the department was as bright as she wanted to make it. Meanwhile, this call could mean only one thing. I looked at my watch. We could probably be back in the city by ten thirty or so. Depending on whether she wanted me to push it, something the R350 could certainly deliver on.

When Bree came out of the tent again, she had already traded in her shorts for jeans, and she was zipping up a hooded Georgia Tech sweatshirt.

'You don't have to come. I'll be as quick as I can. Back by breakfast, if not before then.'

I'd already begun gathering up our things. 'And the check's in the mail, and it's only a cold sore.'

She laughed, sort of. 'I'm really sorry about this. *Shit*, Alex. I can't tell you how sorry I am. And pissed off.'

'Don't be,' I said. 'This was the perfect day.' And then, because I couldn't help myself, and because I knew Bree wouldn't be insulted by the change of subject, I asked, 'So what's the case?'

Chapter Nine

Talk about a disorienting change of pace and venue, and definitely not a pleasing one, to put it mildly. We reached the Riverwalk apartment building at 10:50 that night, which made the murder scene about six hours cold. Bree had offered to drop me at home on Fifth Street, but I knew she was eager to get here. This was a headline case, that much we knew for sure.

Things were still very busy, and eerie. There were about as many reporters and news vans as I'd expected. The case already had *feeding frenzy* written all over it: a wealthy victim, a bestselling author, killed in a supposedly safe neighborhood, in a most horrifying way.

Bree's ID got us as far as curbside, where the tall building's U-shaped driveway was cordoned off. Technically, it was part of the crime scene, given that the murder victim had actually landed there after she'd been thrown from her terrace in full view of dozens of witnesses.

A team of white-suited techs was still going over the ruined van where she'd landed. It was parked near the entrance. To my eye, the technicians looked like ghosts in the bright lights. Across the street, well over a hundred people stood crowded behind a double line of police barriers. None of the faces jumped out at me, but that didn't mean anything. *This isn't your case,* I reminded myself.

Bree got out of the car and walked around to my side. 'Why don't you go sleep at my place? Please go, Alex. No one's expecting you home, anyway, right? Maybe we can pick up later where we left off.'

'Or I could wait here and get you back ASAP,' I said, and reclined the driver's seat for her benefit. 'See? Nice and comfortable, sleeps five. I'll be fine here in the car.'

'You sure?' I knew Bree had to be feeling guilty about tonight. I had been there before, many, many times, only maybe now I knew how my family felt.

'You'd better get going. You've probably got half the MPD up there, drooling all over your crime scene.'

A couple of uniformed officers stared our way as Bree leaned in and gave me a good-bye kiss. 'What I said before?' she whispered. 'I meant it.'

Then she wheeled around on the uniforms. 'What the hell are you two doing? Get back to work. Wait! Scratch that. Somebody show me where to go. Where's my crime scene?'

The transformation in Bree was a thing to behold. Even her posture changed as she strode toward the murder scene. She looked in charge, reminded me of myself, but she was still the sexiest woman I'd ever met.

Chapter Ten

That night, a man and a woman in jogging outfits were hidden deep in the crowd gathered on Connecticut Avenue, across from the Riverwalk apartments. As police cars continued to arrive, they were there, admiring their handiwork.

The brilliant creation, Yousef Qasim, was no more. *Poof* – gone but not forgotten. The male had played Yousef brilliantly, and the audience had been held spellbound from the moment he stepped out on the terrace, his stage. Apparently, many of these onlookers were still in awe of the bravura performance, still talking about it in hushed whispers.

What a fitting encore this was. Hours and hours after the show, all these looky-loos remained outside the luxury apartment building. New admirers arrived every few minutes. The press was all over it – CNN, the other majors, newspapers, radio, video artists, bloggers.

The man nudged the woman with his elbow. 'You see what I see?'

She craned her neck, looking left, then right. 'Where? There's so much to look at. Help me out, here.'

'Four o'clock. Now do you see? That's Detective Bree Stone getting out of the car. And the other one – that's Alex Cross. I'm certain it is. Cross has come, and it's only our first show. We're a hit!'

Chapter Eleven

For the first half hour, I tried to convince myself that I was content just sitting in the car, staying on the sidelines. The Mercedes, half station wagon, half SUV, was as comfortable as the easy chair in my living room. A copy of *The History of Love* by Nicole Krauss sat on my lap while I flipped through various stations on satellite radio, then listened to the local news. I had been savoring the Krauss, because it reminded me of how it was when I first fell in love with fiction. I had another good one at home, *Winter's Bone* by Daniel Woodrell, that I was equally enthralled with.

Plenty of time for reading now that I was out of the game. *But was I out of the game?*

Listening with one ear, I picked up on a few obvious inaccuracies in the news coverage, the worst being a report that the killer at the Riverwalk was some sort of terrorist. It was too early to jump to that kind of conclusion. Every news outlet in town was on this story, though, the nationals too, all scrambling for a unique angle. That usually led to mistakes, but the media didn't seem to care as long as they could attribute a theory to some kind of 'expert,' or even another news outlet.

Not that the killer would care about accuracy. It seemed obvious to me that what he wanted more than anything was simply attention.

I wondered if any Metro Police personnel had been assigned to follow the news coverage itself. If it were my case, that would be one of the first things I took care of. Emphasis on the *if*. Because this wasn't my case. I didn't have cases anymore. I didn't miss them either, at least that's what I told myself as I watched the action from my car.

There was something about being at the busy homicide scene that kicked in my instincts, though. I'd been formulating theories and running different scenarios in my head from the moment I got there – I couldn't help myself.

The killer had obviously wanted an audience; he'd been consistently described as looking 'Middle Eastern,' which added up to . . . what? *Was it possible that this was a new kind of terrorism – the door-to-door variety? How did a bestselling crime writer fit in? There had to be some tie-in. Was the killer acting out a brutally sadistic scene he had imagined many times before? Was it something the author had written about? What kind of psychopath wanted to throw victims off twelve-story buildings?*

Eventually, my curiosity moved me to my feet. I got out of the car and gazed toward the top floor. I couldn't see Bree or anyone else up there.

Just a quick look around, I told myself. *For old times' sake. No harm in that.*

Chapter Twelve

Who was I trying to kid, anyway? The Dragon Slayer was on the prowl again, and it felt natural, like I had never been away. Not even for the months I had been.

Most of the television-news cameras were set up around the MPD street-level command center. As I walked nearby, I recognized the captain of Violent Crimes, Thor Richter. Richter was standing behind a bouquet of microphones that had been stuck in the middle of all the chaos, and he was handling the interviews himself.

That probably meant Bree was still upstairs. Fine by her, I was sure. She didn't like police politics, or Richter in particular, and neither did I. He was too much by-the-book, a ruthless prick and shameless ass-kisser. Plus, who the hell was named Thor? I was being unkind, I knew, but I just didn't like the captain.

The lobby of the apartment building was relatively quiet, and I was recognized by a couple of uniforms who didn't seem to know that I wasn't on the Job anymore and hadn't been for a while. As I rode the elevator to twelve, I didn't really expect to get much farther than the primary perimeter. Somebody would be checking badges there.

Somebody was – an old friend, it turned out, Tony Dowell, who used to work in Southeast. I hadn't seen Tony, or heard from him, in years.

'Look who it is. Alex Cross.'

'Hey there, Tony. I thought they retired cops as old as you. Bree Stone around anywhere?'

Tony reached for his radio but then changed his mind. 'Straight down the hall,' he said, and pointed. Then he handed me a pair of latex gloves. 'You'll need these.'

Chapter Thirteen

I felt a little shiver of anticipation, then kind of an unpleasant chill. Was it that easy to step back into the line of fire, or whatever this was? At the front door to apartment 12F, a small Asian man I recognized as an MPD techie was dusting for prints. That told me it would be relatively calm inside. Chemical elements aren't introduced until the evidence-collection teams are finished.

I found Bree standing all by herself in the middle of the living room, looking pensive and far away.

A line of dark streaks, probably the victim's blood, ran across the ivory carpet. A sliding glass door was open to the terrace, and a light breeze rustled the curtains.

Otherwise, the living room looked pretty much undisturbed. There were built-in bookshelves on every wall, and they were filled with hardbacks, mostly fiction, several of them by the victim herself, including foreign editions. *Why a crime writer?* I wondered. There had to be a reason, at least in the killer's mind. Was that train of thought correct? Maybe, maybe not, but I was definitely analyzing the scene.

'How's it going?' I finally spoke.

Bree's eyebrows went up in a *How did you get in here?* kind of way, but she skipped the chitchat entirely. I had never seen her on the Job before, and she was a completely different person.

'Looks like he came in through the front door. No sign of forced entry anywhere. Maybe he posed as a serviceman of some kind. Unless she knew him. Her clothes, and her purse, are here.'

'Anything missing?' I asked the natural question.

Bree shook her head. 'Nothing real obvious. Doesn't look like she was robbed, Alex. She was wearing a diamond bracelet and earrings when she went over the railing. So maybe you *can* take it with you.'

I pointed at the streaks on the carpet. 'What do you know about these?'

'The ME says the victim's *knees* were bloody before the fall – and get this: she was wearing a dog leash when he tossed her off the balcony.'

'Somebody on the radio said it was a rope. I was thinking noose, but that didn't totally make sense to me either. A dog leash? That's interesting. Bizarre, but interesting.'

Bree pointed toward an archway and a formal dining room beyond, with lots of glass cabinets full of dinnerware. 'Bloodstains start back there and then end here in the middle of the room. She was crawling, and she was under duress.'

'Like a dog. So he needed to humiliate her, and in public. What could she possibly have done to him? How could she deserve this?'

'Yeah, sure feels like it was personal. Maybe a boyfriend, or some- body who fantasized about her?' She breathed in and out slowly. 'You know, this probably would have been your case if you were still on the force. High profile, high crazy factor.'

I didn't tell her that the same thought had occurred to me about a half dozen times already. The weird cases usually funneled my way. *So was Bree the new me?* Suddenly I wondered if our meeting at the party had been as 'accidental' as it had seemed at the time.

'Anyone else live here?' I asked.

'Her husband died two years ago. There's a housekeeper, but she was off this afternoon.'

I rocked back on my heels. 'Maybe the killer knew that.'

'I'll bet he did.'

It was interesting, the way Bree and I fell into it. The really strange part was that it *didn't* feel strange at all. I kept noticing different little things. A needlepoint pillow that said *Mirror, mirror on the wall, I am my mother after all.* A Hallmark greeting card propped up on the mantel. I looked at it, saw it was unsigned. Was that anything? Probably not. But maybe. You never know.

Bree and I walked out on the terrace together.

'So, he's got every opportunity to kill her in private, but he marches her out here, throws her off the balcony instead,' Bree said, talking more to herself than to anyone else. 'That is *so* messed up. I don't know where to go with it.'

I looked out at the view – a couple of other luxury apartment buildings across the street; the National Zoo down a bit to the left; more trees than you would see in most big cities. Very pretty, actually – the twinkling lights at night, the patches of dark green dramatically lit.

Straight below us was the U-shaped driveway, a working fountain, and a wide sidewalk out front. Plus hundreds of spectators.

Then something hit me. Or, rather, something I suspected suddenly felt true enough to say out loud.

'He didn't know her personally, Bree. I don't think so. That's not what this is about.'

Bree turned and looked at me. 'Keep going.'

'He didn't *kill her* personally, if that makes any sense. What I mean is that this was a public execution right from the start. It was all about having an audience. He wanted as many people as possible to watch him kill her. This was a performance. The killer came here to put on a show. At some point, he may have even stood down there and picked this terrace out for the murder.'

Chapter Fourteen

A nd then there were three of us.
My friend Sampson had walked into the living room, all six foot nine, 240 pounds of him. I knew Sampson was probably surprised to see me, but he played it deadpan, the usual for the Big Man.

'You looking to rent?' he asked. 'Place is available, from what I hear. Probably go cheap after today.'

'Just passing through. Neighborhood's a little too rich for my pocketbook.'

'Passing through doesn't pay the same as consulting, sugar. You need a better business plan.'

'So what have you got, John?' Bree asked. She called him John; I'd been calling him Sampson since we were kids. Both ways worked fine, though.

'Nobody seemed to notice our boy come in or out of the building. As we speak, they're running all of today's surveillance tapes. Such as it goes, this place is fairly tight, securitywise. Unless he can walk through walls, I'll bet he's going to show up somewhere on one of the tapes.'

'For what it's worth, I don't think this one minds having his picture taken,' I said.

Just then, a uniformed cop called from across the room. 'Excuse me, Detective?'

All three of us turned.

'Uh, *ma'am*? Detective Stone? There's a question for you. From CSI in the back room.'

The three of us followed the uniform down a narrow hallway into a den. It was lined with more books, and French lithographs in expensive-looking frames, plus several vacation photos. The apartment seemed to have quality furnishings everywhere – everything highly polished, oiled, or fluffed. A cardboard box full of liquor delivered from Cleveland Park was sitting by the door. *Was the killer the delivery guy? Was that how he got in here?*

A tapestry love seat was arranged in the corner, along with a television on a console. The cabinet doors were open to show a combination DVD player and VCR underneath.

I noticed another Hallmark greeting card on a shelf. I looked, and this card was also unsigned.

'Somebody should maybe bag these greeting cards, Bree. Unsigned. Could be nothing. But there was another one in the living room.'

A young woman in a crime-scene Windbreaker was waiting for us by the TV. 'Over here, Detective.'

'What am I looking at?' Bree asked.

'Maybe nothing . . . but there's a tape in the player. No other videos on display in the room. Do you want me to play it, eject it, or what?' Obviously the CSI techie didn't know whether to wind her watch or shit.

'Latent prints all done in here?' Bree asked in a kindly manner.

'Yes, ma'am.'

'Were the cabinet doors open or closed to begin with?' I asked.

'They were definitely found open, just like you see them now. You're Dr Cross, aren't you?'

The young cop's tone was a shade defensive, but Bree seemed not to notice. She flicked on the television and then the tape machine.

At first there was just static. Then came a flash of blue screen. *Here we go,* I thought.

Finally an image came up. Disturbing one too, right out of the box.

It was a medium shot of a dark-blue wall with a flag hanging on it. A plain wooden chair was the only other item in the picture.

'Anyone recognize that flag?' Bree asked. It had bars of red, white, and black, with three green stars across the middle.

'Iraq,' I said.

The word dropped like a heavy weight in the room.

Bree did the smart thing, then. She paused the tape. 'Everyone out,' she said. 'Now.'

A handful of other cops had gathered at the door to see what was up in the den. 'Detective,' one of them said, 'I'm D-2 on this case.'

'That's right, Gabe, so you know how sensitive this tape might be. I want you to talk to everyone who was just in here. Make sure this stays tight.'

She shut the door to the den without waiting for a response from the D-2.

'Do you want me to go?' I asked her.

'No. I want you to stay. John too.'

Then Bree flipped the tape back on.

Chapter Fifteen

A man walked out of the shadows and directly into the frame. *The killer? Who else would it be? He'd left us this tape, hadn't he? He wanted us to see it.* He wore a plain oatmeal-colored robe and a black-and-white kaffiyeh, and appeared to be incredibly pissed off at the world. He carried an AK-47, which he draped across his lap as he sat to address the camera.

Now *this* was stranger than strange. It took my breath away, actually. The style of video was immediately familiar. We'd all seen tapes like this before, from Al Qaeda, Hezbollah, Hamas.

My gut tightened another notch. We were about to find out something about our killer, and I was willing to bet it wouldn't be good news.

'It is time for the people of the United States to listen for a change,' the man said in heavily accented English. The skin on his cheeks, forehead, and prominent nose was heavily pockmarked. The skin color, mustache, and apparent height matched the eyewitness accounts from that afternoon at the Riverwalk.

This was our guy, wasn't it? The one who'd thrown the author Tess Olsen twelve stories to her death? And before that, seen fit to humiliate her with a dog leash?

'Each one of you watching this film is guilty of murder. Each one of you is as guilty as your cowardly president. As guilty as your congress and your lying secretary of defense. Certainly as guilty as the pathetic American and British soldiers who defile my streets and kill my people, because you believe that you own the world.

'And now, you will pay with your lives. The blood of Americans will be spilled in America this time. Blood that I will spill myself. Make no mistake, there is much that one man can do. Just as none of you are innocent, *now none of you are safe.'*

The man got up and approached the camera, staring out at us as if he could see right into the den. Then he beamed with the most horrific smile. A second later, the screen went back to static.

'Christ,' Sampson said into the ensuing silence. 'What the hell was that crazy piece of shit? Who was that maniac?'

Just as Bree was reaching for the 'stop' button, another image came up on the screen.

'A double feature,' said Sampson. 'Man believes in giving us our money's worth, anyway.'

Chapter Sixteen

A t first, it was a blur – someone standing in front of the camera. When he stepped back, we saw that it was the same man, only now dressed in plain green coveralls and a black baseball cap that said MO.

The scene was obviously Tess Olsen's living room. *Today*. Mrs Olsen was in the background on all fours, naked and visibly trembling. Her mouth was taped shut. And around her neck was the red dog leash.

He had filmed everything, playing to an audience the whole time he was here.

The feeling in the den went from bad to a lot worse. The killer – or the terrorist, as I'd already begun to think of him – approached Tess Olsen. He pulled hard on the leash, and she struggled to her feet. The woman was sobbing uncontrollably. Possibly she knew what was going to happen now. *Did that mean she knew the killer? How would she know him? Because of a book she was writing? What was her latest project?*

Seconds later, the man had pulled her out on the terrace. He first peeled, then ripped the tape off her mouth. We couldn't hear much from this distance – not until he grabbed Mrs Olsen and hung her over the edge. Then her piercing screams reached the camera's microphone, which was set up maybe twenty feet away.

All the while, the killer kept checking over his shoulder, looking toward the camera every few seconds.

'See that? How he moved back into the frame?' Bree said. 'He wasn't just putting on a show for the crowd on the street. This was meant for us as well – for whoever found the tape, anyway. Look at the bastard's face.' Now he was smiling. Even from this distance, his eerie grin was clear and unmistakable.

The next few seconds seemed to stretch on forever, as I'm sure they did for Tess Olsen. He pulled her back inside and then set her down on the floor. *Did she think there would be a reprieve? That she was to be spared?* Her shoulders heaved once, then she began to cry again. A minute or so later, he brought her out on the terrace again.

'Here it comes,' Bree said gravely. 'I don't want to watch this.' But she did. We all did.

The killer was a powerful man, probably over six feet tall and well built. He shocked me by lifting Tess Olsen like a barbell, straight up over his head. He looked back at the camera one more time – *Yes, you bastard, we're watching* – then winked and threw her off the balcony.

'My God,' Bree whispered. 'Did he just wink at us?'

He didn't leave the terrace, though. Or the picture frame. I could see by the angle of his head that he wasn't looking straight down to where she fell. He was looking out at his audience, at the people down on the street. He was taking chances that he didn't need to take.

In the scheme of things, that was good for us. Maybe that's how we'd find him, catch this bastard. Because he was reckless – and liked to preen in front of an audience.

Then I analyzed my own thought: We, *not* they, *were going to get this sonofabitch.*

And then, the killer spoke to the camera, and this was the eeriest part of all. 'You can try to capture me,' he said, 'but you will fail . . . Dr Cross.'

Sampson, Bree, and I turned to one another. John and I were speechless, and all Bree could manage was 'Holy shit, Alex.'

Ready or not, I was back in the game.

Chapter Seventeen

Well, I *wasn't* ready. Not yet, anyway. Four days after the Riverwalk murder, I was thinking about my patients. I was already conflicted, though. I was trying *not* to focus on Tess Olsen's murder, and who the maniac killer might be, and *how* he could possibly know me, and what the hell he wanted from me.

I couldn't help starting my day by checking the latest news on washingtonpost.com. Nothing further had happened during the night, thank God. No more murders, so at least he wasn't on a spree.

The morning's sessions would keep me on my toes, anyway. It was my biggest day of the week, the one I looked forward to but also dreaded in some ways. There was always the hope that I might do somebody some good, have a breakthrough. Or, possibly, I could fall right on my ass.

It started at seven with a recently widowed DC firefighter who was in conflict between a sense of duty to his job and kids, and a growing sense of meaninglessness about life that produced daily thoughts of suicide.

At eight I saw a Desert Storm vet who was still wrestling with demons he'd brought home from the war. He was a referral from my own therapist, Adele Finally, and I was hopeful that I could help him eventually. Still, this was the crisis stage of his treatment, so it was too early to tell if we were really communicating.

Next came a woman whose postpartum depression had left her with a lot of ambivalence toward her six-month-old daughter. We discussed her little girl and even talked about my feelings – just for a minute – about Damon possibly heading off to prep school. Same as in police work, I was usually unorthodox in the sessions. I was there to talk to people, and I talked freely, for the most part.

I had a half-hour break, during which I checked in with Bree, then glanced at the news on washingtonpost.com again. Still nothing new, no further attacks, no explanations for the death of Tess Olsen.

The morning's final patient was a Georgetown law student whose mysophobia had become so intense, she'd begun incinerating her own underwear every night.

Quite a morning. Satisfying in a strange way. And relatively safe – at least for me.

Chapter Eighteen

B ree called the office while I was eating an unbuttered hard roll before my one o'clock. 'We did some close-up work on the tapes,' she said. 'Tell me what you think of this, Alex. There's a scar on the killer's forehead. Shape of a half-moon. It's fairly pronounced.'

I thought for a moment before answering. 'Could mean head trauma at some time. This is a shot in the dark, but he could have damaged frontal lobes. People with frontal-lobe damage can display bad tempers and impulsiveness.'

'Thanks, Doc,' Bree said. 'Nice having you on the team.'

I was on the team? Since when? Had I agreed to that? I didn't think so.

After lunch, and the very nice homicide-case chat with Bree, I had my last client of the day, also my favorite, a woman in her mid-thirties named Sandy Quinlan.

Sandy was a recent transplant to DC from small-town life in northern Michigan, not far from Canada. She'd accepted an inner-city teaching job in Southeast, which had endeared her to me immediately.

Unfortunately, Sandy didn't like herself very much. 'I'll bet you have a dozen clients like me. All these lonely, depressed single women in the big, bad city.'

'Actually, I don't.' I told her the truth, a terrible habit with me. 'You're my only DSW in the BBC.'

Sandy got the joke and smiled, then went on. 'Well, it's just . . . pathetic. Nearly every woman I know is looking for the same dumb-ass thing.'

'Happiness?' I asked.

'I was going to say a man. Or a woman, I suppose. Somebody to love.'

I definitely saw a different person in Sandy than she saw in herself. She chose to appear as the classic loner stereotype, nice looks hidden behind black-rimmed glasses and dark, baggy clothes. As she'd grown comfortable with me, she'd proven to be personable, interesting, and funny when she wanted to be. And she cared deeply about the children she taught. She talked about them frequently and in the warmest terms. No ambivalence whatsoever.

'I have a real hard time seeing you as pathetic,' I finally said to her. 'Sorry, it's just an opinion. I could be all wrong about that.'

'Well, when your therapist is probably your best friend, call it what you want.' Before I could respond, she laughed self-consciously. 'Don't worry, I don't mean that as psycho as it sounds. I just mean that . . .'

My human impulse was to reach out to her, but as a therapist, I couldn't, or shouldn't, anyway. There was something in her eyes, though – they were so needy – that I couldn't help having a dual response. I wanted her to know that I cared about how she did. And I wanted to make sure that our relationship was clear. Maybe Sandy's tone and that expectant glance of hers hadn't meant anything. Then again, *everything means something*, or so I've read in a lot of very thick books used at schools like Georgetown and Johns Hopkins.

I'd have to be careful with Sandy. We got through the session okay, and once she left, I was done for the day. *Or was I? Did I have a second job to go to now?*

I was just coming down the stairs of my building when my cell rang. I didn't recognize the number. *Now what?*

I put the phone to my ear.

'I'm calling for Kyle Craig,' a male voice said. He was breaking up some but had my full attention. 'He can't come to the phone right now . . . because he's in solitary confinement in Colorado. But he wanted you to know he's thinking about you every day, and he has a surprise planned for you. A terrific surprise, right there in Washington, DC. Remember, Kyle is the *man with the plan*. Oh, and he also wants you to know that he hasn't seen the sun in four years – and it's made him stronger and better at what he does.'

The phone went dead in my hand.

Kyle Craig – Jesus, what next?

And what was that message supposed to mean? 'He has a surprise planned for you.'

Chapter Nineteen

I tried to tell myself that I couldn't spend a lot of time worrying about the homicidal maniacs I had already put away in jail. Not when some others were still walking free. Besides, nobody had ever come close to breaking out of ADX Florence. And this wasn't the first time Craig had threatened me from his jail cell.

Also, I wasn't on the Job anymore. Of course, I *was* going out with the head detective on a very big, very nasty case.

The Riverwalk homicide was already a media sensation. Everybody seemed to be talking about it. Even my patients had brought it up. The more hysterical news outlets spun some absurd theory every couple of hours. They were selling fear 24-7, doing a brisk business, and I had to admit I dealt with that particular commodity myself. Except that I tried to *relieve* the fear, as best I could, anyway; I had always attempted to stop the panic and make it go away by taking killers off the streets.

All the MPD theories about the killer seemed to be going nowhere, or at least Bree thought so. The facial image from the video had no match in the FBI's Terrorist Screening Database. The voiceprint had been contracted out to the same agency that worked with the Bureau on Osama bin Laden's recordings after 9/11. So far, no luck there either, but it was too soon to expect much.

Also, the killer hadn't identified himself with any jihad or cell. And no one had stepped up with information about him after seeing – on repeated news broadcasts – still pictures made by spectators of the murder.

Bree shared every shred of information with the Feds, but she also continued her own investigation. That meant sixteen-hour days for her.

On Thursday evening I stopped by her office, hoping to coax her out for a bite to eat. The MPD's Violent Crimes Unit is fairly inconspicuous, located behind an ordinary-looking strip mall in Southeast. There's more than enough parking, though, which some cops joke is the real reason everybody wants to work there. It just could be.

I found Bree's cube empty. The computer was still on, with a yellow sticky note on the monitor that said *Call Alex* in Bree's handwriting. I hadn't heard from her, though – not all day. *So what was she up to now?*

'You looking for Bree?' The detective from the next cubicle gestured with his half-eaten sub. 'Try the conference room. Down that hallway to your left. She's been camping out in there.'

When I entered the room, Bree was sitting with her feet up and a remote in one hand, scratching her head with the other. The killer's video was playing on the television. Open files, pages of notes, and crime-scene photos were spread out everywhere. And still, just seeing her there turned me on more than I cared to admit.

'Hey, you. What time is it?' she called when she spotted me hovering across the room.

I closed the door before kissing her hello a couple of times. 'Dinnertime, break time. You hungry?'

'Starved, actually. Just watch this with me a few more times? I'm going cross-eyed in here by myself.'

I was happy to help out and then not terribly surprised when 'a few more times' became dozens of viewings, and dinner at Kinkead's turned into take-out empanadas from around the corner.

The grisly murder tape from the Riverwalk never got any easier to watch. Neither did hearing my name spoken on it. I compensated by lasering in on the killer. Maybe there was some nuance of his speech or behavior, something nobody had noticed yet. I knew this exercise wasn't about giant leaps right now; it was about making small connections. Like Tess Olsen being a crime writer. Or maybe even the Hallmark greeting cards I'd noticed in the apartment. The killer's need for an audience.

So it surprised us both a few minutes later when we found something important, something that might be huge.

Chapter Twenty

It started out as a barely discernible flash, something almost sublim-inal in the static just before the second half of the tape began. Bree and I had been staring so much at what the killer wanted us to see, we hadn't really looked anywhere else.

'Hold it a second,' I said.

I picked up the remote and rewound the tape a bit, then froze it.

'There,' I said to Bree. 'See it?'

It was almost nothing. More like the suggestion of an image, almost too fast for the human eye or even the slow-motion feature on the VCR. A ghost is what it was. A clue. *Left there on purpose?*

'This tape's been used before,' I said.

Bree was already putting on her shoes, which were size-ten black flats. 'You know anyone at the Cyber Unit over at the Bureau?' she blurted out.

The police department relied heavily on the FBI for video-forensics assistance. I knew a few names over there, but it was now nine o'clock at night. That didn't seem to matter to Bree, who was up out of her seat and pacing.

She finally picked up the phone herself. 'Let me try Wendy Timmerman. She works late.'

I raised my eyebrows at her. 'Wendy Timmerman works late? Someone's been paying attention.'

Wendy was ostensibly an office manager for the department, but she was also something of a secret weapon for anyone who wanted to bend the rules a little without breaking the law. She knew everyone, and everyone, it seemed, owed her one kind of favor or another.

Plus, she had no life. She practically lived at her desk.

Sure enough, Wendy talked for a couple of minutes to Bree, then called back with a name and number.

'Jeffery Antrim,' Bree said, hanging up. 'Lives over in Adams Morgan. Supposed to be a genius at this stuff. I guess he moonlights out of his apartment, but Wendy said bring him a six-pack, and we'll be admitted to his lair in a flash. Hey – remind me to send Wendy some flowers.'

'Don't bother,' I said. 'She'll call you when she wants a favor. It'll be more than some flowers.'

Chapter Twenty-One

As Wendy Timmerman had suggested we should, we stopped at a convenience store on our way over to the Adams Morgan neighborhood. We sneaked a couple of tantalizing kisses in the store, then in the car, but now we were on our way again, back to business, damn it. Jeffery Antrim, who seemed closer to Damon's age than my own, was friendly enough and let us right in when I showed him the beer. I had my doubts about the 'boy genius' label until I saw his home setup. The small apartment – laboratory, 'lair,' whatever – barely had room for furniture. I wondered if any of the expensive equipment, piled everywhere, had been pilfered from the Bureau.

We sat on mismatched kitchen chairs for a few hours, drinking the second six-pack we'd brought, while Jeffery worked in the other room. Sooner than I expected, he called us in to look at what he had found.

'Here's the scoopy-doopy-doo. There wasn't much more than shadow images on the underlying track. So I captured everything I could. Then digitized it. I'm assuming you won't mind a composite of deinterlaced frames?'

'I guess it depends,' Bree said.

'On what?'

'On what the hell you just said, Jeffery. You speak English? Or maybe Spanish? My Spanish is serviceable.'

Jeffery smiled at Bree. 'Well, here you go. Take a look for yourselves. I can always break it back down if you want.' He tapped out a few more commands. 'It's printing now, but you can see it here. Take a good look at this.'

We leaned close to watch one of the small monitors in a tower of gadgetry stacked on his desk.

The image was indeed shadowy, more dark than light, but still discernible. In fact, it was immediately familiar to both of us.

'Holy shit,' Bree said under her breath. 'Suddenly, it all becomes clear as mud.'

'Isn't that *Abu Ghraib*?' Jeffery asked from where he was stationed behind us. 'It is . . . right?'

The Abu Ghraib prison scandal in Iraq was some years old now but was still a sore spot in a lot of Washington circles, and elsewhere, of course. Apparently with the Riverwalk killer as well.

The image was either a still photo or a news-video capture. It didn't really matter which at this point. Whatever details were unclear, I could pretty much fill in from memory. A female American soldier stood in a wide cell-lined corridor. On the floor at her feet was a hooded, naked Iraqi prisoner.

The man was on all fours, just as Tess Olsen had been.

Around his neck was a dog collar attached to a leash, which the soldier held.

Bree's eyes stayed locked on to the image, and she slowly shook her head back and forth. 'So, Jeffery, you keep any coffee in that tiny kitchen or should I go pick some up?'

Chapter Twenty-Two

The killer's second story was one of his favorite genres, science fiction.

Oh yes, this was delicious. The plan was working just right so far.

The killer wasn't playing the Iraqi soldier anymore, but this was a better story and a much juicier role for him: Dr Xander Swift. *What actor wouldn't kill for the part, so to speak, and to do this particular scene?* In the *thea*ter, of all places. *Delicioso!*

The sidewalk in front of the august Kennedy Center was quickly filling with people that night. The crowd was mostly young, urban eclectic, confident, slightly obnoxious. Just about what you'd expect at a science-fiction stage adaptation of a short story, already once turned into a Hollywood movie. The difference was that the play had a big star actor in it. Thus the sizable crowd, though it wasn't quite a sellout.

The killer – who *wasn't* a star himself, not yet, anyway – assumed his role as Dr Xander Swift as he approached the Kennedy Center. *It was never too early to get into a part, was it?*

A row of six swinging doors opened from the street onto a tiled ticketing area. Then four interior doors led farther into the theater's carpeted lobby. He noticed everything and wouldn't forget a single detail.

Almost believing that he was Dr Xander Swift now, getting more deeply into the role, the killer moved no more quickly or slowly than the crowd surrounding him. Thick, tinted glasses, a gray-flecked beard, and an unassuming tweed jacket helped to keep him undetected. *Just another theater lover,* he was thinking.

Still, he couldn't help having the slightest doubt about the rehearsal.

What if he blew it? What if somehow he was captured tonight? What if he made a mistake at the Kennedy Center?

His eyes loitered, taking in a metallic silver poster in a glass case as he passed.

Matthew Jay Walker
in
We Can Remember It for You Wholesale

The hot-shit Hollywood actor, with his name in black type above the title, was known for shoddily made but highly successful films. Absurd live-action comic books that cheated the customers out of ten bucks. He was the sole reason for the nearly sold-out performance tonight. Women especially loved Matthew Jay Walker, even though he'd recently married a beautiful actress with whom he'd adopted children from third world countries, the latest Follywood trend. They were living in Washington now so that they could 'influence the government on matters important to the children of the world.' Did some people really talk – and worse, think – like that? Yes indeed, they did.

Inside the auditorium, synthesizer music set the tone for the evening. Dr Xander Swift easily found his seat, 11A, on the far left aisle.

He was definitely getting into the part – good stuff, and very well played – if he did say so himself. He was positioned only steps from one of the four illuminated fire exits, but almost immediately, the location was irrelevant to him. He knew instantly that he would *not* be using the ticket he'd already bought for the same seat on Saturday night.

This was the wrong vantage point! All wrong! Dr Swift had needed to see it firsthand to realize what was now so clear to him.

The symbolic murder had to take place not here but up on the stage itself.

That would be best – for the audience. *And the audience was everything, wasn't it?*

At five minutes past eight, the theater went dim, then black. The synthesizer music swelled, and a heavily brocaded curtain rose slowly.

A wash of red light hit the stage, enough to send a collateral haze over the audience, where seat 11A was now empty.

Dr Xander Swift had seen all that he needed to see for tonight – so he had left the theater. The murder was on – for tomorrow. Tonight was only a rehearsal, a walk-through. He wanted to play to a full house, after all. That was a requirement.

All in his honor, of course.

Chapter Twenty-Three

The next day's Violent Crimes meeting had only one, very important agenda item, at least from my point of view. Bree asked me to sit in, and I'd be lying if I said I didn't want to be there. The meeting was heavily attended, standing-room only, and the place was buzzing with hot rumors.

Captain Thor Richter held up the start for the arrival of the deputy mayor, who was twenty minutes late and who spoke not a word the whole time he was there. The fact that Larry Dalton attended, however, sent a clear message on this one: *Everyone's watching the case.* This was just what the maniac killer seemed to want, but it couldn't be helped. No way could we disinvite the deputy mayor.

Bree started off by telling the group everything she and I had recently established. Our late-night stint with Jeffery Antrim had yielded a few more Abu Ghraib images but nothing else of real substance. Still, it was a good start, I thought. I assumed the killer had left it as a message for us. *Or me?*

'So then we opened our lens a little wider, for derivative elements elsewhere,' Bree said, and brought up a PowerPoint slide.

'Here's a transcription of the speech the killer gives in the first half of the videotape. And this' – she changed slides – 'is a speech from a 2003 video made by someone calling himself the Sheik of America.'

'Is it the same guy?' somebody in the back asked.

'No,' Bree said. 'Actually, it isn't. But he's obviously borrowing from more than one source. Abu Ghraib. Now this. Statistically, the two speeches are about sixty percent similar.'

'Hang on a minute. Why do you insist it's not the same guy?' Richter wanted to know. He had a snide way of making his questions sound like accusations.

I saw a brief flash of annoyance on Bree's face, probably invisible to everyone else. 'Because the Sheik was *arrested* last year. He's cooling his heels in a New York prison,' she said. 'Let's move on, shall we?'

Another detective raised his hand like a schoolkid. 'Do we have a bead on nationality one way or the other at this point?'

Bree nodded in my direction. That was my cue. 'A lot of you know Dr Alex Cross. I'm going to ask him to run down the basic points of our profile as it stands now. The killer knows about Dr Cross. In case you haven't heard, he was mentioned by name on the tape.'

'How could I resist an invitation like that?' I said, and got a few laughs.

Then we went right into the heavy stuff.

Chapter Twenty-Four

As I stood at the front, I actually recognized about half the people in the room. I'm not sure how many of the rest of them knew me by reputation, but probably most of them did. I'd worked the high-profile cases in DC for years, and now here I was again. *Doing pro bono work? Helping out Detective Bree Stone? What was this, actually?*

'One thing's pretty clear,' I began. 'He's going to *want* to kill again, whether or not he actually does it. His signature aspect is terrorist, but there are also serial tendencies here. There's already a recognizable pattern that I see.'

'Can you clarify that, Alex?' someone asked. I looked over at Bree, but she raised her chin at me in a go-ahead signal.

'His opening bid, so to speak, was an individual homicide. It's possible he's warming up to something bigger, but I don't think so. He just might stick to one victim at a time.'

'Why?'

'Good question, and I think I might even have the answer to that one. My guess is that he doesn't want to be eclipsed by his own work. This is about *him*, not the victims. Despite what he says on the tape, he's a narcissist at heart. He badly wants to be a star. Maybe that's why he 'invited' me onto the case. He may have even left some greeting cards at the crime scene – a couple of unsigned Hallmark cards. We're still checking into that one and what it might mean if he did. And we're checking on the books Mrs Olsen had written.'

'What about his motive?' Richter asked. 'Are we still thinking this could be political?'

'Yes and no. Right now, our working theory is that he's Iraqi-born, or descended, with some kind of law-enforcement or military background, or both. The FBI thinks he's lived in the US for at least a few years, if not his entire life. Above-average intelligence, highly disciplined, and yes, probably anti-American. But we also think the political agenda could be more a means of expression than an end in itself.'

'Expression of what?' Richter pressed, even though he had to know we didn't have a lot of answers yet.

'A need to kill, maybe. He seems to like what he's doing. But, more important, he likes being in the spotlight.'

Just like you do. Thor.

And maybe *just like me.*

Chapter Twenty-Five

Several people scribbled or typed out notes in the deepening and troubling silence that followed. I didn't want to dominate the meeting, so I handed it right back to Bree for the rest of the Q&A. Richter grilled her hard, but she never backed down from her domineering boss. Sampson was right about Bree – she was going places in the MPD, or she was going to get tossed by some jealous superior.

Afterward, we were gathering up our materials in the empty briefing room when she stopped and looked at me. 'You're pretty good at this,' she said. 'Maybe even better than your hot-shit reputation.'

I shrugged her off with a smile, but deep down I enjoyed the compliment. 'I've done a lot of these meetings. Besides, you carried it, and you know it.'

'Not the meeting, Alex. *This.* This work. You're the best I've seen. By a lot. If you want to know the truth, I think we're pretty good together. How scary is that?'

I stopped organizing the files in my hands and stared at her. 'Then, Bree, why do I feel like we're headed in the wrong direction on this thing?'

She looked stunned by what I'd said. 'Excuse me?'

It had been bugging me since just before the meeting ended. Everything had been moving so fast. This was really the first opportunity to hold our stuff up to scrutiny. And now I felt as if we were missing something important. I was almost sure of it. I hated the timing, but I couldn't help the feeling I had. *My famous goddamn feelings!* My gut was calling out to me to review all the bidding so far, everything that we thought we believed.

'Maybe this all makes sense because it's what he wants us to think,' I said. 'That's just a hunch I have, but it bothers the hell out of me.'

I'd been burned like this before, not too long ago. We'd spent a lot of time on the Mary, Mary case in LA, running down an obvious but misleading person instead of the actual killer. More people had died while we figured that out.

Bree started pulling papers from the briefcase she'd just packed. 'Okay, fine. Let's break it apart again. What do we need to know to nail this thing down the right way?'

The obvious answer to her question was that another murder would provide a hell of a lot more information for us.

Chapter Twenty-Six

I t was time for the *second* story to unfold.
Nine hundred fifty-five brave souls were filing toward and into their plush seats at the Kennedy Center that night. The Grand Foyer was lit by eighteen one-ton crystal chandeliers that resembled . . . what? Giant stalactites? The foyer was huge, more than six hundred feet in length. At its center was an eight-foot bronze bust of the great Kennedy himself, never more august and serious in his life.

A crew of thirty-seven worked behind the scenes here. Impressive. Expensive too.

A cast of no fewer than seventeen trod the boards.

And one lone figure waited, quietly, underneath the stage.

Dr Xander Swift.

At three o'clock that afternoon, he'd come in through the stage door. A large toolbox in hand and a few rehearsed phrases about the boiler were all it took. Inside the toolbox were his props.

Pistol.

Ice pick, just in case.

Butane torch.

Supply of ethanol.

Now it was more than five hours later and almost time for the main act. Above his head, the play was in progress. The house was full, theater lovers one and all, drama and suspense fans.

Matthew Jay Walker was well into a scene in which he talked somewhat robotically with another character on a monitor. Walker was excessively handsome, of course, a little shorter than expected, and quite the spoiled brat, if truth be known. His agent had made demands for fresh exotic fruit, a supply of Evian water, a personal makeup artist. Now it was time for Walker to meet his costar.

'Hello, Matthew Jay! Greetings,' said Dr Swift. 'I'm here . . . *behind* you.'

The actor looked around, surprised – no, *shocked* – when the trap-door in the stage floor, normally used only in the second act, flew open.

'What th—'

'Ladies and Gentlemen, I am so sorry for the interruption,' said Dr Xander Swift in a loud, clear, commanding voice that could be heard way up in the cheap seats. 'But please, may I have your attention, your *full* attention, your undivided attention? This is a matter of life and death.'

Chapter Twenty-Seven

At first, the only noticeable stir in the audience was that of riffling pages as dozens of people looked to their programs to see *who* this was up on the stage.

Matthew Jay Walker turned his back to the audience and spoke in a whisper. 'What the fuck do you think you're doing? Who the hell are you? Get off the stage! Now!'

Suddenly, Dr Xander Swift held forth a pistol until it nearly touched the actor's face. He let his hand shake, as if he were nervous – which he was not. 'Shhh,' he said in a stage whisper. 'You don't have any lines here.'

He continued to push the gun at the actor until Walker went down on his knees. 'Please,' Walker said on mike. 'I'll do whatever you want. Just calm down.'

'Call nine one one,' someone yelled out in the front row. The audience was finally beginning to get it.

The killer addressed them. 'I am Dr Xander Swift, from Immunization and Control. I must inform you that this man has been tagged for extinction,' he explained. 'Frankly, I'm as shocked and saddened as you are.'

'He's crazy! He's not an actor!' cried Matthew Jay Walker suddenly.

'I'm *not* crazy. There's a very sensible plan,' replied Dr Swift.

Holding his gun on the actor with one hand, Swift began to swab Walker with ethanol gel from an industrial foil pouch in one of his pockets. He plastered the gel down the actor's chest, through his wavy blond hair, under his chin. The smell was so intense that Walker gagged and choked. 'What are you doing? Please, stop!' he cried out.

Now the audience was on its feet. Shouts came from the wings. 'Stop him! Somebody get up there. Where is security?'

The doctor's voice boomed from the stage again. 'Anyone who comes up here will be shot dead. Thank you for your attention and your patience. Now please, watch closely! This will be indelible in your mind's eye. Never to be forgotten by any of you, so help me God!'

A butane torch sparked in his hand. Then ethanol exploded into flame all over Matthew Jay Walker's body. The actor's face seemed to melt away, and he screamed in terrible pain. He began to whirl around in circles, trying to beat out the fire that was crisping his skin.

'You're watching the rapid disintegration of flesh,' Dr Swift explained. 'Happens all the time in war zones. Iraq, Palestine, distant places like that. Fairly routine, this. Nothing out of the ordinary, I assure you.'

Then he ran swiftly across the stage, away from the screaming actor, who was now rolling on the floor. He used his torch to ignite the black masking drapes that hung there. They caught immediately, with a dramatic *whoosh.*

'Hold your applause! Please, hold your applause,' he called to the audience, *his* audience now. 'Thank you so much! Thank you! You're fabulous!'

He did a half bow, then disappeared from sight off the stage. Next, he nearly flew down a steep flight of stairs to a fire exit and out into an alleyway in back. A high-pitched door alarm screamed behind him.

Dr Swift moved aside an empty crate in the alley and picked up an expandable nylon duffel he'd left there earlier that day. He deposited his gun, torch, and coat inside. Then the thick glasses, the contact lenses, the beard, the prominent forehead. Finally the shock of salt-and-pepper hair he'd worn for the role.

Once again, he was himself, and he exited the alley onto the street, where he turned away just as the first fire truck was arriving.

It was done, his mission accomplished, his part played very close to perfection. Now Dr Xander Swift could disappear from the earth forever, just as the Iraqi had after he murdered the crime writer in front of all those appreciative fans.

My God, I'm good, he thought, and his chest swelled with genuine pride. *After all these years, I'm making it big.*

A few blocks away from the Kennedy Center, a woman was waiting for him in a blue sports car.

'You were *won*derful.' She beamed and kissed the killer on the cheek. 'I'm so proud of us.'

Chapter Twenty-Eight

'Alex, come and look at this. It's unbelievable. Actually, it's *insane.* Look at this, will you?'

Bree was holding up something in a clear plastic evidence bag when I found her and Sampson on the stage of the main theater at the Kennedy Center. One whole side of the play's set was charred black. Another dark patch on the floor showed where the actor Matthew Jay Walker had died in front of an audience of nearly a thousand.

I had assumed even before I got there that this was the same crazy perp as at the Riverwalk. *Why else would Bree have called me?*

'Show him the card,' Sampson said. 'Found it underneath the trap-door where he came in. Looks like this freak watched too much TV in the '90s.'

Bree handed over the evidence bag, and I took it reluctantly.

Inside was a handmade postcard. One side was black, with a large, bright-green letter *X,* in what looked like a degraded close-up of an old typewriter font. On the other side, in letters clipped from magazines, ransom-note style, were the words *The Truth Is Out There.*

'*The X-Files.*' Bree said what I was already thinking. 'Tagline from the TV show. "The Truth Is Out There." We don't know if this murder was based on a particular episode, but it might have been.'

'The same killer,' I said. 'Has to be him.'

'Supposedly this guy was white. Older too, in his fifties or sixties,' said Sampson.

I swept my arm around the stage. 'You've got a dozen expert witnesses to talk to here. If anyone can recognize makeup, it's going to be actors. Two murders based on specific source material, though. Both with some kind of calling card left behind for us to find.'

'Different methods,' Bree said. 'Could be coincidence. I'm not saying it is, but could be. Maybe there's more than one perp? Possibility?'

'We've got a unifying signature, Bree. Public executions in front of an audience. Maybe we ought to call him the Audience Killer. That's the heart of it for him.'

'Audience Killer? Is that in the DSM-IV?' Sampson's smile was grim. He coped through humor. A lot of homicide cops did, myself included.

Bree ran a hand over the top of her head. 'I'm with you all the way, but . . .'

'But what?'

'Richter. Thor the Bore isn't going to let me rule out any possibilities without further cause.'

'What about the ones that make perfect sense to rule out?' I asked.

This was the kind of bureaucratic logjam I associated with my time at the FBI, not Metro. Things sure had changed since I'd been away. Or maybe it was just me who had changed.

I sighed out loud, looked around the stage. 'What else do we have?'

Chapter Twenty-Nine

I took my work home that terrible night, and this wasn't even my case. Yet.

It was two in the morning, and I already had the makings of a revised profile spread out on the kitchen table in front of me. I couldn't get the Audience Killer, as we now thought of him, out of my head. Or Kyle Craig, for that matter. *What the hell did he want with me? Why was he making contact now?*

When the light under Nana's door came on, I flipped the pages over so she wouldn't see them. As if a bunch of upside-down paper wouldn't look suspicious to her, or could fool the old night owl in the slightest.

'You hungry?' was the first thing she said. It had been a long time since she'd asked what I was doing up in the middle of the night.

A few minutes later, she had a couple of grilled apple-and-cheddar sandwiches going on the stove – half for her and one and a half for me. I cracked a beer and poured a small amount into a juice glass for her.

'What's on those pages there that you don't want me to see?' she asked, her back still to me. 'Could it be your last will and testament?'

'That supposed to be funny?'

'Not at all, sonnyboy, not funny in the least. Just sad, very sad.'

She put down our plates and sat across from me at the kitchen table. Just like it'd been for years.

'I don't think you're going to like what I have to say,' I told her.

'And that's stopped you when?'

'I've been in private practice for a while. It's been good for me – the change. I like it most days.'

Nana bowed her head and clucked a couple of times. 'Oh, Alex.

I'm not going to like this one bit. Maybe I should go back to my room and sleep.'

'But,' I said, then corrected myself. '*And* something's missing for me.'

'Mm-hm. I'll bet. Getting shot at, and missed. Getting shot at, and hit.'

I didn't know what she could have done to make this easier, but she sure wasn't trying.

'I left law enforcement for some good reasons.'

'Yes, you did, Alex. They're all sleeping upstairs.'

'Nana, I've never been someone who works for a paycheck. My work, for better or worse, is part of me. And part of me is missing lately. That's just the way it is.'

'I can't say I haven't noticed. But I'll tell you something else. There's a lot of other things missing around here these days. Things like phone calls in the middle of the night. Things like wondering when you'll be home again – *if* you'll be home again.'

We went back and forth like that for a while. The thing that surprised me was that the longer it went on, the stronger I felt about what I needed to do.

Finally I pushed back from the table and wiped my hands on a paper napkin.

'You know what, Nana? I love you dearly. I've tried keeping the peace. I've tried doing things your way, and whether or not it shows, it's not working. I'm going to live my life the way I have to.'

'Oh, for heaven's sake, what does that even mean?' she asked as she threw her hands into the air.

I stood up. My heart was racing. 'Whatever it means, I'll let you know when it's done. I'm sorry, but that's as much as I can give you right now. Good night.' I gathered the papers, turned, and walked away from her.

Her laughter stopped me. It was just a soft chortle at first – the kind of feather that can knock you over, though. I turned back again, and something in my expression sent her into a full cackling belly laugh.

'*What?*' I finally had to ask.

Nana gained control of herself, mostly, and slapped both hands down on the kitchen table. 'Well, look who's back from the dead! *Alex Cross.*'

Chapter Thirty

It was business as usual the next day, or maybe I should say business as unusual. Sampson and I were canvassing the neighborhood around the Kennedy Center that afternoon when Bree called.

'You will not be sorry if you drop whatever you're doing and come back over here.' She hung up without a hello or good-bye.

'What happened?' Sampson must have seen the confusion on my face.

'Something. That's all I know. Let's go.'

We found Bree parked at a computer terminal when we got to the office.

'Please tell me we didn't come back here to play solitaire,' Sampson said.

'Guess who's got a blog?' Bree said. 'I actually got a call from a reporter on this. She didn't even know it was the first time I was hearing about it.'

She sat back to make room as we crowded in.

The home page she showed us was both simple and impressive. It had an all-black background with white writing. In the upper-left corner, there was an animated graphic of a television set with what looked like live static on the screen. White block letters that read MY REALITY faded up, then out, then back again, like credits on a TV show. Underneath that, there were menu options for 'Channel One,' 'Channel Two,' down through 'Channel Eight.'

Weblog entries took up the bulk of the page, with the most recent one on top. It was marked for 12:30 a.m., only fourteen hours prior. The title on it was simply *Thanks*.

'Death is more universal than life; everyone dies but not everyone lives.' – A. Sachs

Thanks for all the comments. I really like hearing from people who appreciate what I do. I read the negative ones too – just don't like them as much (grin). So to most of you, I say keep it coming. To the rest, I say get a life.

Some of you have asked why I'm doing this. I am doing it for myself. Let me repeat that. I am doing it for myself. Anyone who says they know what I'll do next is full of shit 'cause even I don't know what I'll do next. Don't be fooled by the police! They have no clue what to do with me because they have never seen anything like me before. The only thing they have control of is their sound bites. Be skeptical.

I can tell you this much: there is more. If that fact pleases you, I can tell you this much again: you won't be disappointed.

Keep on living, fuckers.

Bree scrolled further down the page. 'The entries go back a way, but they're not all this directed. Sometimes he talks about his day. What he had for lunch. It's a little bit of everything.'

'Does he talk about the murders?' I asked.

'Only indirectly. The entries from those days are all, like, "Had a good time tonight" and "Did you see the news?"'

'What about these?' Sampson touched the screen where the menu of channel numbers was.

'Oh, you'll like this.' Bree clicked on Channel One. The little television screen in the corner switched from static over to a grainy still image. I recognized it as one of the phone-camera captures from Matthew Jay Walker's murder, taken by someone in the audience and already shown on several news broadcasts.

'And then there's this.' She clicked another one, and an audio file opened. Now the little screen showed a horizontal green line that jumped and spiked with the recorded sound of a woman screaming. I recognized Tess Olsen's voice right away.

'That's her,' I said.

'Definitely?' Sampson asked.

'Definitely.' Bree and I said it at the same time. We had watched the videotape of her murder so often, the individual modulations of every scream were familiar, like some sick song we knew by heart.

The recording that now played had to have been made separately, we realized, given that the video was left behind in the apartment. That fact went a long way toward authenticating this site.

'Little handheld recorder in the pocket? Easy.' There was a kind of grudging respect in Sampson's voice. 'It's all elaborate, but within that, he's using the fewest possible strokes. Like a big, efficient machine.'

'Otherwise, we'd have his ass in custody,' Bree said. 'He knows how good he is.' She grunted in disgust.

This was the admiring/hating phase of the game. His methods were undeniably bold and well executed. On the other hand, you can start to hate a killer, and even yourself a little, for every day that he gets to be free in the world. I think all three of us felt it.

'Well, the good news is that he likes attention,' Bree said.

'I thought that was the bad news,' Sampson said.

'Both.' They looked at me. 'He's going to be out there in the world more, which means that his reactivation time could be a lot quicker. But at some point, his confidence is going to outpace his skill. That's when he'll blow it. Has to happen.'

'Because you say so?' Sampson asked me with a grin.

'That's right,' I said. I wadded up a page and shot it across the room into the garbage can with a metallic swish. 'Because I say so.'

PART TWO

INFAMOUS!

Chapter Thirty-One

The lawyer Mason Wainwright arrived for his meeting with Kyle Craig at four o'clock sharp, as he always did. Kyle insisted that he be punctual. But this visit wasn't to be like any of the past ones. This would be his final time with Kyle Craig, and that was cause for some sadness but also celebration.

He wore his usual cowboy boots and hat, an oversize buckskin jacket, the horn-rimmed glasses, the snakeskin belt, his Far West professorial look. As soon as he entered the space, he and Kyle hugged, as they always did. 'The beauty of rituals,' said Kyle.

'Everything is ready,' the lawyer whispered against the prisoner's cheek. 'No cameras permitted. We're alone in here. As you know, Washington is under way.'

'Then let's get started here. Nobody will believe this . . . nobody. This is greatness, Mason.'

The two men pulled apart and immediately began to shed their clothing, stripping down to shorts. Kyle's were off-white prison issue with yellow stains. 'They're not from piss. It's burn marks from the laundry,' he told the lawyer.

'Well, *these* are from piss.' Wainwright laughed as he pointed to his own shorts. 'That's how frightened I am.'

'Well,' said Kyle Craig, 'I can't really blame you.'

The lawyer opened his briefcase next. He pried apart the top of the case and took out what first appeared to be molded flesh. Actually, it was a custom-made prosthesis, a realistic face mask originally developed for skin burns and cancer victims, and occasionally used in Hollywood films like *Mission: Impossible.* The mask was made of silicone rubber, and every detail had been hand painted by a renowned costume artist in Los Angeles.

There were two prosthetic applications: one of Mason Wainwright, the other of Kyle Craig.

Once the masks were fitted properly, Kyle spoke to the lawyer. 'Yours looks perfectly fine. Very good, actually. And mine? How do I look?'

'You look like me.' The lawyer grinned crookedly. 'I think I got the better of the deal.'

'Are there any problems inherent with the masks?' Kyle asked next, as thorough as ever.

'Only one flaw with these prosthetics, from what I've been told. The likenesses are perfect. That's not a problem. But the eyelids don't blink.'

'Important to know. Let's finish dressing, then.'

Kyle put on the lawyer's clothes quickly – just in case a guard came by, which happened occasionally, though not usually during the legal sessions, when Kyle and the lawyer were left alone by law.

Mason Wainwright had worn clothes a couple of sizes too small that day, including his trademark cowboy hat. When Kyle got to the boots, he inserted two-inch lifts from out of the briefcase.

Now he stood at a little over six two, close enough to the lawyer's height.

Dressed in the prison jumpsuit, the lawyer was still taller than Kyle, but he would walk with the prisoner's habitual slump, so it wouldn't matter that much, if at all. They were ready now, but the plan called for them to stay together for the full hour. Just as they always did. Everything exactly the same. Rituals to be observed.

'Do you want to ask your questions – the eight?' the lawyer said. 'Or should I ask them?'

Kyle went through the usual questions. Then neither of them spoke for the remainder of the time they had together. Kyle Craig seemed to be almost in a trance. But he was just thinking ahead, making plans.

Finally, when only a minute or so of the meeting remained, Kyle rose first, looking like the lawyer, of course.

Then the lawyer stood, looking like Kyle Craig.

Kyle extended his arms, and Mason Wainwright moved into them. *'In your honor,'* the lawyer whispered. 'I apologize that this took so long to arrange.'

'Masterpieces take time,' said Kyle Craig.

Chapter Thirty-Two

M ason Wainwright was slumped over slightly and looking down at the floor when the guard opened the door to the small meeting room. 'Let's go, Craig,' the guard ordered. 'Play period's over. Time to go back to your suite.'

Wainwright muttered his assent, then he moved down the hallway in front of the ill-tempered turnkey. He was bent over and shuffling like the 'dead man walking' he was supposed to be. *Just don't let him see you blink,* he reminded himself.

This was the time when the whole plan could go up in flames. Everything could be lost in the next few minutes. His part was an easy one to play, though – stay calm, keep quiet, head down – unless the guard noticed some change, some error on his part. The lawyer had studied Kyle Craig's mannerisms for months and believed he pretty much had everything down. Still, he couldn't be certain until this was over.

Suddenly the guard's nightstick was in the small of his back. *What was this? Shit, no!*

He'd obviously made a mistake and wondered what it was. *Where had he messed up and ruined the escape Kyle Craig had been planning since the first day he arrived at the supermaximum-security prison?* Maybe even before then, since the Mastermind seemed to anticipate everything that could possibly happen.

'*This* way, Mastermind. You forget the way to your own cell, genius?' the guard said, and laughed derisively. 'C'mon, let's move it! Gotta get back to my Court TV.'

The lawyer didn't look around at the prison guard, didn't acknowledge him in any way, just turned down the indicated corridor and continued to slump along.

Fortunately nothing else went wrong on the way back to Kyle Craig's cell. Finally the guard slammed the door, and Wainwright was alone. *He'd done it!*

Only then did the lawyer raise his eyes and dare to look around. So, this was where the Mastermind had lived, and *how* he had lived for the past several years. What a disgrace that such a fine mind would be trapped in a space with virtually no stimulation and that Kyle had been subject to the urges and whims of bestial prison guards and slow-witted administrators.

'In your honor,' the lawyer whispered again, then he prepared himself to follow the rest of Kyle Craig's instructions.

The lawyer checked out the small cell, which was made of poured concrete. The bed, desk, stool, and bedside table were screwed into the floor as a safety precaution. The toilet had an automatic shutdown so cells couldn't be flooded. Kyle had 'earned' a black-and-white TV, but it only played self-help and religious programming, so who would want to watch it?

The lawyer felt claustrophobic, terribly so, and thought that it would be difficult not to lose one's sanity in this tiny hellhole. Mason Wainwright finally had to laugh at that. Most people would feel that he had lost his sanity a long time ago, even before he became one of the Mastermind's disciples.

When a guard did a check just before mealtime at six that night, he couldn't believe what he saw. He immediately pushed the panic button on his belt. Then he waited for help to come running. Still, the guard couldn't take his eyes away from the jail cell.

Kyle Craig had hanged himself!

Chapter Thirty-Three

The sun was shining in Kyle Craig's eyes, and what a glorious thing that was. *The sun! Imagine.* He drove Mason Wainwright's Jaguar coupe a couple of miles over the speed limit to a mall outside Denver, where a Mercedes SUV was waiting for him. Now this was more like it, power and comfort. Plus, nobody would be looking for the Mercedes.

Kyle Craig had doubters to confound and frustrate.

Followers to delight.

Promises to keep, promises written in blood, promises recorded in the august *Washington Post* and the *New York Times.*

Yes, he would see the sun again, and he'd see a whole lot more than that too.

He was traveling to Washington, but he thought he'd take a round-about route, visit a few enemies, maybe kill them in their own homes.

He was going to make a name for himself again, and he had a plan on how to do it.

Not a word of it on paper, though – everything in his head.

'My God, just look at that sun!' he exclaimed.

Chapter Thirty-Four

I was home on Fifth Street and had just finished eating a late dinner with Nana and the kids when the phone started to ring off the hook. Most of us were in the kitchen doing a family cleanup. Damon, Jannie, and I were taking care of everything; Ali was supervising; and Nana was reading the papers in the living room – the *Washington Post* and *USA Today*, her favorites.

Her TV show was on tonight too, *Grey's Anatomy*. Nana loved the series because she felt there were three very bright and true-enough-to-life black characters in the ensemble cast, which she believed was a first for TV. *Grey's Anatomy* was one thing that she and I agreed on. We were both addicts of the medical drama, and we were rarely disappointed for our devotion and attention.

Jannie frowned when she answered the phone and discovered, to her amazement, that it wasn't for her. 'It's for you, Daddy.'

'What a surprise,' I said. '*Major* upset.'

'It's not a girl,' Jannie came right back, 'so you can forget about that. It's not Bree.'

I don't know what I was expecting, but it wasn't what I heard during the next few confounding seconds on the telephone.

'Alex, this is Hal Brady.' Brady was the chief of detectives these days at the MPD, an old friend, the boss of Thor Richter and all the rest of us.

'Hi, Chief.' I managed a few words, but mostly I was in an intent listening mode. The fact that Brady was calling me at home wasn't a good sign.

'This isn't about Bree, is it?' I suddenly had a premonition.

'No, no. Bree is fine. In fact, she's in the office with me now. I'll let you talk with her in a minute,' Brady said, then continued. 'Alex, the reason I'm calling is that Kyle Craig escaped from ADX Florence sometime today. They're still working out the details of how he did it, but this can't be good. Not for you, not for any of us. He's on the loose. They have no idea where he went.'

I didn't hesitate for a second. 'I need a favor,' I told the chief. 'A big favor.'

Chapter Thirty-Five

I'd been out to the supermaximum-security prison in Florence a couple of times since Kyle Craig had been incarcerated there. On the flight, I made a few notes about him from the papers I'd collected over the years. Even as I scribbled the notes, I was recalling certain incidents between us. At one time, Kyle had been a friend, at least I'd thought so. He'd fooled a lot of people along the way, and I have always been a terrible sucker for those who seem to lead a good life.

I wrote in my notepad:

Expects to be recognized as superior; has a grandiose sense of his own self-importance; narcissistic to an extreme.

Interpersonally exploitive; complex thinker.

Superficial charm. Can turn it on and off at will.

Sibling rivalry (probably killed one brother).

Severely abused, physically and emotionally, by his father. Or so he claims.

Duke University undergraduate and law school. Top of his class. Made it look easy.

IQ: 145–155 range.

No conscience.

Father, William Hyland Craig, former army general, chairman of two Fortune 500 companies, now deceased.

Mother, Miriam, still living in Charlotte.

Former FBI DIC, trained at Quantico, where he also taught new agents.

Highly competitive, especially with me.

I arrived in Florence, Colorado, around noon the day after Kyle's escape, and very little seemed to have changed about the super-maximum-security prison. I spent the first hour talking with two of the guards who knew Kyle Craig particularly well; then I interviewed Warden Richard Krock. The warden seemed more shocked than any of us that Kyle, or anybody else, could have escaped from Florence. No one ever had before; no one had even come close.

'As you now know,' Krock told me, 'the lawyer went back to Craig's cell, wearing a prosthetic mask, and then hanged himself there. What you don't know is that we videotaped some of his early visits with Craig. Would you like to see them?'

I sure *would*.

Chapter Thirty-Six

For the next few hours, I sat and studied tapes of some of the early meetings between Kyle and Mason Wainwright. The lawyer hadn't invoked his lawyer–client privilege until the third week he'd spent with his client. *Why was that? Because Kyle wanted us to see something? Or maybe because the lawyer did.*

What, though? The first visit was virtually the same as the others that were taped.

Wainwright entered the meeting room wearing a very memorable outfit, which no doubt helped with the eventual escape: cowboy hat and boots, buckskin jacket, horn-rimmed eyeglasses that clashed with everything else he had on.

He and Kyle hugged as soon as they met. Kyle said something that wasn't caught on tape.

Then came a series of eight questions – always the same ones, or very close.

Some kind of code? Or was Kyle playing games? Or simply crazy – he and *the lawyer?* I couldn't tell at this point. About anything, really. Except that Kyle Craig was the first prisoner ever to escape from ADX Florence. The Mastermind had done the impossible.

Finally Kyle and the lawyer hugged each other again. Wainwright said something to Kyle that wasn't picked up on tape. *Was this how they exchanged information – whether they were taped or not?*

I expected that it was. We would certainly try to find out.

Next, I went to Kyle's cell, but there wasn't much to see in there. Prisoners weren't allowed many personal possessions at ADX. The small room was neat and orderly, as Kyle was himself.

Then I saw the message he'd left.

A greeting card was propped on the table that was bolted down next to his bed.

It was a Hallmark – unsigned – just like the ones at Tess Olsen's penthouse.

Minutes later, I was back at Warden Krock's office. I needed some answers to questions that had developed in the past few hours.

'Visitors?' I asked. 'We know about the lawyer, though we have no idea what his real relationship to Craig was. Were there other visitors? Anyone who came around more than once?'

Krock didn't have to consult his files to answer. 'In the first year, there was a persistent reporter from the *Los Angeles Times* named Joseph Wizan, whom Craig refused to see. Repeatedly. Several others contacted Craig through my office but didn't bother to come out here because he wouldn't see them either.

'The only one who did visit, and this was just a few months ago, was the author Tess Olsen. You know, the woman who was killed in Washington recently? Kyle surprised us. He agreed to meet with her. She came here three times. She planned to do a book on Craig, another *In Cold Blood*, if you listened to her talk about it.'

'You spoke with her, then?' I asked.

'I did. On all three of her visits. Half an hour or so the first time.'

'How did she seem to you? What was your impression?'

Warden Krock moved his head back and forth as if he were weighing his answer. Finally he spoke. 'She seemed like a fan. Honestly, I wondered if she and Craig had something going before he was caught.'

Chapter Thirty-Seven

I returned to Washington early the following morning, having already passed along the news about Tess Olsen, the Hallmark card in Craig's cell, and the possibility that Kyle may have had a relationship with Olsen, or even with the killer in DC. But more than anything else, I wondered what Kyle was planning.

Bree had pulled together a small forensic team focusing on the blog leads she was chasing down. An agent named Brian Kitzmiller from the FBI's Cyber Unit had been assigned to us and was more than willing to come on board. The Audience Killer case had already caught his attention.

Bree asked Kitzmiller for the earliest possible meeting after he'd had a chance to go over the blog. Kitzmiller gave us a four-hour turn-around, which meant he was fast. Another good sign that we had everybody's attention on this case.

We showed up at the Hoover Building close to three. I certainly knew my way around there, though I'd never done much work with the Cyber Unit and had never met Kitzmiller – I'd heard of him, however, and knew he had a reputation as a puzzle-solver.

'Come on in.' Even seated in front of a work terminal, he was obviously very tall and gawky-looking, with the brightest orange hair I had ever seen in my life.

This part of the unit was a low-ceilinged room on the second floor, a few levels below my old office. Everyone sat in wide stall-like cubicles with their backs to the center, where a large octagonal conference table was strewn with papers, files, and laptop computers. *People did work here* – good sign.

A glass wall separated the unit from the busy corridor outside.

Bree, Sampson, and I grabbed chairs and sat down in Kitzmiller's stall. He was about my age, fit, and with that blinding head of hair.

'I can't really source any of the audio,' he said, 'but I did compare the screams on what the blogger calls Channel Two against the video-tape from the original crime scene. It's almost definitely a match. But that's not quite the same as a forensic link between the blog and the killer. Theoretically, anyone could have posted this.'

'You mean, if someone else had access to the recording,' I said. 'We're all in agreement that the audio is original, right?'

'Sure,' he said. 'So it's either your suspect or someone who was given access by the suspect. Hard to tell about that for sure yet.'

'Let's focus on one thing at a time,' Bree said. 'You told me on the phone that the blog was posted from Georgetown University? Is that right?'

'Or, at least, *through* Georgetown. That's the basic problem I'm seeing already, Bree. Whoever put up the blog knew how to cover his or her tracks fairly well.'

'Proxy server?' Sampson asked. His little niches of expertise always surprised me.

Kitzmiller smiled appreciatively at Sampson, but then he shook his head. 'Negative. *Worse,* actually. He used an open proxy. Universities are notoriously easy marks for this kind of thing. Any boob can remotely attach their IP address from anywhere, and wham – you've got an untraceable site. All I can get you is a location. Nothing about identity.'

'Any suggestions at all?' Bree asked. 'We really need your help on this.'

'Sure. I understand your frustration, Detective. My suggestion is that you get totally involved on your end. Jump in the deep water with me. We'll keep paddling around here, but you'll be glad if you do some stirring of your own. Believe me, a whole lot of detritus turns up online. You'd be surprised what you might find.'

'Honestly, I don't know the first thing about cyberforensics,' Bree said.

'You don't have to. I'm not talking about cracking code, here. I'm talking about a large community that needs to be canvassed. The whole blogosphere.'

'Blogosphere?'

Kitzmiller started pulling up several new windows at once, layered over one another on the screen to show us what he was getting at.

'First of all, we've got everyone who posted responses to the original blog. There was the MY REALITY site, for example. It's already been taken down, but there were more than three dozen separate screen names for people who had replied to at least one of his entries. So that's a pretty good start. You remember the old shampoo commercial? "You tell two friends, and they tell two friends, and so on and so on"? Same thing here. Some number of people read this, then turn around and talk about it on their own blogs, and the scope goes up exponentially. Chat rooms too.

'Now add to that the fact that you've got a killer who apparently likes to be in the spotlight. There's a good chance he'll stay a part of the community in some way. People intersect. You find the right intersection, maybe you solve your case, find your killer, go into the Detectives' Hall of Fame.'

'That's a lot of *ifs*,' Bree said. 'I don't like *ifs* and *maybes*.'

People had been talking about cyberspace as the new frontier in law enforcement for years now. It looked like I was about to get my first extensive taste of it.

Kitzmiller ran a simple Google blog search for us to illustrate his point. He searched *Audience Killer* and got a whole screenful of responses.

'Wow,' said Bree. 'I'm kind of impressed already. Or maybe I should say *depressed*. That's a lot of detritus.'

Sampson added, 'Fuck! It's an epidemic.'

'You notice he never uses that full title on his own site. That's probably why you hadn't found it earlier. Even so, right here you've got more than eighty other strands that mention him, and two specifically dedicated to the subject. And he presumably hasn't even hit three homicides yet.'

'Does the fact that he's courting the attention speed all this up?' I asked.

'Sure, it does. There's a voracious audience for all this stuff on the Internet. Most people say they abhor the killing, and a lot of them actually do, I'm sure. What you end up with is a mix of folks with legitimate forensic interest, people who want to know more but maybe for the wrong reason, and then people who just plain get off on it all. This guy is their dream come true. No one's ever been so accessible, not while he was still this active.'

Bree spoke quietly, working it out in her head. 'So . . . he uses other people to help turn himself into the thing he wants to be.'

Kitzmiller nodded and pulled up another window, the 'official' Jeffrey Dahmer fan club site. 'Pick your poison. He wants to be Dahmer. He wants to be Ted Bundy. He wants to be the Zodiac Killer.'

'No. He wants to be a much bigger star,' I said. 'I think he wants to be bigger than any of the others.'

Including Kyle Craig? I had to wonder. *How the hell does Kyle fit in?*

Chapter Thirty-Eight

I was already frustrated about the case, plus I was suffering from Bree deprivation. I was concerned that I'd have trouble focusing at work that week, so I decided to tape my sessions. Just in case, just to be safe.

Anthony Demao, the Desert Storm vet, did something unusual for him, which was to talk in depth about his combat experience. I sat and reviewed the tape again over lunch at my desk. As I listened, I could picture Anthony: ruggedly good-looking, still in shape – a quiet man, though.

'We didn't have sufficient support on the ground. The CO didn't give a rat's ass. We had a *mission*. That's all he cared about,' he said.

'How long had you been there at that point?'

Silence. Then, 'Ground attack started end of the month, so a couple of weeks, I guess.'

I was becoming more and more convinced that something really bad had happened to him during Desert Storm, something that could be a key to Anthony's difficulties, maybe even an incident he'd repressed. The balance in this case was between not wanting to push too hard and a gut feeling that he wasn't going to stick with the therapy for long, especially if he didn't think we were making enough progress.

'I did some research,' I said on the tape. 'You were Twenty-fourth Infantry Division, right? This was just before you all started toward Basra.'

'How did you know that?'

'It's part of history. You were part of history. The information isn't very hard to find, Anthony. Is there anything that happened there that you don't want to talk about? To me . . . or anyone else?'

'Maybe there is. Probably some stuff I don't want to get into. I don't blame anyone for what happened, though.'

His speech was faster now, and clipped, as though he wanted to get past this part.

'Blame anyone for what?' I asked.

'For any of the shit that happened. You know, I enlisted on my own. I wanted to go.'

I waited, but there was no elaboration.

'That's it for now,' Anthony said then. 'A little too much, too soon. Next time. I need to ease into this, Doc. Sorry about that.'

I clicked off the tape recorder and sat back in my chair, thinking. I knew he was losing ground lately, even with the subsidized housing he had. Another month or two of unemployment could be a real problem for him. People like Anthony Demao slipped through the cracks all the time.

I rubbed my eyes hard and poured myself another cup of coffee. There was a lot to think about, maybe too much. I had one more client coming – and then later that afternoon, a meeting at police headquarters.

A big one.

Chapter Thirty-Nine

It was time to trade on my reputation and laurels in a way I'd never done before. I knew that Chief of Police Terrence Hoover would take a meeting if I asked, especially since I had cleared it through the chief of detectives first. I was less sure if Hoover would agree to the ridiculousness I was about to propose to him. We'd have to see about that.

'Alex, come in. Sit down,' he said as I stood like a moke in his doorway. A college wrestling photo on the wall behind him showed the younger Hoover at the University of Maryland and explained where that crushing handshake of his came from. 'I haven't heard from you in a long time.'

'I appreciate you seeing me, Chief. Needless to say, there's something on my mind.'

Hoover smiled. 'So we're skipping the idle chitchat, huh? Okay. What are you after, Alex?'

'Nothing too complicated. Just a job.'

Hoover blinked and ducked his double chin. 'A job? Well, shit, Alex, that is a surprise. I thought you were coming to ask me for something. Instead, you're here to *offer* me something.'

That was a relief to hear. 'Thanks for saying that, Chief. I guess I'll keep offering, then.'

'Please do. You're on a roll. I definitely want to hear the rest of the pitch.'

Here it went.

'Some cops talk about wanting to make a difference. I guess I would say that I believe I can do more good than harm, and that's a reasonable objective. I want to come back on the force but in a limited capacity. I'd like to work the Major Case Squad, but outside of the regular rotation. Specific assignments only. I've been consulting on the Kennedy Center and Connecticut Avenue murder cases already, and if any of this is agreeable to you, it would be a seamless reentry for me. I know the team, and I think I could be an asset.'

Hoover laughed out loud. 'I've heard some pretty good speeches in here, but that one goes on the short list.' He pointed at me. 'You know you can afford to be this cocky 'cause you know damn well I'm gonna say yes.'

'Just figured I'd lay it out there.'

He stood up, and so did I. 'Well, the answer is yes. Let me have Arlene call recruiting, and I'll speak to the superintendent myself. We'll work something out.'

Superintendent of Detectives Ramon Davies, I knew, would be my boss on the Major Case Squad. Davies was above Thor Richter, and if I could get this investigation taken out of Richter's supervision, we'd be able to move a lot more freely on it.

'I think I just cashed in every chit I've got,' I said, shaking Terrence Hoover's hand again.

'It'll be good to have you on this one,' he said. 'I hear they're calling him the Audience Killer.'

Since I had come up with the name, I was tempted to smile but didn't. 'Audience Killer, huh? I guess that sounds about right.'

Chapter Forty

I hooked up with Bree and Sampson back at the Daly Building that evening. I'd already been given an office there, and it was doubling as a nerve center for the Audience Killer case. It felt a little like a college dorm room, with the three of us crammed in there together.

I'd never worked this way before, quite so cooperatively. There was no tension about our roles, though, no debating how the work would get done. There was just the case. And, of course, the proximity of Bree's long legs and other parts, her fetching looks, and so on and so forth.

She was searching through the drawers for something when I came in. Sampson stood behind her, reading a file on the desk over her shoulder.

'Check this out.' He held up a mug shot. 'Meet Ashton Cooley.'

'What's his deal?' I asked, glancing at the file upside down from where I stood.

'Ashton is a stage name,' Sampson said. 'He tried out for, but *didn't get*, Matthew Jay Walker's part in that sci-fi play at the Kennedy. The producers went with the big Hollywood name over the local talent. Typical, right?'

'That could piss you right the hell off,' Bree contributed. 'Don't you think so? I do.'

I took the picture and looked at it. The actor was in his twenties, white, dark-haired, kind of pouty-looking.

'I'm guessing a lot of actors would have wanted that part. Play could've been headed for Broadway,' I said.

'Sure,' Sampson said. 'But how many of them were suspects in a *previous* homicide?'

Chapter Forty-One

Sampson was working another murder case in the projects, so Bree and I went to see the actor. We cut over to Massachusetts Avenue, then up Sixteenth Street to Cooley's Mount Pleasant address. The neighborhood is still remembered for the 1991 riots, sparked by charges of anti-Hispanic racism among DC's black cops.

Cooley, I read on the way over, had been – and technically still was – the primary suspect in the shooting death of a girlfriend, Amanda Diaz, two years earlier. The DA had been forced to give it up for lack of evidence, but apparently it had been a close call.

Cooley still lived in the same apartment where the shooting took place. Not the sentimental type, I guess.

The apartment was on the second floor, above a Central American grocery, in a building not yet reached by any neighborhood-improvement effort. Bree and I took the stairs and arrived at a dank, tiled hallway with one translucent window at the far end.

Cooley's was the middle of three metal-faced apartment doors. We knocked and waited.

'Yeah, who is it? I'm busy.'

'Mr Cooley, I'm Detective Cross, here with Detective Stone from the MPD.'

To my surprise, the door flew open, and he ushered us inside. 'Get in, get in.'

Bree scratched her ear and gave me a look.

'Do you have some particular concern about the police being seen at your door?' she asked.

'You mean because that always works out so well?' he said. 'Last I checked, cops at the front door is not good news.'

We walked into a narrow hallway with two closed rooms along the left side and a row of framed headshots – maybe Cooley's actor friends – hanging on the other chipped and peeling wall. I wondered if one of them was the dead girlfriend.

'Could we sit down?' Bree asked.

He didn't move. 'Not really. What do you want? Like I said, I'm busy.'

Cooley was already one strike away from finding out what it's like when I lose my patience. 'We have questions about two Saturdays ago. Just for starters, can you tell us where you were?'

'Okay.' He started toward the back room. 'Let's sit down. I was right here that Saturday. Never left the apartment.'

Once we were in the living room, Bree stayed on her feet. I sat down across from Cooley on a tall, wobbly stool. He had one very old easy chair, a coffee table, a half-decent home-theater setup, and another stool as the balance of his furniture.

'How long have you lived here?' I asked.

'Ever since I won the lottery,' he deadpanned. His manner was cocky and full of hard eye contact.

Bree stepped in. 'Mr Cooley, can anyone verify that you were here that night?'

He sat back in his chair. 'Yeah. The good ladies at 1–900–FUCKYOU can do that.'

With two quick steps, she was on him. She jerked the handle on the side of his La-Z-Boy and laid him out flat. Then she leaned in close. 'This isn't funny, asshole. *You* aren't funny. Now talk to us, and keep it straight. I don't have much of a sense of humor lately.'

She'd gone further than I would have, but it worked out.

The actor put his hands up in mock surrender. 'I was just kidding around. Damn. Chill, girl.'

Bree stood up but stayed close. 'Talk. I don't feel like chilling, dude.'

'I rented a movie, ordered Chinese from Hunan Palace. Somebody delivered the food. You can talk to them.'

'What time did they deliver?' I asked.

He shrugged.'Seven? Eight? Somewhere in there. Hell, I don't know.' Bree barely moved toward him, and he flinched before recovering again.'I'm serious. I don't know what time it was. But it doesn't matter. I was here the whole night.'

I didn't say so out loud, but I felt inclined to believe him. Despite his show of testosterone, everything about him was *weak* – the way he moved, the way he talked, the way he had folded so fast when Bree got a little aggressive.

We were looking for someone much more in control than this guy, someone who was stronger in every way.

And probably a better actor too.

Bree must have felt it.'Let's go, Alex,' she said. She turned back to the actor, smiled.'Sorry, you're not right for the part. Bet you hear that a lot, smart-mouth.'

Chapter Forty-Two

At nine thirty on Sunday morning, *church day*, a mild-mannered type named David Hayneswiggle, an accountant, and not a very good one, gazed down and saw that the George Washington Memorial Parkway was filling up with traffic. Both northbound and southbound lanes were crowded – though not enough to keep anyone from doing at least sixty and often eighty or more.

Once in a while, a northbound car would honk loudly as it approached the usually deserted pedestrian bridge that ran across the highway. Made sense to Hayneswiggle.

The people riding along below him had to be wondering what some guy in a droopy Richard Nixon mask was doing up there all by himself. And if they did wonder, they were only half right.

It *was* a Nixon mask, but he *wasn't* alone. David Hayneswiggle had plenty of company.

The *third* story had begun, and it was a doozy – very imaginative, high profile, dramatic as hell.

Another terrific role to play too. The accountant with nothing to live for, nothing to lose. Huge chip on his shoulder. Payback time long overdue for this guy.

An eighteen-year-old high-school boy lay motionless on the cement at his feet. The poor lad was dead, his throat slit and already bled out. The boy just couldn't get it in his head to cooperate and do as he was told. Next to him, a teenage girl sat with her back against a wall that also hid her from view of the cars passing below.

The girl was still alive. One of her small hands was in her lap; the other hung limply overhead, where she was cuffed to the bridge's railing. A line of sweat beads showed on her upper lip, just above the duct tape that was wrapped all the way around her mouth and head.

David Hayneswiggle looked down at the girl, who was all bug-eyed and shaking like an addict. 'How you doing? You still with me?' he asked.

She either ignored him or didn't hear what he'd said. *It doesn't matter what the girl thinks, or how she acts,* David Hayneswiggle thought to himself. Once again, he watched the traffic down below on the George Washington, gauging for speed and distance, and just the right moment. The third story was going to be something else.

Whenever some total jackass honked at him, he held up the double peace sign. 'I am not a crook,' he said in his best croaky Nixon voice. He identified so much with Nixon, another loser with a chip on his shoulder.

When he had seen enough, had memorized the scene for future reference, he knelt down next to the girl. She scrambled, moving away maybe a foot, all that she could manage on account of the handcuffs attached to the railing.

'Save your strength,' he said. 'You're safe, right? As long as you're cuffed to the rail. Think about it. Everything is cool.'

He squiggled his arms under the boy's body, then strained to get himself into a half-kneeling position. The kid couldn't have been more than 150 pounds, but it seemed like a ton. *Deadweight,* no joke.

David Hayneswiggle flexed his leg muscles, keeping them ready as he eyed the highway from a squatting position. He saw his target. A white Toyota minivan had come into view about a quarter mile away. There were no trucks allowed on the parkway, so a Hummer, or something like the minivan, was as big as he was going to find. The van stuck to its lane, possibly hemmed in by other cars.

He scootched over to the right a bit, lining himself up as best he could.

When the van was about a hundred yards off, he secured his grip on the boy.

At fifty yards, he rose. In one powerful motion, he came to his full height. And then he chucked the body over the rail, watching it tumble like a heavy sack. It hit the minivan's hood and windshield with a smash of glass, followed by a fast squealing of tires. *Holy shit!*

The van swerved and skidded underneath the narrow bridge and back out the other side – then it tipped over. Steel groaned against concrete, and two more crashes sounded from behind the minivan as other daydreaming drivers failed to stop in time.

Traffic was backed up almost instantly.

The northbound parkway would soon be the northbound parking lot; southbound cars would be stopped too, as the rubbernecking set in.

He had their attention now.

Finally someone was noticing David Hayneswiggle.

Hell, it was about time.

Chapter Forty-Three

D avid Hayneswiggle addressed the girl now, and he had to speak loudly over the thrum of traffic still headed south on the parkway. He actually had to shout to be heard. 'Ready? Are you ready? Hey, I'm talking to you. Don't act like I'm not here!'

The girl's boot heels scraped concrete as she tried to get farther away from him – from this madman who had already killed her boyfriend. The handcuff on her wrist cut deeply into her skin, but the pain didn't seem to matter. She was focused only on getting away from the weirdo in the Richard Nixon mask, that being him.

She was pretty enough, in a suburban-cheerleader kind of way. Lydia Ramirez, according to her driver's permit. Seventeen years old, but he took no pity on her. Adolescents were the most wretched humans of all. 'Okay, now don't move. I'll be right back for you. Hold that deer-in-the-headlights look.'

Hayneswiggle stood up again and checked out the scene below. The audience was assembled, and they seemed impatient for the show to continue. The highway was complete chaos now. Northbound traffic was already backed up along the Potomac.

The tipped van at the head of the line ensured that nearly all the stopped cars were on the south side of the walkway, facing him. A smashed Volvo directly below let out a hissing cloud of steam. A few of the onlookers were yelling up at him, but he couldn't tell what the hell they were saying. Probably just pissed because they'd been inconvenienced. *Well, screw them.*

'Can't hear you!' he shouted back. And that reminded him.

He picked something up from the sidewalk, one of the items he had brought with him for the show – a twenty-five-watt bullhorn with about a thousand-yard range.

He pointed it at the crowd. A few of the jackasses down there *ducked.* '*I'm baaa-acck!*' he announced. '*Did you miss me? Of course you did.*'

Several motorists who weren't already out of their cars got out now. A woman with a bloody forehead looked up at him in a daze.

'And you thought this was going to be an ordinary day, didn't you? Guess again, folks. Today is real special, one you'll never forget. You'll tell your grandchildren – that is, if this messed-up world of ours lasts that long. Hey, speaking of the world lasting, how many of you voted for Al Gore?'

He set down the bullhorn and took something out of his pocket, something that glared in the sunlight. Then he hunched over the girl, shielding her from view. A moment later, he stood again – with the girl in his arms.

'Here she is! Let's hear it for our little star, Lydia Ramirez.' Then, smiling broadly, he casually flipped her over the edge of the overpass. Just like that, like nothing.

The girl's legs and feet flew up into the air ahead of the rest of her. Then a metallic ringing sang out as the handcuff spun on the rail and caught hold. The audience gasped.

The girl crashed back against the bridge, her feet dangling directly over the highway.

'Fake out!' David Hayneswiggle said into the bullhorn. 'Look closely now. At *her,* please. Not at me. I told you, she's our star today. Pretend I'm not even here. That's how it's supposed to work. Look at her!'

As the audience stared, a dark curved line appeared on the girl's exposed throat. Then it became a sheet of red that ran down her neck and over her T-shirt. The people down below were finally beginning to realize what had happened – her throat had been cut.

Then she was still, other than the slightest rhythmic sway of her body.

'Okay, she's gone. Show's over. For today, anyway. Thank you all for coming. Thank you so much. Drive safely.'

People started honking their horns, and there was angry screaming. A police siren finally sounded from somewhere, but it was far off, unable to get through the backed-up traffic.

David Hayneswiggle started to run in a funny duck waddle. He bobbed around the hairpin turn at the far end of the ramp and disappeared into the bushes.

He knew that it didn't matter how many people saw which way he went. Hell, let them search for him all they liked.

Who were they going to look for, anyway – Richard Nixon?

Chapter Forty-Four

This was as sad and disturbing a homicide scene as I'd ever worked in my years with Metro or the FBI. Two young people were dead, and the murders seemed arbitrary and just plain cruel. The kids were definitely innocents in whatever was going on here.

The GW Parkway had been rerouted, but not without stranding at least a mile-long queue of cars still backed up on the roadway. They were now waiting for a flipped minivan to be cleared away by the police. That required a sign-off from Bree, who needed the medical examiner to finish with the two bodies. She had established Metro's jurisdiction here, but not without a heavy dose of animosity from the Arlington County Police Department, which didn't bother Bree in the least.

Helicopters flew overhead every few minutes, police and media, the latter always coming too close for comfort. I saw them as Peeping Toms with a license to look and to shoot film.

The crowd, many of whom had witnessed the actual murders, was a strange mixture of angry-aggressive and scared silly. They were a captive audience, though. We needed to identify some of them as our witnesses, then try to get everyone else moving again. The title of an old Broadway show popped into my head: *Stop the World – I Want to Get Off.* I really did.

The Virginia Highway Department was there in numbers, the state police too, and they were showing their impatience and ire with body language, if nothing else. Bree, Sampson, and I had divided our part of the workload as best we could. Bree was on the immediate crime scene, checking out all the physical evidence. Sampson had the killer's entry and exit from the scene, which had created a huge extended perimeter from the Potomac all the way into Rosslyn, Virginia. He had a team of Arlington cops working with him on-site.

My focus was on the killer and his mind-set at the time of the two murders. To ascertain this, I needed the best witnesses I could find, and I needed them in a big hurry. With a scene as sprawling as this one, I had no guarantee that the traffic wouldn't start moving again. For the moment, at least, the killer had stopped the world, and nobody was getting off unless he wanted them to.

Chapter Forty-Five

I did a quick assessment of the cars nearest the bridge, looking for solo white males. Make no mistake about it, I believe in profiling during emergency situations like this one. *The more a witness has in common with the criminal they've seen, the more reliable their testimony will be* – at least statistically speaking. That had also been my experience at homicide scenes again and again. So I was looking for white males, preferably alone in their vehicles.

I settled on a black Honda Accord about five car lengths back from the overpass. The man inside was sitting sideways to avoid looking ahead, and he had a cell phone pressed to his ear. His engine was running, with the windows rolled up.

I rapped hard on the glass. 'Metro Police. Excuse me, sir? Sir? Excuse me!'

He finally held up his index finger without actually looking around at me. *One minute?*

At that point, I opened the car door for him and showed my creds. '*Now*, sir? Please hang up the phone.'

'I gotta go,' he said to whoever, and stepped outside, full of piss and vinegar, I could tell. 'Officer, can you, or somebody, tell me how long we'll be stuck here?'

'Not long,' I said, rather than lecture him about the two kids who had just died. 'But I need you to tell me exactly what you saw happen on the overpass.'

He talked fast, with an irritating nonchalance, but his story corroborated what we'd gathered so far. The driver of the Honda had come to a halt seconds after the young male had been thrown down into traffic.

'At first, I didn't realize what the accident, or whatever, was all about. I just saw cars suddenly stopping in front of me. But then I saw the dead kid.' He pointed to the bridge. 'And the one up there. The girl who got her throat cut. Terrible shit. Tragic, right?' He asked the question as if he couldn't figure it out for himself.

'Right. Can you describe the man who was on the overpass? The killer?'

'Not really. He had on one of those Halloween masks. The rubber kind you put over your whole head? I think it was supposed to be Richard Nixon. I'm pretty sure. Does that make any sense?'

'It does. Thank you for your help,' I told the man. 'Another officer will come by to take down a few more particulars.'

The next eyewitness I spoke to was a limo driver, who told me the killer looked taller and much heavier than the female victim. Also that he wore a dark Windbreaker with no insignia that the driver could make out. And then a few vaguely recollected bits of what had been said over the bullhorn. 'That sonofabitch bastard yelled, *"I'm back!"* Those were his first words.'

'Did you notice if he had any kind of camera or recording device up there?' I asked.

The limo driver shook his head. 'I'm sorry, I honestly don't know. Not that I saw, anyway. There was a lot of confusion.'

'Still is,' I said, and patted the guy on the shoulder. 'Anything else you remember?'

The limo driver shook his head. 'I'm sorry.'

I managed to squeeze in four more witnesses before the GW was opened to traffic again. Any further accounting would have to come later; I'd gotten as much during the critical first hours as I could get. I hoped it would help, but I didn't think so. For someone who was putting on live shows, the killer was covering his tracks very well.

A few minutes later, Bree, Sampson, and I reconvened at the west end of the pedestrian bridge, where the killer had apparently fled, at least according to several of the witnesses.

'The bushes over there are all trampled down,' Sampson said, pointing to a stand of high grass out of sight from the road. 'For all we know, he had a motorcycle or something stashed away. So far, we've got nothing more on him.'

Bree added, 'No calling card, by the way.'

'That's a little weird,' I said. 'He forgot about his signature this time? Since when does that happen?'

'Or he changed his pattern,' said Sampson. 'Again, since when does that happen?'

'Or' – I finally said what had been bothering me for a while – 'this wasn't the same guy.'

Then Bree's cell went off. She listened, and her face couldn't have been any more grim.

Finally she looked at the two of us. 'Well, he's struck again. There's been another murder.'

Chapter Forty-Six

They weren't going to know what hit them this time. The killer had arrived at FedExField in Landover, Maryland, about two hours before kickoff for the first football game of the season. He grabbed a soda and a hot dog, then browsed the Hall of Fame Store, not really interested in buying – he wasn't a Redskins fan, not his hometown – but he wanted to blend in with the rest of the sports crowd.

For a while, anyway.

And then – he wanted to stand out. Really stand out. Make his bones. Play his role *in the fourth story.*

Out of the corner of his eye, he could see some of the football players warming up – kickers booming high, long punts and making field-goal attempts. It was going to be another sellout crowd – there had never been a Redskins home game that wasn't. There was about a thirty-year waiting list for season tickets.

And, man, did he love sellout crowds for his stories.

Some particularly high-spirited fans, the Hogettes, were singing 'Hail to the Redskins' slightly off-key and with off-color lyrics liberally sprinkled in, which seemed weird since there were lots of kids in the crowd. The so-called superfans wore bright-colored wigs and polka-dot blouses and plastic hog snouts. Some of them were smoking extra-long cigars, which enhanced their piggy image.

He hadn't gone quite that far with his outfit, but he was wearing a Redskins cap and jersey, and he had his face painted red and white, the home team's colors. His persona was that of a disgruntled fan named Al Jablonski. A good, solid role to play.

Ninety-one thousand fans packed the stadium, all waiting for Al Jablonski. They just didn't know it yet.

Close to game time, the First Ladies of football scampered onto the Technicolor-green field – masses of flying hair and pom-poms, skimpy red halter tops and white short shorts. *Family entertainment at its most all-American,* the killer couldn't help thinking.

'Are you ready for some *foot-ball?'* he shouted from the stands.'Some foos-ball!' A few fans around him joined in or laughed at the familiar line from the *Monday Night Football* TV show. Al Jablonski knew his audience, and his game.

The control booth for the stadium scoreboard was located underneath the huge sign. He knew the way and arrived there in time for the national anthem to be sung by a soprano marine from the base down in Quantico.

Al Jablonski knocked on the metal door, said, 'Couple of messages from Mr Snyder's office. Vanessa sent these down.'Vanessa was actually the name of one of the owner's assistants. Easy enough to find out.

The door opened. There were two guys inside – stat geeks, from the looks of them, real antiques. 'Hi, I'm Al Jablonski.' He shot them both, and the sound of the gun was completely lost under loud cheering from the crowd as the national anthem ended. Sort of took away his thunder.

So he sat at the geeks' computer and put a message up on the big stadium screen for all to see.

I'M BACK! AND I JUST WANTED TO MAKE THIS SUNDAY A REAL KILLER FOR EVERYBODY.

THE GUYS WHO USUALLY SEND OUT THESE ANNOYING MESSAGES AND PLUGS ARE DEAD INSIDE THE CONTROL BOOTH. SO ENJOY THE GAME WITHOUT ANY FURTHER INTERRUPTIONS FROM MANAGEMENT OR CORPORATE SPONSORS. PLEASE WATCH YOUR BACKS, AND YOUR FRONTS TOO. I'M IN THE BUILDING, AND I COULD BE ANYWHERE, AND ANYONE.

THIS IS SO MUCH BETTER THAN FOOTBALL, DON'T YOU THINK? *GO, SKINS!*

Chapter Forty-Seven

Kyle Craig had just heard the latest good news from Washington, DC, when his mother slowly opened the twelve-foot-high front door of the vacation house near Snowmass outside Aspen. When she saw who it was, the old woman fainted like somebody had hit her 'off' switch.

Kyle managed to catch dear old Mom before she struck the stonework floor, and he smiled to himself. *It was good to be home again, wasn't it?*

Moments later, he was reviving the old woman in the cavernous kitchen of the twelve-thousand-square-foot house. 'Are you okay? Miriam? Mother?'

'William?' she groaned when she looked up at the face staring down at her. 'Is that William?'

'Now how could that possibly be?' Kyle asked, and he frowned deeply. 'For once, just once, use the intelligence that you were given, that you *must* have been given. Your husband, my father – *William* – has been dead for a long time. I helped you bury the general in Alexandria. Don't you remember the glorious day? Sunny skies, crisp cool breeze, smell of burning leaves in the air. Good Lord, you're losing it, woman. People sent all those flowers – congratulating you on gaining your freedom from that hypocritical tyrant and bastard.'

Suddenly, Kyle clasped both hands to his face. 'Oh, my God. My fault! This is all my fault, Mother. *The mask!* These prosthetic masks are so damn realistic. I look just like Father in this one, don't I? Finally I'm living up to the old man's image for me.'

His mother began to scream, and he let her go on for a bit. There was no one around to hear her raving, anyway. His father had never allowed her household help when he was alive, and she still didn't have any staff. How typical was that? She had all the money in the world and nothing to spend it on.

He watched the pathetic old woman shake and twist her head back and forth. Ironically, her face was more masklike than his, a mask of one family's tragedy.

'No, it's just me. It's Kyle. I'm out and about again. I wanted to see you, of course, to visit. But the other reason I came – I need some money, Mom. Won't be here for more than a couple of minutes. You'll have to give me the numbers for the overseas accounts, though.'

After Kyle had finished at the computer in his father's old office, he felt like a new man. He was wealthy now, nearly four million trans-ferred into his account in Zurich, but even more important, he finally felt free. That didn't happen just because a man got out of prison. For some prisoners, the sense of freedom never came again, even if they did get to see the sun.

'But I'm free, free at last!' he shouted to the high rafters of the Colorado house. 'And I have important things to do. I have so many promises to keep.'

Chapter Forty-Eight

When he came back downstairs to say good-bye to his mom, he had discarded the rubber mask. He'd worn it on most of the drive from Florence to Aspen, but it probably wasn't wise to push his luck too far. The same could be said for being here at the house – except that few people knew his mother stayed here – and he did need the money after all, needed it for his plan, to make all his *nightmares* come true.

He snuck up on Miriam, whom he had hog-tied to his father's old lounge chair in the family room. Right in front of the twelve-foot-high fireplace. God, how many memories were here – his father screaming at him until his veins looked like they would burst, the general striking him so many times he lost count. And Miriam – never saying a word, pretending that she didn't know about the beatings, the tongue-lashings, the years of constant abuse.

'*Boo – Mommy!*' Kyle said as he popped up behind the old girl. He wondered if she remembered how he used to do this when he was just a little boy, five or six years old at the most. *Boo – Mommy! Pay attention to me, please?*

'Well, I'm through with the bulk of my business here in Colorado. I'm a wanted man, y'know, so I'd best hit the road. Oh dear, you're shaking like a leaf. Listen, sweetie, you're perfectly safe here in this house, this fortress of yours. Alarms everywhere. Even a snowmelt system on the walk and driveway.'

He leaned in close to her – smelled lavender, and it was like reliving a nightmare of things past, things gone terribly, terribly wrong in his life.

'I'm *not* going to murder you, for God's sake. Is that what you were thinking? No! No! No! I want you to watch what I do from now on. You're an important witness for me. I'm working to heap honor on you and Dad too.

'Speaking of which, tell me one thing – did you *know* that he struck me almost every day when I was a boy? Did you know that? Tell me that one thing. It will stay between the two of us. I won't tell Oprah or anything like that. No memoirs for me. I'm no James Frey or Augusten Burroughs.'

It took her nearly a minute to get the words out. 'Kyle . . . I didn't, I didn't know. What are you talking about, anyway? You always made things up.'

He smiled down at her. 'Ahhh. That's a relief.'

Then he pulled out a Beretta, one of the guns Mason Wainwright had left for him in his car.

'Changed my mind, Mom. Sorry. I've wanted to do this for so long. I've ached to do it. Now watch this. Watch the little black hole at the end of the barrel. You see that? Tiny eternal abyss? Watch the hole, watch the hole, watch the abyss, and—'

Bang!

He shot his mother right between the eyes. Shot her a couple of times for good measure. Then he left a few clues behind for the investigators who would show up at the house eventually.

Clue #1: In the kitchen – a half-finished bottle of Arthur Bryant's barbecue sauce.

Clue #2: Propped on the bedroom dresser, a Hallmark card with no handwritten message.

Not easy clues but clues all the same. Something for the hunters to go on.

If they were any good at their jobs.

If Alex Cross was one of those hot on his trail, anyway.

'Catch me if you can, Dr Detective. Figure out all the puzzles, and the murders will stop. But I doubt that's what is going to happen. I could be wrong, but I don't think anybody could catch me twice.'

Chapter Forty-Nine

When Bree Stone arrived at work on Monday morning, the phone on her desk was already ringing. She set down an empty Slim-Fast can – she'd downed two on the way to the office – and snatched up the receiver. She'd been thinking about Alex, but now that nice thought was gone.

'Bree, it's Brian Kitzmiller. Listen, I have something pretty neat to show you.'

'Something pretty *neat*, Kitz? What might that be? A new game for your Wii? You are a piece of work, you know that?'

She shrugged her work bag back onto her shoulder. 'I can be there in a few minutes.'

'Not necessary. Stay right where you are. Do you happen to be near a computer?'

'Of course I am. Who isn't nowadays?'

As soon as she was online, Kitz directed her to a site called Serial Times.net. Bree rolled her eyes as she brought up the site. *What now?* The home page was a crowded and sloppy-looking collection of thumbnail images, 'unofficial' updates, and actual news items. Really sick, gross stuff. Right up there with the worst she'd seen.

The most prominent item was a red-bordered box with the headline

Exclusive! Don't miss this!
Message from DCAK!
Click here.

'And I'm supposed to believe this is for real?' she asked, then added, 'Is it, Kitz?'

'Just click it. Then you tell me.'

The next window had a black background with a short message in the same white typewriter font as the killer's original blog, which was one of hundreds of leads she had followed that didn't seem to go anywhere.

The familiar look of the site wasn't what definitely answered Bree's question, though. It was the two images pasted in at the top of the screen: a small Iraqi flag and a bright-green *X-Files X* – symbols from the first two homicides.

Yeah, they seemed to say, *it's me.*

'Those two items aren't public knowledge yet, are they?' Kitzmiller asked. 'Am I right?'

Bree shook her head as if he could see her, then mumbled, 'No, they aren't, Kitz. We've kept them to ourselves.' She was already reading the message below. The latest mindblower.

'Imitation is the sincerest form of flattery,' – Charles Caleb Colton

I'm setting the record straight for everybody who cares, or ought to care, about these things. That piece of shit work out at the George Washington Memorial Parkway? Someone else did that, not me. I'll take the flattery, but don't try to pin that one here, 'cause I don't want it. I mean, 'Nixon' just copycatted what I did at the Riverwalk! Didn't even have the nerve to show his face. Plus, the work itself was amateurish. Not worthy of me or those I model myself on.

FedExField – that one was yours truly. Took some balls to get in and out of there. Imagine making a kill in a closed-in public area like that.

Make no mistake. There is only one DCAK. When it's me, you'll know it. You'll know because I'll tell you.

And the work will be done with some imagination and flair. Give me a little respect. I think I've earned that much.

At least now the police have someone they can catch – this imitator! Isn't that right, Detective Bree Stone? 'Cause you're not even close to catching me, are you?

Keep on living, fuckers.
—DCAK

For the next few seconds, Bree stood there, shaking her head back and forth. Alex had been right about the parkway murders . . . and probably everything else.

Chapter Fifty

P *lus, DCAK had used her name.*

Bree finally sat back in her chair and tried to process that little nugget. She couldn't believe how brazen and arrogant this prick was, and how completely messed up. And scary.

'Bree? You still there?' Brian Kitzmiller asked over the phone.

'Yeah. I'm here. Just having a depressed-cop moment. That was pretty neat, all right.'

'You okay? Other than the obvious?'

She focused on her hands, which were shaking only a little bit. 'Yeah, Kitz. Thanks for asking. It's creepy, but it makes sense to me. He's probably a total junkie for his own coverage. Of course he knows who I am. And of course he knows about Alex. He's watching us, Kitz.'

'In one way, that's good news, isn't it? We wanted to make sure we were in the same communication stream as the killer. I think we're there.'

'Ya think?' Bree's mind was racing with all kinds of questions. 'When was this posted?'

'Eleven twenty last night. It's already burning up the chat rooms. It's everywhere, and I mean everywhere.'

'That might explain *these* calls.' She picked up the stack of pink message slips already in her in-box. The top one was from Channel Seven news. 'Listen, I need a name to work with. Something solid. Whose site is this?'

'Still working on that. I've got an IP address, and I'm checking all the major registries. With any luck, I'll have a name for you soon. Operative word – *luck.*'

'I hear you. Soon is good, though. Thanks, Kitz. We need you on this one.'

'Yeah, I agree. You definitely do. I wonder who he "models" himself after? You got any ideas?'

'No, but I bet Alex will.'

Bree hung up, then tried Alex and Sampson. She reached voice mail for both of them and left the same message: 'Hey, it's me. Something just came up. Another posted message from our Audience Killer, now signing off with the shortened form "DCAK". I'm moving on it as soon as I have an address. I hope one of you will get this before then, but I'm lining up a backup unit in the meantime. Call me ASAP.'

Bree knew she'd work better with her partners than with a couple of uniformed cops, but the second she had a name and address, it would be *go time*.

DCAK wanted to know her better – well, he just might get his wish soon.

Chapter Fifty-One

I saw the light on my phone flashing, but I didn't answer calls during therapy sessions. So I let it go for the moment, and then I worried about it.

'Who was that I saw on my way in here?' Anthony Demao was asking. I had to juggle my clients' schedules around some to accommodate my new lifestyle. 'Another cuckoo clock like me?'

I smiled at Anthony's usual irreverence. 'Neither of you is cuckoo. Well, maybe a little.'

'Well, she may be crazy, a *little* crazy, but she sure is good-looking. She gave me a smile. I *think* it was a smile. She's shy, right? I can tell.'

He was talking about Sandy Quinlan, my schoolteacher patient. Sandy was attractive, a good lady, maybe a little cuckoo, but who wasn't these days?

I changed the subject. Anthony certainly wasn't here to talk about my other patients. 'Last time, you started to tell me about your army unit's push toward Basra,' I said. 'Can we talk about that today?'

'Sure.' He shrugged. 'That's what I'm here for, right? You fix cuckoo clocks.'

After Anthony Demao left, I checked my voice mail. *Bree.* I caught up with her on her cell.

'Good timing,' she said. 'I'm in the car with Sampson. We'll come get you. Guess what? It looks like you were right again. Must get boring.'

'What was I right about?'

'Copycat. On the GW Parkway with those kids. That's what DCAK says, anyway. Says he did FedExField but not the two murders on the overpass.'

'Well, he would probably know.'

I met Bree and Sampson on Seventh Street and climbed into the back of her Highlander. 'Where are we going?' I asked as she pulled out in a hurry.

Bree explained as she drove, but I had to interrupt her halfway through. 'Hold on, Bree. He used your name? He knows about you too? What are we doing with that?'

'Nothing, for now,' she said. 'I'm feeling pretty *special*, though. How 'bout you? You feeling honored?'

Sampson shrugged at me in a way that said he'd already had the same conversation with her and obviously with the same result. Bree showed no fears, at least I'd never seen any.

'By the way,' Bree said, 'he claims he models himself after people. Any ideas on that?'

'Kyle Craig,' I said. It just came out. 'Let me think about it some.'

Kitzmiller had provided Bree with the name Braden Thompson, a systems analyst with a firm called Captech Engineering. We double-parked outside Captech's dull, modern-looking building, then took the elevator up to the fourth floor.

'Braden Thompson?' Bree asked the receptionist, and held up her MPD badge and card.

The woman picked up her phone, her eyes still on Bree's creds. 'I'll see if he's available.'

'No, no. He's available, trust me. Just point the way. We'll find him. We're *detectives*.'

We walked calmly and quietly through the bustling office but didn't make any less of a scene for it. Secretaries' heads turned, office doors opened, and workers checked us out as if we were here with the take-out food.

A white plastic plaque etched with Thompson's name marked a windowed office on the north side of the building. Bree opened the door without knocking.

'Can I *help* you?' Braden Thompson was about what you'd expect for somebody working here: paunchy, fortysomething white guy in a short-sleeved shirt and tie, possibly a clip-on.

'Mr Thompson, we'd like to talk with you,' Bree said. 'We're Metro Police.'

He looked past her at me and Sampson. 'All three of you?'

'That's right.' Bree was inscrutable. And the truth was, none of us wanted to miss this interview. 'You're an important guy.'

Chapter Fifty-Two

'**B**rady, is everything *okay*?' a high-pitched female voice asked Thompson from behind us.

'It's fine, Ms Blanco. I don't need any help. Thank you, Barbara.' He motioned for us to come inside. 'Close the door, please.'

As soon as we were alone with him, his voice went up a step too. 'What are you people doing? This is my place of business.'

'Do you know why we're here?' Bree asked.

'I know exactly why you're here. Because I exercised my First Amendment rights. I didn't break any laws, and I'd like you to leave. *Now*. You all remember the way to the door?'

Sampson stepped forward. '*Brady*, is it?' He looked over the things on Thompson's desk as he continued. 'I was just wondering how your bosses here might feel about that creepy little Web site of yours. You think they'll be cool with it?'

Thompson pointed an index finger at him. 'I haven't done anything illegal. I'm well within my rights.'

'Yeah,' Sampson said. 'That really wasn't my question, though. I just wondered how your employer might feel about SerialTimes.net.'

'You have no right to use that information if I haven't broken the law.'

'In fact, we do,' I put in. 'But we're assuming we won't have to, because we're assuming you're going to tell us where that message came from.'

'First of all, Detective, I couldn't tell you if I wanted to. DCAK's not an idiot, okay? Haven't you figured that out for yourselves by now? And second, I'm not fifteen years old. You'll have to do better than you're doing. A lot better.'

'Do you mean like a subpoena for your home system?' Bree asked. 'We can do that.'

Thompson adjusted his glasses and sat back now, beginning to like the position he was in. I could see why. I wasn't sure that we could get a subpoena for his home system, much less arrest him. 'Actually, no. Assuming you don't have your subpoena with you – probably because you were just too damn eager to get over here – I can make sure that my server doesn't have anything more than *Peanuts* cartoons on it by the time you get there. And I don't even have to leave this chair to do it.'

He looked up at us, calm as could be now. 'You obviously don't know much about information transfer.'

'Do you know what the hell is going on out there in the real world?' I finally said. 'Do you have any interest in seeing someone like that murderer stopped?'

'Of course I do,' he snapped back. 'Stop insulting my intelligence and think about it for a second. *The big picture?* Constitutional rights – your rights, my rights – hinge on exactly this kind of thing. I have the right to do everything I did, and I don't just mean that morally. It's your job to uphold the constitution, Detectives, and it's our job, as citizens, to make sure that you do. See how it works?'

'See how *this* works?' Sampson lunged, but we caught him in time. Everything on one side of Thompson's desk went flying.

Brady stood up, a bit brazen even, as Sampson stared at him. 'I think we're done here,' he said.

But Sampson wasn't. 'You know what—'

'*Yes,*' Bree said. 'We're done, Brady. For the moment, anyway. We're leaving.'

As we turned to go, Thompson spoke again, more conciliatory than before. 'Detectives? You obviously think my little posting is real or you wouldn't be here. Will you just tell me if it has something to do with the iconography?' This guy was a true fan, a real freak. He couldn't help himself, could he?

Bree couldn't help herself either. With the door halfway open and a small crowd of office workers gathered behind her, she turned to face Braden Thompson.

'I can't comment on that, sir. Not at this time. But let me reassure you that we won't mention your Web site, SerialTimes.net, anywhere outside this office unless it's absolutely necessary.'

Bree smiled at Braden Thompson, then lowered her voice. 'Keep on living, fucker.'

Chapter Fifty-Three

Pissed off at the world in general, and at Braden Thompson in particular, the three of us showed up at the Daly Building. We didn't get very far before Superintendent Davies headed us off. 'Over here,' he barked, then turned and walked back to his office. 'The three of you, *now.*'

We looked at one another, not liking the vibe.

'Why do I feel like I'm about to get detention and miss football practice?' Sampson muttered.

'Yeah,' Bree said, 'and cheerleading practice too. Oh, wait, I wasn't ever a cheerleader.'

Bree and I wiped the smirks off our faces before we went in.

'Can you explain *this?*' Davies flipped a newspaper around on his desk.

There was a story above the fold in the *Post*'s metro section, 'Audience Killer Copycat Theory Surfaces.'

I wasn't surprised by the headline so much as reminded about how fast these stories can spread and get out to the press.

Bree answered for the group. 'We just learned about it this morning ourselves. Even right now we're coming from—'

'Don't give me a lot of explanations, Detective Stone. In my book, that's only a step up from an excuse. Just do something about it.' He twisted his neck a few times, as if he were trying to undo the pain we'd put there.

'Excuse me, sir,' Bree said. 'This isn't the kind of information we can control. Not once it's been—'

Davies cut her off again. 'I don't need a lesson in damage control.

I need you to take care of the mess. This is Major Case Squad. Your superiors aren't a safety net. You need to respond to the problems *before* I ask you to respond to them. Do you understand me?'

'Of course I understand you,' Bree said. 'I don't need a lesson in damage control either. Apparently, neither does DCAK.'

Suddenly, Davies smiled, and it was totally unexpected. 'You see why I like her?' he asked Sampson and me.

Yeah, I was pretty sure that I did.

Chapter Fifty-Four

There was no new part for DCAK to play today, no gruesome murder planned. So the killer was just being himself. He decided to go online again before dinner, couldn't resist hearing about himself. And he wasn't disappointed.

The message boards on the Internet were full of chatter about DCAK! True, much of it was tabloid or fantasy stuff, but that didn't matter. The point was, *they were talking.*

SerialTimes didn't have anything new. Neither did Sicknet or SKcentral. That made sense. His fans were waiting for his next move.

Finally he clicked into a couple of the chats. It was good to be among 'his people' at the end of a long day. He even used a first name here, as a 'gift' to them. Not that anyone would know that he did, but the contact felt more personal. Besides, he was into dropping clues.

In his honor, of course.

AARON_AARON: What's up, DCAK lovers?

GINSOAKED: Copycat, duh. Where you been?

AARON_AARON: No shit, duh. What else? Anybody? Anything?

REDRUM5: Been quiet. Busy weekend. He deserves some rest, right? Any day now, bet. Watch his smoke!!!!

DCAK-FAN: How do you know so much?

REDRUM5: I don't. Just a theory of mine. Just my opinion. Okay with you?

AARON_AARON: Maybe he's been busy already today.

DCAK-FAN: Busy, like what?

The killer sipped the white wine he'd poured for himself, a nice chardonnay. He deserved it. He didn't like to brag, but then again, that's not what this was. More like stepping into the light. Or having a curtain call after a brilliant performance.

AARON_AARON: Okay, what if he copycatted himself? Think about it for a sec.

GINSOAKED: You mean, like, he did the parkway and FedExField and then said he didn't do it?

AARON_AARON: Yeah, exactly. What if?

GINSOAKED: Freakin' brill.

ADAMEVE: I'm all over that too.

REDRUM5: No way. Did you read the public file? Any of you?

AARON_AARON: So what? I wouldn't put it past him. This dude is a total master mindfucker. I'm sure we won't be able to guess what's coming next. Hey, by the way, what does everybody think about that dude Kyle Craig getting out of stir early?

DCAK-FAN: KC is so yesterday, man. Who cares?

The killer looked up from his computer. He was being summoned. 'Dinner's ready! Come and get it or I'll throw it away.'

Chapter Fifty-Five

The press conference scheduled for this afternoon was Bree's first as lead investigator on a murder case anywhere near this size. She'd spoken with reporters plenty of times, just not a room filled with every media type in the city and several national outlets too – which was what we were expecting today. At least that.

'Will you go up there with me?' she asked. We were working over the prepared statement in her office. 'The press knows you, and the public has seen you before. I think it'll send the right signal to keep things a little calmer.'

I looked up from the draft in front of me. 'Yeah, sure. If that's what you want.'

'Yeah, that's what I want. Okay, I'm nervous,' Bree said next, surprising me with the admission.

'You'll do great,' I told her, because I believed it to be true. 'Introduce me at the beginning, and then you'll have a seamless pass-off if there's anything you want me to take. I'll just be there for backup.'

Bree finally grinned. 'Thanks. You're the best.'

Right, and isn't that what got me involved in this mess?

But then she gave me a big hug and whispered, 'I love you. And I look forward to paying the debt. I *really* look forward to that.'

We got to our improvised pressroom at four thirty, plenty of time to make the six o'clock news, which was the whole idea. Every seat was already taken, plus there were reporters and cameras gathered in a *U* around the perimeter. 'Dr Cross! Detective Stone!' The photographers called out our names, trying to get a good shot.

'Never let 'em see you sweat,' I said to Bree.

'Too late for that.'

She stepped to the podium, introduced me, and began her statement without using notes. *She's smooth, good at this,* I thought, *very poised and confident.* The press liked her too. I could tell that right away.

I stood to the side, just close enough to be in Bree's peripheral vision when the questions came.

The first couple were softballs that she handled easily. No hits, no runs, no errors.

Tim Pullman from Channel Four got in the first toughie. 'Detective, will you now confirm the existence of a copycat killer? Or is it just conjecture?'

The question made me wonder if he had even listened to her initial statement, but Bree patiently went over it all again.

'Tim, the evidence points that way – toward a copycat – but we're not in a position to rule anything in or out conclusively, pending further investigation of the message that was sent. We're on it. The FBI is involved too. Everybody is working overtime, believe me.'

'When you say *message,* do you mean the posting on SerialTimes?' someone yelled out from the back.

'That's right, Carl. Like I said a minute ago. If you were listening?'

The same reporter continued, undeterred by Bree's mild zinger. He was a short redheaded man whom I recognized from one of the cable channels. 'Detective, can you explain how this Web site has remained online despite the strenuous objections of the victims' families? What's with that?'

We hadn't actually been briefed on this – the families – so I watched Bree closely, ready to jump in if she wanted me to. That would be her call.

'We're trying to leave open the possibility of dialogue with all suspects in these killings. We'd welcome their direct communication, and for the sake of resolving this as quickly as possible, we've decided not to close any established channels. Including the Web site.'

'*Why the hell not? Why not close it down now?*' An angry shout came from the back of the room. Heads and cameras swiveled around. I caught sight of a man, Alberto Ramirez. *Oh, brother!* It was his daughter Lydia who had been killed on the parkway overpass.

Chapter Fifty-Six

The grieving father's voice was tight but unwavering. 'What about what's best for my daughter Lydia? And for her poor mother? And her three sisters? Why do we have to be subjected to that kind of filth after everything else that's happened to our family? What's the matter with you people?'

No reporter jumped in with another question, not while the father had the floor. This was as good for them as it was bad for the MPD.

'Mr Ramirez,' Bree said. I was glad that she recognized the slain girl's father and used his name. 'We're all terribly sorry for your loss. I would like to meet with you about this matter immediately after the press conference—'

Some invisible barrier of restraint and protocol broke then, and a barrage of questions came firing at Bree from every direction.

'Is it the policy of the MPD to disregard community input?' asked some young wise guy from the *Post*.

'How do you plan to keep *additional* copycats from cropping up?'

'Is Washington safe for anyone right now? And if not, why not?'

I thought that I knew what we ought to do next. I leaned in toward Bree with a slightly exaggerated finger to my watch. 'Time's up,' I whispered by way of advice. 'Feeding time at the zoo is over.'

She nodded in agreement, then held up her hands to be heard. 'Ladies and Gentlemen, that's all the questions we can take right now. We'll work to keep you as informed as possible, as frequently as possible. Thank you for your patience.'

'My daughter is dead!' Alberto Ramirez was shouting from the rear. 'My little girl died on your watch! My Lydia is dead!'

It was a terrible indictment, and I knew it rang true, at least for the press. Most of them knew that we were looking for a needle in a haystack, how impossible this kind of manhunt was, but they wouldn't report it that way. They preferred their own bullshit act, sanctimonious and dumb.

Chapter Fifty-Seven

Kyle Craig was on the road again, and he was excited to be moving fast through time and space and fantasy. For a while during the car ride east, he let the sameness of the farms and fields rush past him and cool his overheated brain. Then – finally – he arrived in Iowa City, which was surrounded by rolling hills and woods and which he knew to be a picturesque and much-loved college town. Just what he needed for the next step in his plan, or his 'recovery program,' as he liked to call it.

It took him another half hour to find the main library building at the University of Iowa, which was situated east of the Iowa River on Madison Street. He had to show one of several IDs and then locate a computer that he could use for a while. A nice, quiet reading room would be perfect for his needs.

At this moment, Kyle knew two ways to get a message to DCAK. The more complicated involved the use of steganography, which would mean sending a message hidden in a picture or audio file. He didn't think he needed to go to that much trouble just yet. Nobody seemed to know about his relationship to the killer in DC. Or, as he knew, *the killers*.

Instead, he chose a faster, low-tech method. He knew how and where to locate DCAK from Mason Wainwright, his former lawyer and loyal fan. He typed in www.myspace.com, then clicked on a name from 'Cool New People.' Easy as that, actually.

He typed a message to DCAK, wanting to strike just the right tone.

It's good to be free again, free in the way that only you and I can understand. The possibilities are endless now, don't you think? I marvel at your art and your exquisitely complex mind. I have followed every event closely – that is, as closely as I could under the circumstances. Now that I'm out and around, I would like to meet with you in person. Leave me a message if this is as desirable to you as it is to me. I believe we could do even greater things together.

What Kyle Craig kept to himself were his true feelings about DCAK. The word he wanted to type and send out to the killer was *amateur.* Or perhaps *imitation,* if he wanted to be kind.

Chapter Fifty-Eight

No one who hadn't spent time in a supermaximum-security prison could possibly understand his feelings now. That night in Iowa City – wearing another of his prosthetic masks – Kyle Craig roamed around, taking in the sights, savoring being there.

He checked out the campus, which was situated on both sides of the river. The school was nicely integrated into the downtown area, and there were lots of quaint clothing, jewelry, and bookstores, and an incredible number of places to eat and drink. He happened on something interesting called the Iowa Avenue Literary Walk, which featured the words of writers with 'Iowa ties' – Tennessee Williams, Kurt Vonnegut, even Flannery O'Connor, one of his favorites because she was so wonderfully wrong in the head.

Just past nine, he stopped into a bar called the Sanctuary. It looked like it might actually cater to some adults, not just college students, so he wouldn't stand out too much. There were oodles of wainscoting inside and booths that looked like old church pews. And, yes indeed, an older crowd.

'Yes, sir. What can I get you?' he heard the very instant he sat at the bar.

The bartender looked as if he'd probably been a student at the university and then had decided to stay in town, which seemed like a reasonable choice. White-blond hair cut short, with a contemporary flip in the front. Probably midtwenties. Depressingly dull from the look of his eyes and his broad, welcoming smile.

'How ya doing, buddy?' said Craig. No more or less than a cordial greeting. He asked about the wines, then ordered a Brunello di

Montalcino that seemed to tower in quality above the other reds served in the restaurant.

'The Brunello is available only by the bottle. I don't know if I made that clear, sir.'

'It's not a problem. I'm not driving after I leave here,' Kyle Craig said, and affected a pleasant chuckle. 'I'll take the bottle. Uncork it and let it breathe for me, please. And I'd like the Brie-and-apple appetizer. Could they please cut a fresh apple?'

'I could help you with that Brunello. If you need help?'

A voice – female – came from Kyle's right. He turned and saw a woman seated a few stools away. She was by herself. Smiling pleasantly at him. *Police?* he wondered. Then – *No.* Then – *Unless she's very good at what she does.*

'I'm Camille Pogue,' she said, and smiled in a manner that struck him as both shy and slightly sly. Dark hair, petite, probably no more than five feet in her stockings. Mid-to-late thirties, he guessed. Obviously lonely, though she shouldn't be, given her looks, which interested him somewhat. He was drawn to people who had a little complexity to them, at least until he had them figured out.

'I think I'd enjoy the company,' Kyle said, and cast a smile back her way. Nothing too aggressive. 'I'm Alex . . . Cross. Nice to meet you.'

'Hello, Alex.'

Kyle moved down the bar and sat beside Camille, and they talked rather easily for the next half hour or so. She turned out to be bright and only mildly neurotic on the face of things. She taught art history at the university, specializing in the Italian Renaissance. She had lived in Rome, Florence, and Venice, and now she was back in the United States but not sure if she wanted to stay here, meaning in America, not just Iowa City.

'Because America isn't as you remembered it or because it is exactly as you remembered it?' Kyle asked.

She laughed. 'I think it's a little of both, Alex. The political naïveté and indifference in the States just drives me crazy sometimes. But what bothers me most is the conformity. It's a cancer, and it appears to be spreading, especially in the media. Everybody seems afraid to have an opinion of their own.'

Kyle nodded. 'You might accuse me of the latter for saying this, Camille, but I couldn't agree more.'

She leaned in close but not in a way that could be off-putting or threatening. 'So, are you different, Alex?' she asked.

'I'm different, I think. No, I'm sure that I am. In a good way, of course.'

'Of course.'

They walked around the town square after they finished off the Brunello. Then she took him home to a pretty gray-and-white Colonial on a side street off Clinton, with window boxes bursting with colorful flowers. The teacher had the entire ground floor, which was decorated with European furniture and art, and was quite spacious and open and welcoming. Another side of her revealed, a nice side too. *Homey? Homespun?*

'Have you eaten, Alex? Other than your apple and cheese? Your freshly cut apple,' she said, swinging toward him, a bit more forward inside her own place. She had soft breasts, but the rest of her seemed firm. Very nice and desirable, and suddenly Kyle knew exactly how he wanted her. Actually, he felt an incredible rush of lust.

But first, he yanked off his mask – and her eyes went wide with wonder and fear. 'Oh no!' she said.

Not wishing to waste any more time, Kyle thrust forward the ice pick that he had palmed in his right hand. The point passed through the front of Camille's throat and slid all the way out the back. Her blue eyes went to the size of silver dollars, then seemed to roll back into her forehead. Then she was no more, submitting to his waiting arms.

'That'll do it. Now let's make love, shall we?' Kyle said to the dead professor. 'I told you I was different, didn't I?'

Before he departed from Camille Pogue's apartment, he left another clue for whoever might come to collect the body. The clue was a small figurine representing a somewhat famous Midwestern statue called *The Scout*. It would be out of place in the art professor's apartment, but he doubted that anyone would get it.

That was fine with Kyle – *he* got it. As Kevin Bacon had so eloquently said in the magnificent movie *Diner*, it was 'a smile.'

Chapter Fifty-Nine

The next day held two very nasty surprises for me, as surprises so often are. The first was news that Kyle Craig had murdered his mother out in Colorado. And he had left a Hallmark greeting card – unsigned – for us to find. That meant either he was getting confidential information from a source inside the MPD or somehow he was communicating with the killer, with DCAK. *Was that possible? And if it was, what the hell was the relationship between the two of them?*

This wasn't the first time Kyle had communicated with other killers, I knew. There had been Casanova and the Gentleman Caller, possibly Mr Smith. *And now DCAK? Maybe even the lawyer in Colorado had been a killer. Or was he just a follower? A devotee?*

Late in the day, I received the second jolt, and it came from Brian Kitzmiller, who called and asked me to check out something on the Internet. He directed me to the site in question. Great news – somebody had set up a blog for me. I began to read and felt a little sick as I did.

You call yourself the Dragon Slayer? What's that about? Fantasy role-playing games? Are you a gamer, Cross? What excites you? Moves you? You've piqued my curiosity. After all, you are the one who caught the great Kyle Craig.

Let's say I'm watching you and your family a great deal these days. And I notice you're spending a lot of 'alone time' in little Ali's bedroom late at night. Am I wrong about that? I don't think so, but feel free to defend yourself from all accusations and rumors.

And Bree Stone – what are we to make of her? Who was the last female you managed to see for any length of time?

You're an insomniac, right? Of course I'm right. Well, wait until you see what's coming soon. And the day after that. And the day after that.

Sweet dreams, Dr Detective Cross

And then there were photographs.

Of the house on Fifth Street.

The cars in the driveway.

Nana Mama leaving the house with Ali.

Bree, Sampson, and me at FedExField after we were called over there.

He was watching us – *we were the ones under surveillance.*

Chapter Sixty

No one exactly gets why Sampson and I like Zinny's, not even us, which is probably one of the reasons we're attracted to it. It's a long black box of a joint in Southeast, just a bar and some booths, with a floor that's never even close to being clean. Sampson, Bree, and I brought Brian Kitzmiller there late that night for a little Southeast initiation, but mostly because none of us could stop working this case.

Things were crazier than ever. There was the possibility that Kyle Craig was involved in some strange way, and maybe DCAK was watching us. *Maybe even tonight?*

Some pieces were starting to come together. Tess Olsen had been writing a book about Craig called *The Mastermind. Was Kyle behind any of this? Or all of it?* It fit his pattern. He had contacted killers before – and used them. *If he was the brain, then what were the roles of DCAK and the lawyer Mason Wainwright? And were there any others in on the game?*

Bree brought over the first round of drinks. 'This one's on me, guys. Thanks for everything so far. I owe you. *You* especially,' she said, and kissed the side of my head. I have no idea why, but just that got me horny for Bree. I wished the two of us were alone now. At her place, in my car, anywhere at all would be just fine.

She sat down beside me and lifted her glass high. 'Here's to a really shitty couple of days. I'd have gone home, but I know Mr Ramirez would still be in my dreams. And his dead daughter too – and her three sisters. And Mrs Olsen.'

'There's a madman running around out there. Couple of them,

maybe. It happens,' Sampson said. 'Not your fault, Bree. I feel for the man, but Ramirez was out of line.'

'Listen,' Kitz said, 'here's an idea. Maybe a little crazy. So it *must* be good, right? Have you guys ever heard of the Unhinged Tour?'

I lowered my beer. 'I've seen a few mentions online. What about it? Speaking of crazies . . .'

'It's one of the touring shows about serial killers. But the point is *it's in Baltimore* in a couple of days.'

'Show?' Sampson asked. 'Like onstage?'

'More like a convention,' Kitz said. 'They call it a "gathering for people with an interest in forensic psychology."'

'Meaning serial-killer *freaks*. And, let me guess, comic-book geeks too?' Sampson said.

Kitz nodded, smiled, sipped his beer. 'You got it right. That's the demo.' He went on, 'We'd have to scramble a little, but I don't think they'd say no to a groundbreaking lecture on an open serial case, especially this one. Dr Alex Cross could probably headline if he wanted to. At a minimum, it would draw a roomful of ideal field witnesses. That alone would get us a broader-based investigation. Maybe open up a few new channels.'

Bree started to laugh. 'You *are* crazy, Kitz. Couldn't hurt, though. And if we're lucky, really fortunate, we'll draw in DCAK himself. He says he likes to watch us, after all.'

Kitz nodded, then grinned mischievously. 'Who the hell knows how his mind works? Something like this could be irresistible to someone like him. Or his copycat. So what do you say?'

We looked at one another, trying to think of a good reason why we shouldn't go ahead with Kitz's idea.

'This isn't really a *Cyber* thing, is it?' Bree finally said. 'How do you know so much?'

'Oh, you know. Word gets around.' Kitz sounded almost breezy.

Sampson's face lit up. He slapped the table and pointed at Kitzmiller. 'You go to these freaky things, don't you? *On your own time.*'

'No, no.' Kitz picked up his drink again, then added quietly, 'Not anymore.'

The three of us started to laugh, which was a good thing, real good, a necessary release.

Bree leaned into him and purred, 'Ohh, Kitzy, you're a full-blown geek, aren't you?'

'And he cleans up so nice,' I said.

'What about you guys?' Kitz asked. 'Anyone remind you lately what you do for a living? Just because you don't go to the public shows doesn't mean you aren't cut from the same cloth as the people who do.'

We gave him about five seconds of respectful silence before we laughed in his face again.

But then I added, 'Folks, I do believe we have an op to run.'

'But not tonight,' Bree said, hooking her arm into mine, then escorting me out of Zinny's. 'All this freaking talk,' she whispered to me, 'it's got me going. Besides, like I said – *I owe you.*'

'And I plan to collect.'

'With interest, I hope.'

We lasted all the way over to her place, but just barely, and not to the bedroom.

Chapter Sixty-One

Incoming! Again. I got the shock of my relatively new private-practice life early the next morning, and I hadn't even made it to my first appointment before it happened. An earlier cancellation had me at the office a little later than usual, just after seven thirty, sipping coffee from Starbucks as I came in through the front door, still thinking about Bree and last night, and what I hoped would be many nights to come.

I'd be starting my sessions with Sandy Quinlan at eight; then the Desert Storm vet Anthony Demao; followed by Pentagon worker Tanya Pitts, who was having recurring suicidal thoughts and who needed to see me five days a week, maybe seven, but could only afford one, so I comped her an extra session each week.

As I turned into the waiting area from the outside hallway, I was surprised to see that Sandy Quinlan was already there.

So was Anthony. He wore a black muscle-T undershirt and had another long-sleeved shirt draped over his lap.

What the hell was going on here?

For the few seconds before they realized I was standing there in the room with them, Sandy's hand was playing underneath the shirt on Anthony's lap.

She was giving him a hand job in the waiting room!

'Hey.' I interrupted the action. 'Hey, hey. That's enough of that. What do you think you're doing?'

'Oh, my God.' Sandy jumped up and shielded her eyes with both hands. 'I'm so sorry. I'm so embarrassed. I have to go. I have to go now, Dr Cross.'

'No. Just stay right there,' I told her. 'You too, Anthony. Nobody goes anywhere. We need to talk.'

Anthony's expression was somewhere between neutral and, for lack of a better word, interrupted. But he wouldn't actually look at me. 'Sorry about that,' he mumbled into his goatee.

'Sandy, would you come on into my office?' I said. 'Anthony, I'll see you when I'm finished with Sandy.'

'Yeah, yeah,' he answered. 'I get it.'

Once I had her in my office, it took a while for the two of us to recover somewhat.

'Sandy, I don't even know what to say to you,' I finally said. 'You *knew* I'd come in and catch the two of you, didn't you?'

'I know. Of course. I'm so sorry, Dr Cross.' Her voice shook as she squeezed out the words. I almost felt sorry for her, but not quite.

'Why do you think that happened in there?' I continued. 'It's not like you, is it?'

'It *is* totally unlike me.' Sandy rolled her eyes at herself. 'I know how this will sound, Dr Cross, but he's . . . cute. I told you I was sexually frustrated. Oh, God.' Her eyes welled up. 'I am such an idiot. This is my pattern. Acting out for attention. Here we go again.'

I decided to try another tack and got up to top off my coffee from the second cup in my bag. 'Let me ask you this. What was in it for you?'

'"In it"?' Sandy asked.

'I think I know what Anthony was getting out of what was happening.' I sat down again. 'What were you getting?'

Sandy lowered her eyes and looked away all at the same time. Maybe the question was too intimate for her. It was kind of interesting that she could give Anthony a hand job in the waiting room but was embarrassed to talk about it now.

'You don't have to answer the question, but you also don't have to be embarrassed,' I told her.

'No,' she said, 'it's fine. I'll talk. It's just that you've given me something to think about. It seems so obvious when you say it, but . . . I guess I hadn't thought about it that way.' She sat up a little straighter and actually smiled at me. *Strange*, I thought. Not very much like the Sandy I knew.

My larger concern was about where things would go from here with the two of them. I had the feeling that Sandy and Anthony were all wrong for each other, but that didn't mean I could stop something from happening.

Eight ten in the morning, and already it was a bad day.

Which got a little worse at nine.

Anthony wasn't in the waiting room. He'd bolted on me. And I wondered if I'd ever see him again.

Chapter Sixty-Two

At a little past nine, Sandy Quinlan and Anthony Demao met at a coffee shop on Sixth. The rendezvous had been arranged earlier. They had known that Dr Cross was going to catch them, because they had planned the whole thing.

Anthony had a latte and a sweet roll as he waited for Sandy, who licked at the whipped-cream topping before she spoke. 'He didn't even offer me any of his,' she said, and frowned. 'And he had *two* coffees.'

'He was angry at you for violating his space. So tell me everything. What did he say? I want to hear the pathetic details.'

Sandy smacked her lips and licked them clean before she spoke. 'Well, as he always is, Dr Cross was very empathetic, maybe even sympathetic. To me – not to you, you cad. And honest, I guess you'd call it. He finally admitted that he has a huge crush on me. Who wouldn't? But here's the real surprise. He wants to suck *your* cock!'

They both laughed and sipped their steaming drinks, then laughed some more. Finally Anthony leaned in close to Sandy. 'He's not alone on that, is he? Hey, you think he has any idea what we're up to? What this whole thing is about?'

Sandy shook her head. 'Not . . . a . . . clue. I'm quite sure of it.'

'You are? And that's because . . . ?'

'We're way too good at what we do. We're just such brilliant actors, you and I. Of course, you already know that. And I know that. Plus, the *script* is fabulous.'

Anthony smiled. 'We are very good, aren't we? We could fool just about anyone.'

'Make them believe anything we wanted to. Watch this.'

Sandy got up and sat on Anthony's lap, facing him. The two of them began to make out, to kiss with their tongues deep in each other's mouth. Their hands wandered all over, and then Sandy began to grind her pelvis against Anthony.

'Get a room,' said a serious-looking middle-aged woman using a computer a couple of tables away. 'Please. I don't need this in the morning.'

'I agree,' volunteered someone else. 'Grow up and act your ages, for God's sake.'

Sandy whispered in Anthony's ear, 'See? They think we're still lovers.'

Then she stood and pulled Anthony up too. 'Don't any of you sweat it!' she said in a loud voice. 'For God's sake – he's *my brother*!'

They were still laughing when they got outside the coffee shop.

'That was great, so much fun!' Sandy howled and did a little victory dance. Then she waved at the people inside, who were still watching through the windows.

'It was a hoot!' Anthony agreed. Then he got more serious. 'I got a message from Kyle Craig. He says he can't wait to meet DCAK.'

'Well,' said Sandy, 'I can't wait to meet the master of disaster.'

They both laughed at that one, then shared another tongue kiss for their audience in the coffee shop.

'We are so *bad*.' Sandy giggled.

Chapter Sixty-Three

Maybe we would finally catch some kind of break tonight, because God knows we needed one. The Unhinged Tour people had been more than enthusiastic about making room for the profiler and psychologist Dr Alex Cross on their schedule, just as Kitz had predicted they would. What I couldn't have anticipated was the kind of reception I would get when we actually showed up.

The event was booked into a worn, barely serviceable Best Western in the southeast police district of Baltimore, just off I-95 and, appropriately enough, across the street from a cemetery. We parked in the back, close to the hotel's conference-center entrance, then headed inside together.

'Safety in numbers,' Bree said with a hollow laugh.

The reception area was crowded with a noisy, carnival-like mix of people. *The majority of them look fairly ordinary, maybe a little redneck,* I thought. The others, in dark clothes and skin art, were like the show that the rest had come to see.

Vendors at tables along the wall hawked everything from mug-shot coffee cups to authentic crime-scene artifacts to CDs by groups such as Death Angel and What's for Lunch?

Bree, Sampson, and I had just gotten in the front door when somebody tapped me on the shoulder. My hand slid down close to my Glock.

The guy behind me, all sideburns and tattoos, grinned and elbowed his girlfriend when I turned around. 'See? I told you it was him.' The two of them were attached by a heavy chain strung between the black leather collars around their necks.

'Alex Cross, right?' He reached out and shook my hand, and I could already feel Bree and Sampson gearing up to give me a hard time. 'There's a picture of you on the poster—'

'Poster?' I said.

'But I've read your book twice, man. I already knew what you looked like.'

'Except older,' the girlfriend added. 'But you still look like your picture.'

I heard Sampson snort out the laugh he'd been trying to hold in.

'Nice to meet you,' I said. 'Both of you.' I tried to turn away, but the man who'd tapped me on the back held on to my arm.

'*Alex!*' he called to someone across the room. 'You know who this is?' Then he turned to me again. 'His name's Alex too. Is that crazy or what?'

'Crazy,' I said.

The other Alex, wearing a T-shirt with John Wayne Gacy in full clown makeup, came closer for a look. Then a small crowd began to gather around us, or, rather, around me. This was getting pretty ridiculous in a hurry. I certainly wasn't enjoying my new celebrity status.

'You're the profiler guy, aren't you? Sweet. Let me ask you a serious question—'

'We'll go and check in,' Bree said up close to my ear. 'Leave you to your fans.'

'What's, like, the gnarliest crime scene you've ever worked?' the other Alex asked me.

'No, wait—' I reached out to grab Bree's elbow, but a black-fingernailed hand landed on my wrist and held there. It belonged to a frail-looking young woman whose hand seemed to have been dipped in pale-yellow wax.

'Alex Cross, right? You're him, right? Can I get a picture with you? It would mean the world to my mom.'

Chapter Sixty-Four

I finally caught up with Bree and Sampson in a cozy spot called Main
Ballroom #1. That's where I'd be speaking tonight at around seven
thirty. We'd agreed that my name would be the biggest draw and also
create the most buzz online, and I guess we had finally been right
about something.

Kitz and his people had been helping get the word out over the
Web – baiting the hook, so to speak. Whether or not DCAK would
bite now was the question. A lot of other geeks and freaks certainly
had.

The ballroom was a long rectangular space that could be partitioned
into three smaller rooms with accordion-style walls. A stage and
podium were set up at the far end. Several rows of chairs sat in the
middle of the floor.

Bree and Sampson were standing near the stage with a short,
paunchy man in a normal-looking dark suit but with red-framed
glasses that brought to mind Elton John. He had a long, thin braid
hanging from his otherwise short salt-and-pepper hair and an
Unhinged T-shirt pulled over his long-sleeved button-down shirt. *Full
geek mode,* I was thinking.

Bree smiled wickedly as she said, 'Alex, this is Wally Walewski. He's
just giving us the full rundown about tonight. Wait'll you hear.'

'It's really most excellent to meet you,' Wally Walewski said, his eyes
never quite making it higher than my shoulder. 'So, anyway, we've got
your slides – check. And there'll be a clicker – check. And a laser
pointer on the podium – check. And some water? Anything else?
Whatever, I'll take care of it pronto. I'm on the case.'

'What's the capacity of the room?' asked Bree.

'Two hundred and eighty is the limit by law, and we'll *definitely* be sold out.'

'Definitely,' Sampson said, just for me to hear.

We waited until Wally Walewski and his braid were gone before we discussed anything further about our own prep. *Check.*

'Where are our people now?' I asked Bree. What the Unhinged folks didn't know was that we had an undercover team working the event. Baltimore PD had provided us with four local detectives who were passing as conference attendees. We had two of our own people from DC embedded in the hotel staff too.

Bree glanced over the program. 'Right now, the Baltimore boys are in either a fingerprinting seminar or, let's see, a "serial-killer breakout session," whatever the hell that is. Later tonight, we'll have them *here* . . . and *here.'*

She pointed to either side of the audience area. 'Vince and Chesney will float. And, Sampson, I think you and I should stay together. That okay?'

'Sounds good to me. I don't want to be alone here, anyway.'

The rest of Baltimore PD was on standby, with at least one extra cruiser in the neighborhood of the hotel at all times. Hotel security had been briefed and wouldn't be doing anything out of the ordinary, with any luck keeping out of our way if and when crunch time came.

This was meant to be a quiet operation, a little desperate for sure, maybe nothing more than information gathering. But if the killer did show up, we'd be ready to grab him. Stranger things had happened. Hell, stranger things had happened to me.

Besides, we already knew DCAK was surveilling us.

Chapter Sixty-Five

'This is *my* audience,' I began, and got some easy laughs from the captive crowd of oddballs stretched across the auditorium. I went on to talk about the known homicides for DCAK but passed on only information we'd already released to the press. Then I did a little damage control on the copycat theories and showed some crime-scene photos that the audience seemed to appreciate. I also gave what the Unhinged people had billed as an 'insider's look' at our suspect profile. It was something I could do in my sleep by now and probably had. If nothing else, details from my talk would wind up on the Internet and possibly get to *somebody* who knew *something* about the killer.

'This is a nearly psychotic man with a deep-seated need for larger-than-life approval,' I told the packed room.

'The expression of this need eclipses everything else in his world to an extreme, sociopathic degree. When he gets up in the morning, if he sleeps at all, he has no free choice except to seek another audience, to plot and obsess on another murder, and this ritual of his may well escalate.'

I leaned forward on the podium, checking out as many faces as I could in the crowd. It was stunning to me how rapt and attentive they were.

'What this maniac doesn't realize yet – what I think he can't permit himself to admit – is that he'll never get what he's looking for. And *that's* what will catch up with him. If we don't bring him down first, he'll do it to himself. He's moving toward self-destruction, toward facilitating his own capture, and he can't help himself.'

Everything I said was basically true – just a little slanted. If the killer

happened to be in the audience, I wanted to make him as uncomfortable as I possibly could. Actually, I wanted to make him sweat like
a pig on a spit.

I spotted a few in the crowd who had a physical resemblance to
DCAK, based on what we knew: tall, powerfully built, male. But no
one had given me any reason to make a move, or to signal Bree and
Sampson. I was concerned that our little plan was a bust, though not
all that surprised. I'd just about run out of things to say at the podium
– and no one had tried to take my audience away, to upstage me at
the 'crime convention.'

Are you watching me, you bastard?

Probably not.

You're too smart, aren't you? You're much smarter than we are.

Chapter Sixty-Six

After the speech, a brief Q&A, and some unexpectedly warm applause, I was installed by Wally Walewski behind a wobbly card table in the reception area. *Check.*

Anyone who wanted to could meet me here, get a book signed, that kind of thing. For the first twenty minutes, I shook hands, made pleasant small talk, and signed everything from books to the palm of one woman's hand. Almost everybody was nice. Polite too. As far as I could tell, not a serial killer in the bunch.

The only request I refused was a T-shirt that said *DCAK* on the front and *Keep on living, fuckers* across the back.

'How's it going over there?' I finally heard through my acoustic earpiece.

I looked down the line, where Bree was standing with dozens of fans who were still waiting patiently, chatting with one another. 'Quiet so far,' I said. 'Strange but nice enough people. Unfortunately.'

Bree turned her back away from the line and spoke low. 'That sucks. Okay, then . . . Sampson, I'm going to take another quick swing through the crowd. I'll check back in with you when we're at the front door. Hopefully, somebody here isn't all that nice.'

I heard John's reply in my ear. 'Sounds good to me. Alex, you riding home with us? Or hoping to get lucky with one of your fans?' I just smiled at the next person in line.

'I'll be back soon,' Bree said, and disappeared into the crowd. 'You be good, now.'

'I'll try my best.'

A few minutes later, as I was signing a book, I felt a presence behind me.

When I looked up, though, no one was there. But I was sure someone had been.

'She left you a note.'

The woman across the table from me pointed to a piece of paper at my elbow. I unfolded it and saw a printout from a Web page.

Black background, bold white letters. I read the message.

Guess again, smart guy. I'm not psychotic! And I'm not dumb!
See you back in DC, where it's all happening.
In fact, you're missing the show.

Chapter Sixty-Seven

What show am I missing? I wondered. I jumped up from the table, my pulse already racing.

'Who left this?' I asked the people in line. 'Did anybody see who put this note down here?'

The woman whose book I'd just signed pointed back into the crowd. 'She went thatta way, Sheriff!'

'What did she look like?' I asked. 'You sure it was a woman?'

'Um . . . straight dark hair. Black shirt. Jeans. I think? Like everybody else here. Looked female.'

'And glasses!' someone else said. 'She had a blue backpack!'

'Alex' – Bree came back in my ear – 'what's going on over there? Did something just happen? What the hell happened?'

'Bree, we're looking for a *woman*. Definitely a female. Black shirt, jeans, glasses, a blue backpack. I need you and Sampson to cover the exits. Let Baltimore PD know what's going on. She left me a note from DCAK.'

'We're on it!'

A ripple of excitement spread inside the crowd as I began to push my way through a tightening knot of people. Not everyone wanted to let me pass, either. Several of them closed in on me, trying to find out what was happening, where I was going, asking me questions I didn't have time to answer at the moment.

I waved them off as best I could. 'This isn't a game now! Anyone see a woman in a black shirt and glasses go this way?'

A kid smelling of marijuana giggled out a response. 'Man, that's half the people here.'

The crowd shifted again, and I thought that I saw her – at the far end of the lobby. I moved the kid and a few others out of my way. 'Let me through here!'

'Bree!' I was running now. 'I can see her. She's tall. White. Carrying the blue backpack.'

'And *female*?'

'I think so. Could be a disguise.'

When I reached the next corner, the suspect was already more than halfway down a long corridor, running toward the exit at the far end.

'Police! Stop! *Stop right there!*' I shouted at her, and I had my gun out too.

Whoever she was, she didn't even look around as she slammed through the door. It swung back hard, then burst into an opaque web of broken glass.

'East parking lot!' I told Bree and Sampson. 'She's outside! She's running! It's a woman!'

Chapter Sixty-Eight

A *strong woman, too!* She'd completely shattered the door on the way out. *What kind of woman was that? A very angry one? A crazy lady? A collaborator with DCAK or another copycat?*

Pellets of glass showered around me as I pushed through the exit door. *Where the hell was she now?* I didn't see her anywhere outside. No one running.

A few streetlamps overhead left plenty of shadow around the narrow parking lot. The row of cars directly opposite me showed no sign of life, though.

On my left, the pavement ended abruptly and gave way to an empty stretch of lawn.

Then I heard a sports-car engine fire up. The revving noise came from somewhere off to my right. I stared hard into the semidarkness.

Headlights blinked on, then two shining eyes came right at me. *Fast!*

My Glock was still out, and I figured I had time for at least one shot. I squeezed the trigger. A bullet punctured the car's windshield with a *pock* sound. The speeding vehicle kept coming. Right at me! I dove and hit the hotel wall, then rolled onto the asphalt. Banged the hell out of my shoulder and my chin.

I fired another shot. A taillight shattered. It was a small coupe, I saw now. A blue Miata. A neighbor of mine had one, and I recognized the size and shape.

The fast-moving car hopped the curb, then bounced forward into the street.

Then it stopped abruptly! A taxi's tires squealed on the pavement.

The cab had just missed nailing the coupe. *Inches from total destruction. And capture!*

By the time I was on my feet and running, the blue sports car had taken off again.

My badge was out, and I threw open the taxi driver's door. 'Police! I need your cab.'

All the cabbie saw was my gun, but I guess it was enough for him. He was out of his seat immediately, hands held in the air. 'Take it!'

The taxi was a V-6. Good, I'd probably need all of that. I clicked off the radio and AC to funnel extra power.

'Alex? Where the hell are you?' Bree's voice sounded in my ear, faint against the straining engine of the cab.

'In pursuit, I hope. West on O'Donnell,' I called out. 'I'm chasing a dark-blue Miata. Maryland plates. One taillight out. I'm looking at it right now. Female driver – though she's big enough to be a man. Strong enough, too.'

'Maybe it's a man in women's clothes. He likes to play roles.'

'Yes, he does. But I think this really is a woman. We have to get her!'

The coupe shot past the ramp for I-95 and straight through another intersection. The driver was doing at least seventy – and accelerating.

'Bree, if you can hear me, we're both going west on O'Donnell. You copy?'

'Okay, Alex. Still got you. We're on it, on our way. What else do you need?'

'*Shit!*' I yelled. '*Shit!*'

'What?' Bree yelled back.

I swerved to miss a yellow VW Bug as it tried to squeak in a left turn. *Idiot.* 'What I need is a siren. Or some backup,' I clarified for Bree.

'Medallion 5C742, what's your location?' The taxi dispatch suddenly crackled at me. 'Come in. Do you hear me?'

'Alex, what's happening now?' Bree asked. 'Are you all right? *Alex?*'

The coupe barely slowed as it pulled around a UPS truck and straight *into* oncoming traffic. Cars swerved to the side as the coupe barreled at them. I gunned the cab and squeezed in behind.

'Maryland 451JZW,' I told Bree. 'I'm fine. So far, anyway. Still in pursuit.'

I kept my foot down – and managed to nudge the Miata's rear bumper. The sports car jerked but then surged forward again.

'Bree? Did you get that license number? Bree? Bree, where are you?'

There was no response from her. Maybe I'd gone out of range. The only things in my ear now were my own pulse and the taxi's racing engine.

Chapter Sixty-Nine

I knew that the sports coupe could outrun me on a long straightaway, but that was the one advantage the driver didn't have here. In fact, I could swear she was letting me get closer. *Was that really happening? Was it a trap? Was that what this was about? Separating, then grabbing me? Was I the target? Kyle Craig would think up something like that. Was Kyle here? Was he involved?*

Then I saw what was actually going on. With no warning or brake lights, the coupe shot left onto a narrow side street, shimmied twice, and kept moving like a Pocket Rocket.

I missed the intersection completely. No way I could have made the turn. Another came up fast, though, and I took it, hoping for a grid somewhere up ahead.

Tall apartment buildings rose on either side of me so that I couldn't see over to the next block. Straight ahead, the road came to a T with another main artery. *Boston Street,* I thought. I knew that beyond Boston was the harbor. That cut off some options, anyway. Made this a little easier. I hoped.

I can get her – take her down. And that'll be the biggest break yet in this case.

The coupe whizzed by as I approached the intersection, and I accelerated blindly around the corner. *This could be it. One way or the other.*

We were in two lanes of inward-bound traffic now. The Miata wove through other cars expertly, passing on both sides, but it couldn't slip away from me. I was holding on so far. And I had my Glock out again.

When the driver tried another surprise right, I was ready for it. The taxi's outside wheels barely held the pavement, but I made the turn with an inch or two of safety.

A tree-lined residential block appeared ahead. I spotted pedestrians.

My chest tightened up. Kids would be out on a nice night like this. The coupe wasn't slowing down. She was barreling straight ahead, even picking up speed.

I laid on the horn! Maybe I could keep the road clear of people. The coupe rocketed up several blocks, and all I could do was follow at a close distance. *If you ain't first, you're last.* Ricky Bobby in *Talladega Nights.*

When the driver tried the next turn, the street was too narrow for the speed. The Miata slowed sharply – and I came up fast on her.

I slammed into the back fender again, not exactly on purpose this time. I knew I'd just messed up the taxi pretty good.

The coupe fishtailed around the corner and hopped up onto the sidewalk, then somebody's lawn. I heard a woman's scream in the darkness. Two people dove out of the way.

My focus narrowed and also intensified. I saw the Best Western up ahead. *What the hell?* On top of everything else, I had just been taken on a giant circle jerk ride around Baltimore and the harbor area.

It wasn't until I saw the highway up ahead that I got it. The driver had figured out how to outrun me.

And I couldn't let her do that!

Chapter Seventy

Bree's voice was back in my earphone. *'Keep all exits secure. Repeat. Keep all exits secure!'* She was obviously in control. I wished I could say the same. *'Alex? Alex? Can you hear me? Alex?'*

'Bree! I'm here!'

'What's going on? Talk to me. Where is *here?* Are you okay?'

The coupe took exactly the turn I thought it would and paralleled the thruway toward I-95. We were only a block from the hotel now, our starting point. *This whole trip had been another game, hadn't it? Was that right?*

'Whoever it is, they're going for the highway! The Miata's headed to I-95! I still might take her.'

'Where, Alex? Which entrance?'

'Right by the damn hotel!'

I gripped the wheel, ready to take the ramp, but then the coupe flew right by it! A second later, so did I.

Now what?

Almost at the same time, the coupe's brake lights showed. I heard the skid and saw the car do nearly a one eighty.

Even as I slammed my brakes, the Miata accelerated back in my direction. It swerved to miss me, and before I could even get turned around, the coupe was up the ramp, still accelerating. And gone in a cloud of dust.

'North on 95!' I yelled for Bree. *'*I'm still on her tail! For the moment.'

I sped up to the highway and maxed out the taxi at close to a hundred for a couple of exits. Eventually, I took my foot off the accelerator and slammed my fist into the passenger seat.

I turned around at the next exit.

Back at the hotel, Bree and Sampson were waiting out front, along with half a dozen Baltimore cruisers, their roof lights flashing in the darkness. Most of the Unhinged crowd was outside too, loving every second of this chaos and madness.

A three-hundred-pound biker with a white beard came charging up to me in the parking lot. 'Hey, man, what the hell happened out there?'

'Get away,' I said without stopping. The biker cut me off again. He had on about a hundred-year-old Grateful Dead T.

'Just tell me—'

I was in his face now, and I wanted to pop someone. I might have if Sampson hadn't grabbed me from behind. 'Hey, hey, hey!' he was shouting – *at me*.

Then Bree came running up to us. 'Jesus, are you okay?' she asked. 'Alex?'

'I'm fine,' I said, trying to slow my breathing. 'Listen, that might have been DCAK I was chasing. Another of his—'

'It *wasn't* him,' Bree said, and shook her head. 'And we've got to go right now.'

'What are you talking about?' I asked as she pushed me away from the crowd and all their eerie questions.

'I just got a call from Davies. Somebody was murdered at the National Air and Space Museum in Washington. Stabbed to death in front of a crowd of people. He punked us, Alex. He got us real good this time. This whole thing was planned.'

PART THREE

THE AUDIENCE IS LISTENING

Chapter Seventy-One

I had visited the National Air and Space Museum many times with my kids but had never seen anything like this. As we arrived, the building looked dark and foreboding from the outside, except for the glass-walled atrium of the cafeteria. Upon entering, though, we saw dozens of shell-shocked people sitting at tables, waiting to go home. *Witnesses,* I knew. To a person, they had seen a horrific event tonight. What made it worse: at least half of them appeared to be children, some just two or three years old.

A bulging army of news reporters and photographers had been cordoned off over on Seventh Street near the Hirshhorn. At least it made the vultures easier for us to avoid.

Sampson, Bree, and I had come in directly from Independence Avenue. Gil Cook, one of our D-2s, met us at the cafeteria entrance. He approached Bree on the run, waving one arm over his head.

'Detective Stone, the museum director would like to speak with you before—'

'After,' Bree said, and she kept walking. She was on the Job now, somebody not to be trifled with. I liked how she worked, how she took control of the homicide scene.

Gil Cook followed her like a chastened pup looking for table scraps. 'He said I should tell you he's on his way out to talk to the press.'

Bree stopped walking and pivoted toward the D-2.

'Oh, for Christ's sake, Gil. Where is he?'

Cook pointed her in the right direction and then kept pace with Sampson and me. The three of us passed by the darkened Milestones of Flight exhibit, with its life-size planes like giant toys hanging from the ceiling. Very cinematic – right up our thrill killer's alley. More and more, his work was reminding me of Kyle Craig's. The theatrics, the viciousness. *Had he studied Kyle's crimes?*

'Victim's name is Abby Courlevais. Thirty-two years old. White woman, tourist from France. Worst thing about it, she was five or six months pregnant,' Cook told Sampson and me.

The murder had taken place inside the Lockheed Martin IMAX Theater, which showed museum fare during the day but sometimes Hollywood blockbuster stuff at night. The actual killing had occurred right in the middle of my Baltimore speech. And then I'd gotten the note: *Guess again, smart guy. I'm not psychotic! . . . See you back in DC, where it's all happening . . .*

He was really going out of his way to mock us now – getting into it good. And the killer seemed to be topping each act with the next. *Who was the woman in Baltimore? The Indy race-car driver who had taken me on a wild-goose chase, only to get away on I-95.*

A pregnant victim, a visitor from another country – and a more 'civilized' one – would capture media attention in a new way, and that wasn't the half of it. The killer had just pulled off another very public execution inside a national institution. In a post-9/11 world, that meant a new level of intensity for everything – press coverage, public paranoia, pressure on the police to get this thing under control, to end it before anyone else died. No one would care that it was an almost impossible assignment. How many *years* had it taken them to get the Green River Killer – and had they ever gotten the Zodiac?

As to where DCAK might try to take things from here, I didn't even want to speculate about it.

Right now, I had a body to see.

Two bodies, actually.

Mother and child.

Chapter Seventy-Two

'**G**oddamn him to hell!' Sampson said in an angry voice that he managed to keep under his breath.'That sonofabitch! That miserable fucker!'

As homicide scenes go, this one was particularly obscene and troubling. This was a place where families went to be entertained. The IMAX theater had soaring walls, textured only with directional lighting. The rows of high-backed seats were steeply raked in a concave arch across the auditorium, like a modern take on an old medical-lecture theater – *right down to the cadaver, right?*

The victim had apparently been killed near the base of the five-story-high movie screen. That seemed odd to me, but it was the advance word we'd gotten from Gil Cook, and no one else was questioning it so far. I probably shouldn't have either. Not yet.

The poor woman's body lay faceup now. Her hands had been tied behind her back, and even from a distance, I could see silver duct tape wrapped across her mouth. *Just like at the Riverwalk.* I also spotted a wedding band on her hand.

As I got closer, I saw that the tape was stained dark over her lips where blood had been unable to escape. Probably after internal injuries. Mrs Courlevais's white dress was discolored and looked rusty brown all over. She'd obviously been stabbed . . . repeatedly.

Next to the mutilated body was an oversize canvas rucksack. There were metal grommets around the top. The sack was laced with a thick cord, presumably for tying it closed.

Another present from DCAK? Another clue for us to follow nowhere?

More bloodstains and several perforations showed me what I already knew instinctively, that the victim had been stabbed *inside* the sack. The vicious killer had left Abby Courlevais in there, either dead or dying. The EMTs had taken her out in hopes of reviving her, but it was obviously too late.

When I lifted the empty bag to look for markings, I found US POSTAL SERVICE and a long string of numbers stenciled on the side in faded black letters.

So was this the latest calling card? Had to be. But what was it supposed to mean? What was DCAK saying to us this time? And was this murder committed by him, or possibly his copycat?

Witness accounts had already described a blue uniform and cap on the killer. Maybe that was DCAK's version of an in-joke – he'd 'gone postal' on us. He had also left us 'holding the bag.'

I walked to the far side of the floor, near the entrance the killer had used to come in. From here, I tried to imagine the events as Detective Cook had described them. The killer had needed to catch Mrs Courlevais unaware – long enough to bind her hands and mouth – and to get the cloth bag over her head. A mat of dried blood in her hair indicated some kind of blunt trauma but probably not enough to knock her out. Conscious would be better, anyway. More effective for DCAK's purposes, for the theater of it.

And, in fact, witnesses had seen the bag moving when he'd dragged it into the theater.

I walked back to the woman's body again and looked around at the empty auditorium. This audience was closer to him than any of the others had been, so he'd needed to work quickly. No time for lengthy speeches or the usual sickening grandstanding. He hadn't been able to make a full star turn tonight. *So what had been so attractive about* this *particular location,* this *audience,* this *French woman?*

The impact seemed to have been mostly visual. He'd shouted, 'Special delivery!' and then got right to it – half a dozen vicious swings with a blade large enough to be seen from the theater's back row.

I looked down at Mrs Courlevais, then back at the empty sack next to her.

Suddenly, another angle occurred to me. *What else might be tucked inside there? Was there something else in the mail sack?*

I worked the bag open, dreading what I might find. Finally my hand touched a flat piece of plastic. *Something was definitely there. What?*

I pulled the object out. *What the hell?* It was a postal worker's ID A second photo had been pasted over the original. The name was changed too. It said Stanley Chasen.

The image on the ID was a match to the preliminary description we'd gotten: elderly white man, possibly in his seventies, silver hair, bulbous nose, horn-rimmed glasses. Heavyset and tall.

'Who's Stanley Chasen?' Sampson asked.

'Probably nobody,' I said. Then it hit me. I knew what he was doing – I was thinking like him, and not liking the feeling. 'It's a figment of this sick bastard's imagination. He's creating characters, then he's playing them, one at a time. And all the characters inside his head are killers.'

And . . . what? He wants us to catch them all?

Chapter Seventy-Three

I didn't get to leave the National Air and Space Museum until five in the morning, *and we weren't even finished with our workday yet.* Bree and I sent Sampson home to his wife and little one, and then we drove back up to Baltimore – where there was still a mess of paperwork to finish up and a situation to try to make some sense out of, if we possibly could.

On the drive, we talked about the woman who had been DCAK's accomplice at the Best Western – the driver of the blue sports car. *Had he hired her just for the night? Or had she been in on the murder spree all along?* No way to tell yet, but the scenario led to lots of speculation on the ride up I-95, some of it connecting to Kyle Craig and his escape from ADX Florence.

When we finally got back to the Best Western, Bree and I hugged for a minute in the car, but that was about all we did – a hug and a kiss. Then we were needed inside. It was too early to call my house, so I waited until later – well into the morning, as it turned out. When I finally called, I got the answering machine.

I decided to keep my message light, the exact opposite of what I was feeling. 'Hey, chickens, it's Dad. Listen, I'm working through the morning, but I'll be home later this afternoon. Promise. Seems like a good night for a movie. That is, if I can convince anyone to join me.' *And if I can stay awake.*

Bree took her tired eyes off some paperwork and smiled over at me. 'You must be pretty exhausted too. You're a real good dad, Alex.'

'Trying. I'm a guilty dad for sure.'

'No,' Bree repeated. 'You're a good dad. Trust me on that. I had a bad one.'

As it turned out, it was past three o'clock when I finally dragged myself home to Fifth Street. A shower and a little something from the kitchen, and I'd be ready to go again. Maybe just an hour or two of nap time.

As I was getting out of the car, I saw Jannie's long face. She was standing on the front porch, watching me come up the walk. Her features were still, and she didn't move or speak when our eyes met.

'What's going on?' I asked as I humped up the steps. 'Something happened.'

'Yeah, Dad, it sure did. Damon's run away.'

My head tilted back involuntarily. *What?* Maybe I was groggy and hadn't heard Janelle right.

'Run away? What are you talking about? Where is he?'

'He left home five hours ago, and he hasn't come back. Never told anybody where he was going. Nothing. Nana's been going crazy.'

This didn't compute. Not with Damon. It just wasn't something he'd ordinarily do.

'Five hours? Jannie, what is going on? What am I missing here?'

Jannie stared hard at me. 'The basketball coach from Cushing was here today – to talk to you. You missed the meeting. The prep-school coach from Massachusetts?'

'I know what Cushing is, Janelle,' I said.

Just then, Nana came out to the porch. Little Ali trailed a half step behind his grandmother. 'I've spoken with his friends and the parents that I can reach. No one's seen him,' Nana said.

I pulled out my phone. 'I'll call Sampson. We can—'

Nana cut me off. 'I spoke to John already. He's out searching the neighborhood.'

Just then, the phone in my hand buzzed. I hadn't known that it had been ringing off the hook for hours. Sampson's name came up on the caller ID.

'John?' I said into the receiver.

'Alex, I've got Damon.'

Chapter Seventy-Four

'Where is he? Where are you?' I asked, paranoia blossoming inside my head. Kyle Craig had threatened my family. DCAK said he was watching us too.

'We're over at Sojourner Truth. Day wandered around town, then he came up here to shoot some hoops. We had a talk. He's ready to come home now. We'll be back there in a few minutes.'

'No. I'll come to you,' I said. I wasn't sure why. I just felt it should be that way. I wanted to go to Damon, not the other way around.

'Can I come, Daddy?' Ali looked up at me, his small hands outstretched, curious brown eyes always ready for the next little adventure in his life.

'Not this time, pup. I'll be back soon.'

'You always say that.'

'I do. And I always come back.' *Eventually I do, anyway.*

I drove over to the school, the same one Damon and Jannie had gone to, and Ali would be attending before I knew it.

Day and Sampson were playing one-on-one, pounding the school's cracked pavement court. Damon still had on the khakis and nice blue dress shirt he'd probably worn for the meeting with the prep-school coach. A red-and-black necktie hung out of his back pocket. He scored easily on Sampson as I approached the court.

I laced my fingers into the chain-link fence. 'Pretty nice move,' I said. 'Of course, you only had to beat an old man to get to the hoop.'

Damon played it cool – cold, really – and didn't even look my way.

Sampson bent and leaned on his knees, sweat dripping off his face, and not just because it was eighty degrees out. Damon was good, getting better too. Bigger and better, and a whole lot quicker than he ever was before. It struck me that I hadn't seen him play ball in a long time.

'I'm up next,' I called to Sampson.

He held up an index finger that clearly said, *I'm out.*

'That's okay. Game's over,' Damon said. He came out through the gate near my car, and I caught his arm. I needed him to look at me, which he did. Daggers. Sharp ones that cut deep.

'Damon, I'm sorry about what happened today. Couldn't be helped.'

'If you guys are all good, I'm going to take off,' Sampson said.

He clapped Damon on the back as he went. The Big Man knows when to hang in and when to head out.

'Let's sit.' I motioned to the stone school steps. Damon reluctantly sat down with me. I could tell he was pissed, but maybe he was confused too. We almost never got this angry, let it get this bad. Damon was a good kid – a great kid, actually – and I was proud of him most of the time.

'You want to start?' I asked.

'Okay. Where the hell were you?'

'Uh-uh,' I said. I knocked the ball out of his hand and stilled it against the step. 'You don't talk to me like that, no matter what, Day. We're going to have a conversation, but it's going to be respectful.'

I put on a tough face; Day would never know how much what he'd said had hurt me. Probably, he'd needed to get even. I understood. But still.

'Sorry,' he mumbled, and made it sound half sincere.

'Damon, I was literally all over the map with this case. Last night and this morning. I haven't slept at all – and someone else died out there. That's not for you to worry about, but it's what happened. People are dying around Washington, and it's my job to try to stop it. I'm sorry, but I guess that's a problem for both of us to deal with.'

'This was important to me. Just like your work's important to you,' Damon said.

'I know that. And I'm going to do whatever it takes to make this up to you. If we have to drive up for a meeting at Cushing, then that's what we'll do. Okay?'

There was so much I wanted him to know, starting with the fact that nothing was more important to me than his happiness, despite how it might seem to him sometimes. But I put a lid on it. Kept things simple. Damon stared at the ground, palming the ball.

Finally he looked up. 'Okay. That'd be good.'

We stood up together and walked back to the car. As he was getting in, I said the last thing I had to say. 'Damon? About running off the way you did, not checking in despite our house rule, worrying your grandmother . . .'

'Yeah, I'm sorry about that.'

'Well, me too. 'Cause you're grounded.'

'I know it,' said Damon, and he got into the car with me.

Before we got back home, I said, 'Forget about being grounded. Just tell your grandmother you're sorry.'

Chapter Seventy-Five

Here was a *clue* that the cops really needed to have, a little bit of homespun reality that they would never find out about. *And if they did, what the hell, he would already be dead, wouldn't he?*

DCAK used a pay phone way out in Virginia to make the same call he made just about every Sunday. Now that he was a full-fledged successful outlaw, there was no sense taking needless risks with his cell phone, especially not to this particular number, which some smart, or lucky, cop might eventually track down, though that was doubtful. *Was there such a thing as a smart cop?*

He heard a familiar voice that only made him grit and grind his teeth. 'It's a great day at Meadow Grove. How may I direct your call?'

'Room sixty-two, if you would, please.'

'No problem.'

The line clicked, then rang again. Just once, though, then it was picked up.

'Hello. Who is this?'

'Hey, Momma. Guess.'

'Oh, my Lord, I can't believe it's you. Where are you calling from? Are you still out in California?'

This was how the conversation began every single time he called. In a way, it made things easier, more comfortable for both of them, completely artificial.

'That's right. Actually, I'm standing on the corner of Hollywood and Vine right now.'

'I'll bet it's beautiful there. It's beautiful, right? The weather, movie stars, Pacific Ocean, everything.'

'It is. Paradise. I'm going to fly you out here one of these days real soon. How're you doing other than that? You have everything you need?'

Her voice dropped to a whisper. 'You know that colored girl who comes in to clean? I think she's been taking my jewelry.'

'Mm-hm.' Not likely. He had sold off the last of his mother's jewelry a long time ago. That's where the money came from to get his acting career started, then to keep it going for a while.

'But never mind about me. Tell me about you. Just everything. I love it when you call. Your brother and sister almost never do.'

The accent seriously grated on his nerves, if only because he'd worked so hard to leave it behind. Unlike either of his parents, he had always intended to be something, to go beyond his humble beginnings. And now here he was at the top of the world, nobody quite like him, a unique creation.

'Well, did I tell you I've got a big movie coming out soon? Everybody is going to see it. The studio sure seems to think so, anyway. Paramount Pictures.'

He heard a quick intake of breath over the phone. 'No such a thing!'

'That's right, Ma. It's got me and Tom Hanks and Angelina Jolie—'

'Oh, I just love her. What's she like in real life? She nice or stuck-up?'

'She's actually real nice. Loves her kids, Momma. I showed her your picture and told her all about you too. In fact, she's the one who said I should call.'

'Oooh! Are you teasing me? That just makes me shiver. Angelina Jolie! And Tom Hanks too. I knew you were goin' to make it. You're so determined.'

The phone call, the acting, was all too easy and was the least he could do; or maybe it was the most he could do. It wasn't like he was ever going back to visit his mother. Not like Kyle Craig had done out in Colorado recently.

'Wait'll I tell your father about this. You know his birthday's coming up, right?'

Crazy really did run in this family, didn't it? She could remember the man's birthday but not the fact that he'd shot himself in the face twenty-some years ago. This conversation was starting to depress the oxygen right out of him. It was time to go.

'Now listen, I have to be on the set soon, so I'm going to say good-bye for now.'

'Okay, sweetheart, I understand. Nice to hear your voice. You keep knockin' 'em dead out there, you hear?'

He had to laugh at that one. 'Yes'm. I'll do just that. In your honor, Momma. I'll give them hell.'

Chapter Seventy-Six

Thursday around noon, I got a call from Bree, and it wasn't exactly what I wanted to hear, not even in the ballpark. 'Alex, don't hate me for this, but there's no way I can get away this weekend. I'm going to be working straight through. Sorry. Sorry. I'm really sorry.'

We'd been hoping to make up for our aborted camping trip, but she was right, of course. The timing wasn't any good. In fact, it probably couldn't have been much worse, given the uproar over DCAK. Not to mention Kyle Craig being on the loose again and no recent word about where he might be.

'How about I make it up to you over drinks tonight?' she said. 'Say, nine o'clock at the Sheraton Suites over in Old Town. You know the place? You remember?'

'I do, of course I do, and I'll be there. Sheraton Suites. Nine o'clock.'

Everyone was a little frustrated right now, but especially the two of us. We'd been working harder than ever on DCAK, and all we had to show for it were a lot of unanswered questions and some very grisly murders. *How had he pulled off the scene in Baltimore – and the Smithsonian hit at the same time? Who was the mystery woman who had helped him in Baltimore? What were those numbers on the side of the mailbag supposed to mean?*

And what would happen if he tried to go one better again? That one hung over our heads like a weight about to drop – probably not *if* but *when.*

The Sheraton Suites over in Alexandria would be a nice trip down memory lane for Bree and me. It was where the two of us had had one very special evening. The Sheraton was right in the middle of the historic Old Town area and a short walk to the Potomac waterfront. It was a good place to end today, and I couldn't wait to see Bree.

A little before nine, I took a seat at the Fin and Hoof Bar inside the hotel and ordered a cold beer on tap. The bartender, a burly, friendly young guy with a heavy mustache, looked me over. 'You Alex?'

My heart sank a little. Strangers almost never give cops good news. 'That's right,' I said.

'Then I guess this is for you.'

He handed me an envelope with the hotel logo. I recognized Bree's handwriting and opened the letter at the bar. I read, *Alex – Change of plans. – B.*

Inside the envelope, I also found a hotel card key.

'Have a nice night, Alex,' said the bartender with a smile that suggested Bree had given him the envelope herself. 'I'm pretty sure you will.'

Chapter Seventy-Seven

I took the elevator to the third floor of the Sheraton Suites and knocked on the door of 3B. Everything was exactly as I remembered it. For starters, there was a nice scent in the air. When Bree answered in jeans and a blouse, however, I was surprised. Actually, I'd been expecting a little less.

'Hope you don't mind spontaneity,' she said, and handed me a glass of red. It smelled spicy – zinfandel? I didn't really care what kind of wine it was, or the brand.

I started to kiss Bree, and my hand immediately drifted down the back of her blouse. Suddenly her arms were around me. I heard the door *thunk* behind us, and we were enveloped in the soft blues and creams of the hotel suite. *Good idea. Keep the world away for a while, as long as we possibly could.*

The drapes were already drawn, and the bed was turned down just so, everything in its place. 'That bed looks inviting. Sleeps nice too. I remember.'

'Get undressed,' she said with a grin. 'Don't even think about sleeping, Alex.'

I looked at her over the top of my wineglass. 'You in a hurry or something?'

'Not at all.'

Bree sank down into a cushiony club chair to *watch*. There was a twinkle in her eyes. 'You can take your time, if you like. Please do. Just take something off, Alex. I'm in no hurry whatsoever.'

So I did what I was told. I went one button, *one kiss*, pair of pants, *two kisses* – that kind of thing.

Then Bree pushed herself up. She came forward and held me in her arms. 'Don't take this the wrong way – I'm *still* in no hurry.' We finally toppled over onto the bed, which definitely was comfy.

'What about you?' I asked her. She hadn't taken off a single thing yet.

'Oh, I'll catch up with you. Eventually. *You* in a hurry for some reason?'

Bree stretched across me, then reached and opened the nightstand drawer. *What was in there?*

She took out the last thing I was expecting to see: *two lengths of rope.*

Hmmm, interesting development. My heart was starting to race.

'Is that for you or me?' I asked.

'Let's say it's for both of us.'

I trusted Bree, right? No doubts, no suspicions? Well, maybe a couple of questions right then. In a few moves, she looped my left hand firmly but not uncomfortably to the bed. Then she kissed me. A reassuring kiss on the mouth, followed by a second, harder one. *Did I really know Bree?*

'Is it getting hot in here or is it just me?' I asked.

'I hope it's getting hot,' Bree said.

She tied my right hand to the bed next. Bree did know her knots.

'This why you became a cop?' I asked. 'You a control freak, Detective Stone?'

'Could be, Dr Cross. We'll soon find out, won't we? You're looking very yummy, there.'

'Your turn,' I said. 'Clothes off.'

She flirted with her big hazel eyes, and I must say, I was definitely starting to enjoy this – whatever it was. 'Say *please.*'

'Please. But can we hurry this up a little?'

'So, you *are* in a hurry?'

'Little bit now.'

'Little bit, huh? I don't know if *little* is the operative word around here right now.'

Bree's blouse went first – slowly – then her jeans, leaving a soft blue lace bra filled to the brim, and matching blue panties I hadn't seen before. Fit right in with the eye-friendly decor of the suite.

I tried to reach out for Bree, but the ropes held me back.

'Come here, Bree. Kiss me,' I said. '*Please* kiss me. Just a kiss.'

'Just a kiss, huh? I'm supposed to believe that one?'

She did finally kiss me – but not until she'd taken her sweet time tasting me all over. I twisted and twined my legs with hers. That was about all I could do. I was getting a little crazy to move around but not totally minding that I couldn't. And I was definitely hot for Detective Bree Stone, beginning to get in a *big hurry* too.

'My, my, my,' she said, and smiled. 'This is working out even better than I thought it would. We should come here more often.'

'I agree. How about every night?'

Finally she lay down on top of me. Bree's lips were an inch from mine; her breasts were warm on my chest; her eyes were beautiful to stare at this close.

'You want me to undo these nasty ropes now?' she asked.

I nodded, breathing hard. 'Yes.'

'Yes, what?' Her nails softly raked down my chest, then my legs, then between my legs. I shuddered at the touch, couldn't help myself if I wanted to.

'Yes, please! *Is* this about being in control?' I asked again.

'No, Dr Cross. It's about *trust*. Do you trust me?'

'Should I?'

'Don't answer a question with a question.'

'Yeah, I do. I trust you. Is that a wise thing to do?'

'Very wise. It's the only way we can be together.'

I laughed. 'Well, I want us to be together. Right now, actually.'

'You do, do you?'

'I see you're into torture.'

'Uh-huh.'

Then Bree finally reached across my body, and with two quick pulls of the rope, she freed my hands. I would have been impressed by her expertise with knots, but my mind was on other things at that moment. I rolled Bree over and kissed her, and then I was inside her. Deep, very deep. '*Slow,*' she whispered. 'Make this last.' It occurred to me only later that that was exactly what Bree had been going for all along. *Make this last.*

Talk about a win-win situation. Talk about a night off from all the craziness.

Maybe we were even ready for whatever might come next. And maybe we weren't even close. But right now, none of that mattered.

'Room has wireless high-speed access. All the amenities you could hope for. Should we check in on the world?' Bree asked after our first time.

'We definitely . . . *shouldn't* . . . check in on anything.'

Chapter Seventy-Eight

E arly the following morning, the great Kyle Craig entered through the gates of the University of Chicago. He was dressed as he thought a college professor might reasonably outfit himself for class these days: khaki trousers and sneakers, a blue denim work shirt, a gray knit vest, a knit tie. Craig found the getup satisfying in a comical sort of way. *The very idea of his teaching the nation's youth. My God!* At least he was amusing himself, if no one else.

He had already studied the school's Web site, so he went directly to the large library, the Regenstein. He checked a few reference files, and within minutes, he was in a reading room attached to the graduate school – leaving another message for DCAK. This time he decided to be more circumspect, hiding the message in a photograph. He'd learned about the process of steganography while he was in jail, planning for his future.

We meet again, my good friend. I hope to be in your neck of the woods very soon. It will be a pleasant walk down memory lane for me. Plus the unique chance to experience your work from a slightly closer vantage point. You are making history, after all. We both are. Everything is working so beautifully. If you would like to meet in person, I will be at X marks the spot, midnight, the second Saturday from now.

If you aren't there. I will understand completely. You are a busy bee, after all. Such a gifted artist too. I stand in awe of your work and look forward to your next play.

Kyle Craig stopped typing, reread what he'd written, and then pressed 'send.' He whispered to himself, 'If he can't figure out X *marks the spot,* then he doesn't deserve to meet me face-to-face.'

Chapter Seventy-Nine

Kyle changed cabs three times on his way back to his hotel, which was just off Michigan Avenue. He was excited about so many things now, even being free in Chicago, which had always been a favorite city of his, so much cleaner and more upbeat than New York or Los Angeles, or even Washington.

Freedom *is a hell of a concept,* he thought as he rode along in the third and final cab on busy Michigan Avenue. Especially after time spent in that seven-by-twelve hole inside ADX Florence. Life at the prison was cruel and unusual punishment, like being suffocated to death, very slowly and painfully, over several years. ADX Florence literally crushed its prisoners to death, as if the jail were a living thing.

But now – *he was out.*

He had important things to do, not the least of which was carrying out a most exciting plan for revenge against everyone who had hurt him in the past. *Everyone!* It had usually been about revenge for him, the idea of hurting – sometimes torturing – people who offended him, and that certainly hadn't changed. This plan – well, it could take years to complete. It was his masterpiece, after all.

He thought about DCAK for a moment. Actually, Kyle had first come across the killer while still with the FBI. The killer had been living and working on the West Coast – an actor – doing small roles and an occasional murder. Kyle had linked murders in Sacramento, Seattle, and LA to the actor. He'd made contact – twice – by email. But then Kyle had been caught himself, something he had never expected. Ironically, it was while he was in jail that he discovered he had so many fans . . . and imitators. It made sense, actually. Once he was in jail, they knew *where* to contact the Mastermind, and a few clever ones figured out how to do it.

But enough ancient history for the moment. That was such a bore. *Just look at the zombies out there on the Midway!* he thought as he cruised along in the speeding cab. He wished he could kill a few of them too, but alas, he was on a schedule, though one of his own making.

No one paid the least bit of attention to him back at the hotel. Imagine that. No respect, no disrespect – which was a good thing. *Wasn't it?* He had cut his hair down to the scalp and usually wore one of the half-dozen prosthetic masks he kept in his suitcase.

He got to the room – thinking about DCAK and what he was planning for him – slid in the key card, and heard someone inside.

What was this? A visitor? He'd left the DO NOT DISTURB sign on the door.

He took out his gun, a small Beretta that was easy to conceal under his loose-fitting clothes.

Yes, somebody was definitely in there. Interesting development. Who was it? Alex Cross? No, that wasn't even a remote possibility. *DCAK? Here in Chicago?* He doubted it. *Chicago police?* That would be more likely.

He turned the corner – and saw a housekeeper, a young black woman. Listening to her iPod. Oblivious to the world, and who could blame her? Not bad-looking, actually. Chesty, long skinny legs, working barefoot on the rug. Smooth skin. Hair in a tight ponytail. Lord, he had missed this – longed for it every day in jail, several times a day.

'I'm sor-ry,' the girl drawled when she saw him standing there, the gun tucked behind his back now. No need to frighten the poor thing half to death.

'Oh, it's not a problem. Just finish up what you're doing,' he said, slipping the gun back into the holster under his vest.

He took out his ice pick instead. Fingered it, like Queeg with those metal balls.

'You're too pretty to be working here like this, cleaning rooms. I'm sorry if that's insulting. I've forgotten my manners lately.'

The girl stammered without looking at him. 'I'll c-come back,' she said.

'No,' Kyle said. 'Actually, you won't. There is no afterlife.' Then, 'In *my* honor,' he whispered as he struck the maid's chest, once, twice – for symmetry, for art's sake, for the joy of it. And he thought, *She reminds me of one of Alex Cross's girlfriends.* And he stabbed her again.

He even left another little clue before he abandoned the room – a bobble-head figure of the great outlaw Jesse James.

Jesse James! Would anybody get that one?

Anybody in their right mind?

Chapter Eighty

Nana swears that good, positive things happen in twos and threes, though I can't remember that actually happening to me. Lately, even *one* positive thing in a row was hard to come by.

In the morning, I spoke with Tess Olsen's editor at a New York publishing house, then to the author's personal assistant in Maryland, and I was able to get a copy of the proposal for the book that Olsen had planned to write about Kyle Craig. A few lines from the thirty-page outline and pitch were particularly interesting to me.

Olsen had written:

It is important that I gain Kyle Craig's trust and confidence so that he believes I will write a flattering book detailing his cunning and his brilliance.

Based on our meetings at ADX Florence, I am fairly certain I can do this. Kyle Craig likes me. I can tell that already. I know the criminal mind as well as anyone out there, don't I?

In my opinion, Kyle Craig believes that he will get out of ADX Florence someday. He is making plans for the future.

He even went so far as to tell me that he is innocent. Is that possible?

Clearly, Kyle had fooled someone else . . . and then what? *Had he arranged her murder? Or had the killer, or killers, in Washington murdered Tess Olsen as some kind of homage to Craig? Was that a possibility?*

Either way, there had to be a connection, and it was one of the few real leads we had toward the capture of DCAK. Or Kyle Craig, for that matter.

The second positive thing happened while I was going over everything about the case again. Suddenly I figured out a piece of the puzzle, and it tied into my earlier findings about Tess Olsen.

The Hallmark card – I finally got it! It hit me that Hallmark's headquarters were in Kansas City – KC.

KC – Kyle Craig.

A couple of other clues quickly became clear.

A figurine of *The Scout* had been left at the apartment of a murdered woman in Iowa City. Kyle Craig was a suspect in the homicide. *The Scout* was a famous statue located in *Kansas City*.

A bottle of Arthur Bryant's barbecue sauce had been left out in his mother's kitchen. Arthur Bryant's was a famous restaurant in KC.

We were finally making some breakthroughs, even if they were clues the killers wanted us to find.

Why was that? Were we proving ourselves worthy? Was I proving myself worthy of this manhunt?

Was I?

Chapter Eighty-One

We found out about DCAK's next move less than three days later. After I saw my slate of morning patients – including the vet Anthony Demao, who was back and who had had a minor meltdown during our session to prove it – I connected with Bree at the Daly Building. My own desk at the Daly was counterproductively stuffed with DCAK case materials, most of them attached to dead leads, unfortunately. Our plan that day was to weed through and archive everything that needed to come off the radar so we could refocus our efforts where they might do some good.

It never happened.

The phone on my desk rang around two thirty. I picked up and heard a voice that I recognized.

'Detective Cross? It's Jeanne Phillips at the *Post*. I'm wondering if you've seen the latest email yet and if you'd care to comment on it?'

'Don't know what email you mean, Jeanne,' I said. Jeanne had funneled some pretty good information my way in the past, which was the reason I was willing to stay on the line with her.

'Trust me on this, you *want* to know. How about if I hold on while you check your in-box?'

Suddenly, I realized that whatever this was, I didn't want to be on the phone with a reporter from the *Washington Post* when I saw it.

'I'll call you back,' I said.

What I found moments later was another stunner. The message was from DCAK and had been sent to my email, Bree's, and what looked like just about every news desk, TV channel, and radio station in the DC metro area. He had authenticated it in his usual way, with an image of his latest calling card scanned right into the message. The image was of the postal ID from the Smithsonian, which we'd kept out of the press like the others before it.

The message was written in his familiar taunting style.

Detectives:

Does anyone besides me think you aren't giving this case the attention it deserves? By my count, it's DCAK six, cops zero. That's right, I said six. Or maybe five and a half – since this one isn't quite dead yet.

I've gone and found that piece of shit copycat, no thanks to any of you. It wasn't hard – just took a little thought. More than you've given it, anyway; more than you're capable of, I suspect.

But here's what I'm going to do for you. In one hour, you'll receive another message – with an address. That's where you'll find your copycat, and if you're lucky, he'll still be alive. I haven't decided yet. My call, of course. Dead or alive? Dead or alive? We'll have to see.

Now do you understand why the public is so scared of me? I'm better at this than you are, and they know it. That's your problem. It will always be your problem. Time and time again. For years to come, since I plan to be at this for a long while. In the meantime, you can do what you do best. Sit on your asses and wait to see what I do next.

Until then . . .

Keep on living, fuckers.

Chapter Eighty-Two

Bree saw to it that just about every available cruiser in the entire city was put on standby. I called Sampson myself and told him to keep his line open. I tried Kitz to see if we could preemptively trace an incoming email, but I got his voice mail – and the same thing when I tried his assistant. I fielded calls from Superintendent Davies, the chief's office, the mayor's office, and then Nana herself. DCAK's story was already out there on the airwaves. Of course it was. He'd put it there to stoke all the fires that he possibly could.

Word from downstairs was that we had a growing press army waiting for us on the street, too. It didn't feel like anything was going our way, probably because it wasn't, and that wasn't likely to change anytime soon, from what I could tell.

Finally Bree and I stopped taking calls altogether. We holed up in the office, *waiting,* just like the bastard wanted us to. We put our energy into examining the latest email, scanning for a hidden meaning, some indication of his state of mind, anything we might use – anything to keep us from spinning our wheels in another wrong direction.

The MO was basically the same. His online stuff was just another kind of disguise – electronic – but it all came from the same narcissistic mind. This was a deeply disturbed person, but that didn't mean he wasn't enjoying himself. He was organized and clever, and he knew it.

Three thirty came and went.

Then four o'clock.

Then five.

He was obviously toying with us, saying in no uncertain terms, *I'm in control here.* Bree and I eventually began to wonder if another email was coming at all.

Then at five thirty, it arrived.

The message we'd been waiting for was all of six words. *He was efficient, wasn't he?*

Nineteenth SE and Independence Ave. Now.

Chapter Eighty-Three

My stomach had never been tied in so many knots, not that I could remember, anyway. DCAK was bad enough, but now I was sure Kyle Craig had been added to the mix, and I couldn't figure out why, or where this freight train could be headed. Nowhere I wanted to go.

The drive over to Nineteenth and Independence was a paparazzi nightmare of the sort that had probably killed Princess Diana and Dodi Al Fayed in a dark, scary tunnel in Paris. We cut diagonally through the city toward Southeast, sirens wailing and an unbelievable entourage following us the whole way. Hell, we were like the pied pipers of DC, with trailing rats that wanted nothing more than to take our picture and run it in the *National Enquirer*. If they were gambling we wouldn't stop to issue traffic violations right now, they had that right.

Six MPD units were already at the scene when we got there, and they had closed off the main intersections to foot and vehicle traffic. *But what exactly* was *this scene? What had happened here?*

No obvious clues. The neighborhood was a mix of residential and industrial. Two lines of newly refurbished row houses extended along both Nineteenth and Independence from the northwest corner. I remembered that I'd actually read about this project in the paper, all primary colors and funky angles. Just the extra touch of visual drama our killer would go for. *The bastard was making a movie, wasn't he? Shooting it all in his head.*

The new St Coletta School was across the street in one direction, and the Armory Building in the other. It was a huge area to cover – a giant haystack, with somebody's body for a needle. Or, God willing, a living victim this time. *Was that a possibility?* Maybe DCAK wanted a change of pace.

More squad cars arrived, over a dozen of them, and then I stopped counting. I wondered when Kitz and his people would get here. We needed the FBI techies on this, all the help we could possibly get.

First thing, we made the residential buildings our priority, working in teams of two and knocking on every door up and down the street. Everything else had to wait, including any attempt at crowd control. The scene was already too crazy – camera crews matched us step for step, shooting from every angle.

We hadn't been searching long when one of the uniformed officers called out, 'Detectives. Something over here. *Detectives!*'

Bree and I ran to see what was up. The house in question was bright yellow, with large single-pane windows facing out onto Nineteenth Street. The front door was ajar and had been heavily gouged around the doorknob and faceplate. It looked like somebody had recently broken in.

'Good enough for me,' Bree said. 'Sufficient evidence of a break-in. Let's go.'

Chapter Eighty-Four

We went in carefully, silently, along with one of the neighbor-hood officers, a scared kid named DiLallo. The other uniforms stayed outside to keep back any particularly reckless reporters, or even a daring looky-loo on the scene.

Inside, the house was perfectly still. The air was stale and thick with heat – no open windows, no air-conditioning. The decor was modern, like the exterior. I saw an Eames-lounger knockoff in the living room to my left, a red lacquered table, mesh chairs in the dining room beyond. Nothing to go on yet, but I sensed something had happened here.

Bree ticked her head to the left – *she'd take the living room* – and motioned for the patrol officer to go straight back, probably to the kitchen.

I took the stairs.

They were solid floating slabs of wood with an iron railing that made no sound as I climbed. The place was too quiet – *dead-body quiet,* I couldn't help thinking, and I dreaded what we might find here.

Were we the audience this time? Was that the big, new twist here? Had this all been staged for us?

A domed skylight overhead let in plenty of sunshine, and I could feel the sweat dripping down my back.

At the top, the stairs doubled around to an open hallway that over-looked the first floor. A door was closed on the left, with an open one closer to me showing off an empty bathroom. It looked empty from this angle, anyway.

Still no people, though, dead or alive.

I could hear more police arriving downstairs, quite the crowd on hand already. Nervous whispers and radio chatter. The high-pitched voice of Officer DiLallo – somebody called him Richard, as in *Richard, calm down.*

Bree reappeared in the hallway below me. She gave an all-clear sign, and I motioned for her to come up.

'You lonely?' she asked.

'For you . . . always.'

When she joined me upstairs, I pointed to the bedroom door. 'Only one that's closed,' I said.

I steeled myself for what we might find, then burst in through the door. I trained my Glock on the far corner, swept left, swept right.

I didn't know whether to be disappointed or relieved. There was nothing in the room. Nothing there that shouldn't be. A platform bed was neatly made in one corner. The open closet held women's clothes.

What the hell were we missing? We were at Nineteenth and Independence, right?

Just then, we both heard the first faint chop of a helicopter, approaching fast. A moment later, it was hovering right over the house.

Other sounds filtered in from the street. One loud shout cut through. It reached us at the top of the stairs.

'It's on the roof!'

I looked up, and that's when I realized the domed skylight was also a hatch.

Chapter Eighty-Five

'We need a ladder up here!' Bree yelled to the cops below. 'We need it in a hurry.'

I could see black scrape marks on the wall where there normally was a ladder of some kind for roof access. Not anymore, though. Somebody had taken it away.

The skylight was out of reach without it, even if I got on someone's shoulders.

Bree and I hurried outside – there was no hiding the situation from the media now. Two other helicopters had joined the first one, circling the house like scavengers overhead. Neighbors, passersby, and more press than I could count were clogging the front walk and the street beyond. What a pain-in-the-ass mess this was turning out to be, and we hadn't even gotten to the punch line yet.

'Clear this whole area,' I said to the nearest officer. 'I'm not fooling around. DCAK has been here!'

Bree and I split up then, and I pushed my way through to get to the first news van I could find with a broadcast tower. It turned out to be Channel Four, parked in front of the armory across the street.

A reporter was already giving her rapid-fire spiel to the camera as I approached on the run. I interrupted her midsentence.

'Do any of those choppers belong to you?' I shouted, and pointed an arm up at the sky.

She was attractive, ash-blonde, twentysomething, and immediately indignant. 'And who are you?' she asked. Whoever I was, her cameraman swung around to get me in the shot.

I didn't wait for the answer that I needed from the reporter. I stepped right past her and slid open the panel door on the Channel Four van.

'MPD!' I showed my badge to the wide-eyed tech sipping a 'vente' Starbucks at his console. 'I need to see exactly what your chopper is seeing.'

Midsip, and without a word, he pointed at one of the screens. A piece of electric-blue tape underneath it said LIVE FEED.

Here was the audience, I realized suddenly.

I'd been wondering how DCAK's next plan would come into play. Now I knew. *Anyone watching television would see this. That sonofabitch had planned everything just so.*

I looked at my watch – just past six o'clock, the evening-news hour. *That's why the killer had waited to send out the second email, wasn't it?*

The helicopter shot wasn't close enough to capture every detail, but there definitely was a body up there. I was fairly sure it was a male, but not 100 percent. Dark pants, light shirt, and what seemed to be blood coming from the neck. The face looked strange, though, distorted in some way that I couldn't make any sense out of yet.

A collapsible ladder lay on the roof nearby. 'Tell your man up there to pan around,' I said. 'Please do it right now.'

'You don't take orders from him.' The young reporter had her helmet of blond hair stuck inside the van now too. It was getting crowded in there.

'You do unless you want to get arrested,' I told the tech. 'I *will* lock you up. *Both* of you.'

He nodded and spoke into his headset.'Bruce, pan around the rooftop, will ya? Get in closer if you can. This is a police request. Roger that.'

Other than the body, the roof looked deserted, at least from the camera angles. 'Okay, that's good,' I said.

'*Back on the body,*' the reporter barked from behind me.'This is *live.*'

'Alex!' Bree was shouting from the sidewalk. 'We've got a ladder. Let's go on up there.'

I took one more glance at the screen, and as I did, I saw the victim's arm move. It was very slight, but discernible. I was out of the van in a hurry, nearly knocking Miss Channel Four right off her high heels.

'Bree! This one's still alive!'

Chapter Eighty-Six

I was the first one up on the roof. Bree was next, with two very nervous EMTs right behind her. After a quick visual scan to make sure the area was clear, the EMTs scampered over to help the victim, who, we hoped, was still alive.

There was a wooden deck next to the hatch. A flat, open area of tar paper stretched beyond that, which was where the body lay. The roof was steaming in the sun. Heat vapors rose up around the body too, and I could see that the pool of blood leaking from his neck had grown considerably.

'Doesn't look very good,' Bree groaned.

'No, it doesn't.'

The most jarring thing of all was the mask over the victim's face. That's why he had looked so strange in the shot from the helicopter. It was another Richard Nixon caricature – like the one used at the George Washington Memorial Parkway murder scene.

'Why do I think this isn't the copycat?' I shouted in Bree's ear over the roar of helicopters swarming above us. 'Or that there ever was one?'

She nodded. 'I suspect you're right.' We were thinking the same thing again. The so-called copycat murders were DCAK's own homage to himself. And this was the moment when we were all meant to know it – with the television cameras rolling overhead. The whole world was supposed to be watching as the bastard put one over on us again.

'Is he alive?' I shouted to the nearest EMT. I hadn't seen any movement from the victim since we'd come up on the roof.

'BP's nonpalpable. Pulse one twenty,' he called to us. Meanwhile, his partner was radioing down for a gurney.

'Get that mask off him!' Bree said.

Easier said than done. Apparently the latex had melted onto the hot roof at the back of his head. Finally the EMTs had to cut the mask up the front.

Then, as the latex pulled away, a familiar face emerged.

Bree gasped, and I took her arm, partly for the support that I needed myself.

It was Kitz!

The FBI man who'd given us so much computer intel was ghostly pale and covered with swollen beads of sweat. His eyes were closed.

I dropped to my knees next to Brian Kitzmiller. The pads at his neck couldn't keep up with the bleeding. It was a sad, horrendous mess.

'Kitz!' I took his hand and applied slight pressure. 'It's Alex. Help is on the way.'

His fingers fluttered in mine, barely a squeeze, but he was still with us.

His eyes finally opened, and he seemed confused at first.

When he saw it was me, though, he tried to say something. His puffy and blistered lips moved, but if he made a sound, I couldn't hear it.

'Hang in there,' I told him. 'We've got you now. You're going to be okay. Hold on, Kitz.'

He tried to talk again, but nothing that I could understand came out of his mouth.

With what looked to be great effort, he blinked twice. Then his eyes rolled back in his head. The EMTs kept at it, but by the time the gurney got there, it was all over.

Kitz was gone. And he had died on camera, just the way DCAK planned it.

I turned to Bree. My mind was working overtime. 'Kitz blinked twice. *Two* killers?'

Chapter Eighty-Seven

Before the police and TV news choppers got there, DCAK had worked his way across two sections of roof. Then he scuttled down a wobbly painting scaffold to a community parking area in the back, where he would be safe.

He was traveling heavy today, with a laptop and camera in a black satchel slung over his shoulder – but it was nothing he couldn't handle. He was jacked up, and he was definitely into this new role . . . and the *story*.

He slipped off the latex gloves, then plucked a silver lighter out of his pocket. Seconds later, the gloves were a lump of melted rubber on the cement. *Let the cops try to print that and trace the puddle back to him.*

Everything else about him stayed as it was: long blond hair in a ponytail, light growth of beard to match the bleached eyebrows, brown contacts, steel-rimmed glasses, and a White Sox cap turned backward on his head.

The name for today was Neil Stephens, he had decided. He was supposed to be an AP photographer based out of Chicago. The camera was a brand-new Leica. He'd blend right in here. No problems about that. Plus, he'd get to watch the whole thing come to a climax. See all the players close-up, check out their reactions under pressure. No one could have done this better, not even Kyle Craig on his best day.

When he came around from the A Street side of the development, the block on Nineteenth looked like a Barnum and Bailey Circus – *in a good way.* He stood on the bumper of a parked car and took several wide-angle shots – police cruisers up and down the block, ambulances, a SWAT truck in the armory parking lot, a dozen or more TV and radio stations on the scene. Hundreds of locals, it looked like. They were loitering up and down the street, trying to figure out what the hell was going down.

Did anybody know yet? Had they figured it out? DCAK was about to put their mopey little neighborhood on the map. Soon they would all start thanking God it hadn't happened to them.

Yes, little minds would be blown sky-high tonight. He was one of the best ever now, wasn't he? Right up there with Kyle Craig.

By the time the helicopters arrived, the police on the ground had gotten their act together enough to wrangle the masses out of harm's way. Alex Cross was on the scene – and Bree Stone too. Actually, she was getting a little too big for her britches, he was thinking. Maybe it was time to do something about that.

That could be his next story.

Chapter Eighty-Eight

Neil Stephens, AP, jostled shoulder to shoulder with the other press, all of them competing for 'money shots' across the street from the yellow house where the FBI man's body had been found. Of course, he already had his million-dollar shot – a nice close-up on Brian Kitzmiller's face. Eyes wide open, neck bleeding out like a stuck pig's.

'Some crazy scene, huh?' Another lensman turned to speak to him. A brown-skinned fireplug of a guy. 'Whole story's unbelievable, right? You been covering it from the beginning?'

You could say that, DCAK thought to himself.

'Just got to town,' he said, making sure to flatten his vowels for a kind of nasal Chicago accent. *Jest gaht to town.* He loved details like that. That's where the grace was, and the devil too. 'Doing a piece on the detectives and CSI. That's my angle here. Folks love their CSI. This little turn of events is just a, uh—'

'Lucky coincidence?'

The killer returned the guy's cynical smile. 'That's right, I guess. Lucky me.'

'Here they come!' someone shouted, and Neil Stephens of the AP raised his camera along with everybody else.

The door across the street opened. Detectives Cross and Stone came out first, ahead of the body. They both looked like they'd been eating the same shit sandwich – and it looked good in telephoto.

Click! Nice little two-shot of the opposition. Beaten to a pulp but not quite defeated. Still standing, anyway.

Cross looked especially pissed off. His hands and shirt were covered in Kitzmiller's blood.

Click!

Another classic shot.

The two of them joined the other cop – John Sampson, Cross's friend – who was waiting on the sidewalk. Stone said something in the big lug's ear – *click!* – and Sampson shook his head. He apparently couldn't believe what he was hearing. Probably the news that it was Brian Kitzmiller up on the roof.

Click, click, click!

This shit was golden.

The little guy next to him kept talking while he worked, a real live chatterbox. 'They say Cross over there is one of our best. Seems like he's getting his ass kicked a little on this one.'

'Looks that way, huh?' Neil Stephens said, and kept snapping away, getting each of the three detectives' faces close-up, as tight as he could go. Nothing too arty, but good stuff. Keeping it real.

Then he pulled back some and got all three of them in one master shot.

Click, click, click!

Then he stopped shooting and just watched their faces through the viewfinder for several heartbeats. *Is that how he'd take them out in the end? All three in one shot heard round the world? Or maybe do it nice and slow – one at a time.*

Stone.

Sampson.

Cross.

He hadn't decided yet. There was no rush – better to enjoy the journey and get there when he got there. However it went down, the ending would be the same: dead, dead, and dead. And he would be a legend – right up there with the best.

'So you say you just got to town?' The little guy was still blabbing his ass off. 'Guess that means you haven't talked to any of them yet, huh?'

'Not yet,' Neil Stephens said. *Naht yet.* 'But I'm definitely looking forward to it.'

Chapter Eighty-Nine

There is a sad little death of hope and optimism that happens every time something tragic and unforeseen like this goes down. It was as if Kitz's murder opened up a little more room for hatred in my heart. *Was that true?* All I could hope for now was that we would get the killer – or killers – and stop all this somehow.

So I did the one positive thing I could do: I kept working the case, harder than ever before. For starters, Bree, Sampson, and I stayed at the house on Nineteenth Street late into the night. We sucked every last drop of evidence out of the crime scene, but truthfully there wasn't much to go on. The place was clean. It turned out that the home-owners were away for the month. None of the neighbors had seen anything unusual. No one had spotted DCAK before or after he murdered Brian Kitzmiller.

I got home around three thirty the next morning and grabbed a few hours of sleep, then pushed myself to get up and start all over again. There were patients to see first thing, but I used my early-morning run to the office to go over everything in my head one more time. Then again. And again.

What was I missing? He was evolving – that much was clear. Just about every successful serial killer does; it's only a matter of how. Certainly his methods were improving, and growing more complex. Everything about yesterday was a little bigger – the news coverage, the derring-do, and the amount of live-television time he'd gotten.

It was about control, wasn't it? That was what was changing most dramatically here. It crystallized for me as I sprinted across the National Mall, my lungs starting to burn. With each murder, DCAK got a little more control, a little more of an edge on us. Which meant – ironically – that time *wasn't* on our side.

I was still thinking of the killer as *he* but that might not be true. A man and a woman were probably working together, leaving a trail of clues for us to follow.

Chapter Ninety

In many ways, I felt like I was leading a double life – probably because I was. After Sandy Quinlan's appointment that morning, I had Anthony Demao on deck, figuring I'd squeze him in for as many sessions as possible following his meltdown. I still didn't know how things stood between the two of them since the scene that I'd witnessed in my waiting room.

So I was relieved when they ignored each other on her way out that morning. Sandy looked uncomfortable; Anthony just seemed uninterested. I was glad, because this wasn't a hookup either of them needed. It just *felt* wrong.

As soon as Sandy was gone, Anthony's demeanor began to change. He was clearly agitated and seemed shakier than usual. Despite the heat, he'd worn long trousers and a camo jacket, the latter held tightly closed as he walked inside my office and plopped on the couch.

Then he stood again and began to pace around the room. Anthony was walking rapidly, hands jammed into his pockets, mumbling to himself.

'What's going on?' I finally had to ask. 'You seem agitated.'

'You think so, Doc? I had another dream, couple nights in a row. Dream about Basra. The fucking desert, the war, the whole nine yards of bad shit, okay?'

'Anthony, come and sit down. Please.' He had tried to tell me about Basra before but hadn't said enough for me to understand where he was going with it. I gathered something terrible had happened to him in the war; I just didn't know what it was.

When Anthony finally slumped down onto the couch, I spotted a lump under his jacket. I knew what it was, and I sat up straight, my blood pumping.

'Are you carrying?' I asked.

He put his hand over the bulge. 'It isn't loaded,' he snapped. 'Not a problem.'

'Please give it to me,' I said. 'You can't have a gun in here.'

He narrowed his eyes at me. 'I said *it's not loaded*. Don't you believe me? Anyway, I have a license to carry.'

'Not in here, you don't.' I stood up now. 'That's it. You have to go.'

'No, no. Here, you take it.' Suddenly Anthony reached under his jacket and pulled out a Colt 9. 'Take the damn gun!'

'Slowly,' I said. 'Two fingers on the handle. Put it on the coffee table. Keep your other hand where it is.'

Anthony stared at me in a new way, as if he'd just figured something out. 'What are you, a cop?'

'Just do what I asked you to do, okay?'

He laid the Colt on the coffee table. Once I had checked that it was empty, I locked the gun in my desk. Took a breath, let it out slowly.

'Now, do you want to talk about your dream?' I asked him. 'Basra? What happened to you there?'

He nodded. Then he began to talk – and to pace the room again. But at least he wasn't armed.

'It started out the same . . . the dream. We got hit, and I made it to a trench. Like I always do. But this time I wasn't alone.'

'Are you talking about Matt?' I asked. We had gotten that far in the dream before.

'He was there with me, yeah. Just the two of us. We got separated from our unit.'

Matt was a buddy of his I'd heard about. They had worked on the same munitions truck, but I didn't know too much more than that.

'He was ruined, man. Both his legs like hamburger, shredded to shit. I had to drag him by his arms. It was all I could do.' He stared at me for help.

'Anthony, are you talking about your *dream* or what really happened that night?'

Now his voice went down to a whisper. 'That's the thing, Doc. I think I'm talking about *both*. Matt was screaming like he was some kind of wild, hurt animal. And when I heard the screaming, *in the dream,* it was like I knew I'd heard it before.'

'Were you able to help him?' I asked.

'Not really, no. I couldn't help, couldn't do anything at all. A medic couldn't have helped Matt, the condition he was in.'

'Okay. So what happened next?'

'Matt starts saying, "I'm not gonna make it." Not gonna make it.' Over and over like that. And this whole time, there's fire coming from every direction. I don't know if it's our guys or the ragheads. There's nowhere the two of us can go – not with him on those shot-up legs and losing his insides like he was. And then he starts saying, "Kill me. Do it. Please."'

I could see that Anthony was into it now, the dream, the horror of what had happened that night in the war. I let him keep going.

'He takes out his own gun. He can barely even hold it. He's crying 'cause he can't do it, and I'm crying 'cause I don't want him to. And mortars are going off everywhere. The sky is lit up like the Fourth of July.'

Anthony shook his head, stopped talking. His eyes were welling up with tears. I thought I understood: there were no words he could use to describe this.

'Anthony?' I asked. 'Did you help Matt kill himself?'

A tear rolled all the way down his cheek.

'I put my hand over Matthew's, and I shut my eyes . . . then we fired. Together.' Anthony stared at me. 'You believe me, don't you, Dr Cross?'

'I should, shouldn't I?'

'I don't know,' he said, and there was anger in his eyes. 'You're the doctor. You should know the difference between bad dreams and reality. You do, don't you?'

Chapter Ninety-One

In our very strange and strangely powerful session together, Anthony Demao had asked me if I was a cop, and it struck me now that I hadn't answered him. I wasn't quite sure myself these days. I was still settling back in with Metro, and my situation was a special one. I knew one thing for sure: I hadn't ever worked any harder on a case – one that seemed more complex and difficult every day.

Frustrating to all of us, but not that unusual under the circumstances, our hands were tied in the investigation of Brian Kitzmiller's death. The Cyber Unit at the Bureau had promised a new contact soon and a full report on everything Kitz had been doing before he died, but in the meantime, it was basically 'We'll get back to you.'

Which is why Sampson and I showed up on Beth Kitzmiller's doorstep in Silver Spring, Maryland, a day later. We didn't want to bother the family, to intrude on their grief, but we didn't have much choice.

'Thanks for letting us come over,' I said as Beth let the two of us into the foyer of the house.

Her face was drawn, and she looked deeply tired – but there was strength and resolve in her voice. 'Brian died looking for this terrible, terrible man. You do whatever you need to do. Stay here as long as you have to. We need closure, Alex. I need it. So do my kids.'

Six-year-old Emily hovered at the top of the stairs, wide-eyed and silent, watching us. I gave her a wink and a quick smile, and finally she smiled back. Brave little girl, but just seeing her put a pain in my heart. I needed closure too.

'We were hoping to take a look in his office,' I told Beth. 'I know he did a lot of work at home.' *And if anyone crossed paths with our killer online, it would have been Kitz,* I thought, though I didn't say that part out loud.

'Of course. Let me show you the Lair.'

Beth led us through a pair of sliding pocket doors at the rear of the homey Colonial that Kitz would never see again. His office looked out onto a backyard with a swing set and a sunflower garden. Life goes on. For some of us, anyway. Not for Kitz, though.

Beth lingered in the doorway. 'I don't know if you'll find anything worthwhile or not, but please, look anywhere you like. Nothing in our house is off-limits.'

'Is this the only computer he used at home?' Sampson asked from where he sat at a large, cluttered desk. I noted that the system was surprisingly low-tech, just a Dell CPU and monitor.

'He had a laptop from the Bureau,' Beth said. 'I don't think it's here, though. I haven't come across it anywhere.'

I looked over at Sampson. We hadn't found a laptop in Kitz's office or his car. 'How about passwords? Any idea?' I asked Beth.

She blew out a mouthful of air. This was difficult, but Beth Kitzmiller was making it a lot easier for us. 'Try *Gummi Worm,* with an *i.* He used that one sometimes.'

The three of us exchanged a kind of shy, painful smile.

'It was his nickname for Emily,' she offered. 'And occasionally for me.'

Sampson tapped in *Gummi Worm.*

Chapter Ninety-Two

It was Kitz's password – at least, on the computer at home – and while Sampson feverishly worked the keyboard, I started in on the desk drawers.

I turned up a thick stack of pending case files, most of them serial-related, and all filled with Xeroxes of original material. I had to wonder if these were 'unauthorized' copies he'd brought home from work. *Kitz had been a 'fan' of this kind of stuff, right?* If he was a little obsessed, it was part of what made him good at his job. Of course, in the back of my mind, I couldn't help thinking, *Kitz was FBI*, and Kyle Craig had been too. Unfortunately, that particular line of thinking also made me a suspect.

The first case I looked at was one I'd heard about before. Someone was breaking into suburban Maryland homes at night and strangling women in their beds. No theft, no vandalism – just the vicious murders themselves. So far, there had been three in a span of five months, one every seven weeks.

The next file was coded 'Mapmaker,' and outlined a series of shootings, always with the same gun. The victims were apparently random, the only consistency being their location. The shootings, four so far, had taken place on street corners along a straight line running through Northwest DC.

Then I discovered a file Kitz had put together on Kyle Craig. It even included information on how I had taken Kyle down. Plus, Kitz had been going through all of Kyle's old case notes, including the ongoing investigations at the time he was arrested.

When I found the DCAK file, it was mostly old information on the Washington-area murders: copies of crime reports, map sections, lab results, interviews – hundreds of them, all tied to the known homicides. Not much that was new or helpful. And nothing directly linking DCAK to Craig.

'How's it going over there?' I asked Sampson. 'Any luck so far? Good or bad?'

'There's a lot to look at,' he said. 'He's got Technorati, Blogdex, PubSub . . . tracking software, Alex. With the right setup, he could ping anyone who commented on a blog or surfed a site.'

'So how do we find out what Kitz knew? Where did he keep it?'

Sampson thrummed his fingers on the desk. 'I could check his Internet history, see if there were sites he went to a lot. Guess I'll start there.'

A few minutes later, Sampson suddenly sat back in Kitz's desk chair. He whistled through his teeth. 'I'll be damned. Come over here, Alex.'

I peered over his shoulder.

'Look familiar?' Sampson asked. 'It should.'

He'd pulled up a long list of sites, many of them with names I recognized from my own surf-sleuthing. But that's not what had my attention now. In addition to the named sites, the list included dozens of numbers. As I looked closer, I saw that it was actually *the same number,* repeated over and over, subdivided in different ways with periods and slashes.

344.19.204.411
34.41.920.441/1
34.419.20.44/11
344.192.04.411

The list continued beyond the figures on the screen, but what we had was our mystery number – *the one from the side of the mailbag at the Smithsonian.*

'It's an IP address, Alex. A Web site. At least, Kitz seemed to think so.'

'Why didn't he tell us about it?' I asked. 'What's going on here, Sampson?'

'Maybe he hadn't found the right combination. Maybe he hadn't gotten around to checking it yet. Or the site could be inactive.'

'One way to find out,' I said. 'Let's start at the top and work our way down the list.'

Chapter Ninety-Three

Bree Stone stood all alone on the roof of the Nineteenth Street house, staring at the spot where the sun had baked Brian Kitzmiller's blood to a cracked black stain. All the wrong questions were running through her head: *Did you suffer much, Kitz? Were you blindsided? Did you even have a fighting chance? Any chance at all? Did you know who did this?*

They were inevitable questions, human ones, but also unhelpful to this investigation. She needed to focus on the killer's methods and then trace any evidence he might have left here.

Tonight, Bio-Tec was coming in to clean the 'yellow house.' The homeowners would be back in town tomorrow. This was the last walk-through, her final chance to find some shred of evidence that everyday life would soon erase.

Every indication was that the killer had come up through the roof hatch and had exited by the scaffold in the back, two houses over. Kitz's postmortem had shown abrasions under the arms and fibers on his shirt where he'd been hauled up with a strong nylon rope, or a cord of some kind. Nonfatal levels of chloral hydrate were in his bloodstream, indicating he'd been unconscious, which was the only good news so far.

No blood was found inside the house, at least none that mattered. Kitz's throat had been cut right here on the roof, not long before the police arrived. The killer probably could have timed it any way he wanted.

The bastard chose the close call, didn't he? He planned everything about this, including that Kitz should die soon after we arrived.

Bree pressed her knuckles into the back of her neck. The pulsing headache she'd woken up with was turning into an all-day event. And the dark shirt she was wearing was a really bad call. It was already soaked through with sweat.

She walked toward the scaffold, past a litter of cigarette butts and half-crushed tall boys that hadn't been there before, which meant that *somebody* had been. 'Psychotourists,' Alex liked to call them, pathetic creeps drawn by a serial-crime scene. And hell, this was probably the most sensational case in the last ten years, unfortunately for everyone involved.

Bree looked straight down from the roof. The parking area below was mostly empty at this time of day. That's where Kitz's white Camry had been found in one of the resident spaces.

The killer either left on foot or had another vehicle waiting for him. *That is . . . if he left the scene at all.*

Had he?

Or had he stayed awhile to watch and collect memories?

Did he always hang around afterward?

The actual murder had taken place in private, an interesting departure for DCAK. The audience was bigger but also more abstract – out there in TV land somewhere. Bree wondered if he'd wanted – *needed* – to check out the 'live' crowd gathered on Nineteenth Street. She'd be willing to bet her shield that's exactly what the bastard had done.

And what about the woman who'd been his accomplice in Baltimore? Had she been here too? Was she part of everything from the start? What was the deal with the two of them? Lovers? Former inmates at some asylum? And what connected them to Kyle Craig?

Bree sat on the edge of the roof, then finally let herself down the scaffold, carefully, because she was feeling a little shaky right now – too much stress, not enough sleep, not enough Alex either. Seconds later, she was on the ground.

From there, she forced herself to follow the killer's most likely path, up the alley to A Street and back around to Nineteenth.

It was quiet now, especially compared to two days ago. A single MPD cruiser was parked in front of the house. Howie Pearsall, the officer she'd brought with her, was leaning against the passenger side. Howie was a good man, a friend of hers, just not the most ambitious guy in the world.

Bringing him was a safety precaution but not one that Bree took seriously. She was more likely to protect Howie than the other way around. He stood up straight and brushed something off his shirt when he saw her coming.

'At ease, soldier. Don't worry about it,' she said. 'Sorry I took so long, Howie.'

'How'd it go in there?' he wanted to know.

'Howie, it didn't. Hold on, I'll be right back.' She went up the front walk and tore the police notice off the door. So much for the crime scene.

'Excuse me. Detective?' The guy behind her on the lawn seemed to have come out of nowhere. *What the hell was his deal?*

'I'm Neil Stephens with the AP. I was wondering if I could ask you a few questions.'

Chapter Ninety-Four

Neil Stephens, or rather DCAK, wanted to shoot Bree Stone full of holes right there in front of the house. Pull the .357 out of his vest. *Bam.* Dumb cop dead on the front walk. Get the uniform sloppily moping around by the squad car too.

But no. This wasn't even a rehearsal, much less a performance. Maybe it was groundwork for later on, though. And a little bit of fun too. Detective Stone was, after all, a stone-cold fox. *And she was Alex Cross's girlfriend, wasn't she?* That made this very cool. Gave it stature and importance in his mind.

Stone kept moving toward the cruiser. 'No comment,' she said, not even making eye contact with him.

So she was a bitch on wheels as well as a mediocre detective! Figured. Cops weren't much of a challenge. Maybe *collectively* they were.

He pulled the Leica around on its strap. 'Just a quick photo, then?'

Like he cared about the picture. What he wanted was for Stone to see him – to *have seen* the character he was playing today, Neil Stephens.

Detective Bree Stone was his audience right now. But she didn't even look. She held up a palm and got into the car – *Talk to the hand puppet.* 'Let's go,' she said to the cop at the wheel, and they pulled away from the curb. End of interview.

Neil Stephens called out to her, 'Having a bad day, Detective Stone?'

It was meant to be in character, the parting shot of a pushy journalist. He wasn't even sure she'd heard it – until the police cruiser suddenly braked. Then the car backed up several feet to where he was standing.

Bree Stone climbed out and gave him a quick once-over. Now he had her attention. *But was that a good thing?*

'What did you say your name was?' she asked. 'I didn't catch the name.'

'Stephens. Out of Chicago. Associated Press.' The worst thing he could do right now was flinch. So he stepped closer instead. That's what Neil would do – get the story. 'I left you a voice mail this morning.' He hadn't. 'Actually, I was hoping to do a piece on your team while I was here in Washington.'

He was handling this pretty well, but his position still wasn't good. The logic wasn't quite right, didn't feel solid to him.

Stone must have thought so too. 'Could I see some ID?' she asked next.

So what did he do now? He stepped closer again and handed the identification to her. He could see the other cop out of the corner of his eye – both hands still on the wheel. Stone's gun was holstered on her right hip, next to her badge. He had her – no doubt about it in his mind. He could take her out right here, right now. He knew that he should too.

She looked at him again, her face more relaxed than before. 'Yeah, okay. We could do a quickie back at the office. I'll introduce you to whoever's around. How's that sound?'

She was almost convincing. *Almost fooled me, Detective.* But her tone told DCAK everything he needed to know, including that he had to act now or he was toast.

His fist flew up and struck Bree Stone in the temple. *Christ, she had a hard head for a woman.* He grabbed her Glock and shot the other cop right through the open window. DCAK fired into the crumpled form again to make sure. Then he turned back to Stone.

She was still down, obviously hurt but not unconscious. One hand was pressed against her forehead, blood dripping between the fingers. She tried to reach for him. He hooked her with his foot and flipped her on her back.

'*Don't move!*' he screamed in her face.

He put the gun inches from her eyes. 'Look at me, *Bree*. Remember my fucking face. And every time you do, you'll know what a total screwup you are. You and your main mount, Alex Cross. *Hey, you just met DCAK.*'

Chapter Ninety-Five

I rushed to be with Bree at St Anthony's emergency room, which was where my wife, Maria, had been pronounced dead, and I couldn't get that terrible, morbid thought out of my head. Bree was getting stitches when I got there. Word was they practically had to drag her into the ER. Unfortunately, an officer named Howie Pearsall was dead. Another cop down.

Bree started talking as soon as she saw me. 'He made a big mistake today, Alex. It wasn't supposed to go down like this, I'm sure of it.'

'He didn't expect to see you there. No, I don't think that he did. But we can't be one hundred percent sure of that, Bree. He's the man with a plan, right?'

She winced at the stitch she'd just gotten. The doctor working on her looked up at me for help, but Bree kept talking. 'He made the best of it, though. Taunted me, Alex. Let me see the character he was playing – some AP reporter. Neil Stephens, he said. Anything in the name? Or that he was playing a reporter this time? He said he was from Chicago.'

'Let's talk about this when you're done,' I said, and squeezed her hand.

She was still for a few seconds but then blurted out, 'Did you know Howie Pearsall just got married? Couple of weeks ago. Wife's a special-ed teacher.'

I nodded, trying to model silence until the sewing job on Bree was finished.

'I didn't see anybody else, Alex. No female in sight. Maybe she was just a one-shot. A distraction. Hey, be *careful* with that knitting needle, will you?'

'Sorry, Detective,' said the ER doctor.

'Don't be sorry. Be careful.'

Afterward, Bree and I sat in the lobby to talk. I had a few things to say to her that I knew she wouldn't want to hear. 'Bree, this thing just turned another corner. We both know it did. If he didn't kill you today, it's only because it didn't fit with a different plan he's already made, a different *role* he intended to play. I'd be more comfortable if you didn't work alone for the rest of the case. Make any sense?'

'Alex, I wasn't alone at the house. I went there with another officer. He's dead now.'

I nodded. 'Okay. I understand. I'm sorry to sound condescending. There's something else I need to say. I want you to come stay with us—'

'No. Thank you, but no, Alex. I'm not moving because of him. I've seen the sonofabitch now. We're going to nail him. He's going down, I promise you that. In flames, if I have anything to say or do about it.'

This was all kind of ironic. *How many times had I been on the other side of the same sort of conversation?* I hadn't really expected Bree to go for my idea, and I respected her too much to even suggest she back off the investigation. Besides, she wouldn't do it anyway.

'I'm fine, Alex. I'm okay. Thanks for being nice. Let's just get out of here. People *die* in hospitals.'

We were on our way to my car when Sampson called. He sounded excited on the phone.

'Alex, we cracked the IP address. I think it just went live. Anyway, he's got a new Web site up.'

'Jesus, you're kidding. Let me get Bree settled, and I'll be right there.'

'Excuse me?' She was already giving me a look. 'Whatever this is, I'm coming with you. Period. End of discussion.'

'Sampson, we'll be right there.'

Chapter Ninety-Six

Homicide was strangely quiet when we got there; the office was virtually deserted, actually. I knew that most everybody was out on the street, looking for DCAK, or leads on him, anyway.

'How you doing, Bree?' Sampson stood to let her sit, but she stayed standing where she was, stayed stubborn and strong, the Rock.

'I'm good. Couldn't be better, Big Man. What have you got?'

Sampson laughed at Bree's bravado, then the three of us cracked up.

'More of his greatest hits,' Sampson said. 'Let me show you the latest.'

We looked at the screen, where the new site had been called up. It had the same headline as the original: MY REALITY, in bold white letters on a black background.

'Give me a break,' Bree muttered. 'I am so going to mess this guy up. Next time I see him.'

'Bree, Bree, Bree,' I muttered, and left it at that.

I took the mouse and started scrolling down. Instead of a blog, or any text at all, it was just images this time. They were stacked in two columns, pictures of his self-created killers on the left, his 'roles' – and the respective victims on the right. The top two were screen captures from the fake Iraqi video. Next came a shot of Tess Olsen on all fours, with a red leash around her neck.

Another row of pictures showed the *X-Files* professor-type from the Kennedy Center and a publicity still of Matthew Jay Walker, but with a green X over his face.

Then came the 'fake' copycat with the Richard Nixon mask – and two pictures of the young kids he'd slaughtered on the parkway overpass.

Abby Courlevais's picture was a family snapshot that had run all over the news, her husband and little boy smiling next to her. The whole world had been exposed to the image.

The last two photos were grainy and blurred but clear enough for us to make out details. Bree recognized the reporter 'Neil Stephens,' even with a White Sox cap pulled down low over his eyes.

Then came Kitz.

His eyes and mouth were open, and there was a spatter of blood across his chin. This shot was obviously taken after he'd been cut but before the rubber mask had been applied to his face. We were looking at a picture of Kitz dying.

Bree banged her fist against the desk. 'What the hell does he want? Is this his idea of fame and goddamn glory?'

She turned and walked out of the office. Better she let the steam out here than somewhere else. I heard her pacing and then the glug of a watercooler.

'Just . . . give me a second,' she called from the hall. 'I'm fine, Alex. Just a little nuts.'

Sampson nudged my shoulder. 'Keep going.'

At the bottom of the page was another familiar icon from the original site. It was an image of a television set with a screenful of animated static, Channel Two. The box was larger than before but otherwise looked the same. Beneath it was a clickable link that read COMING SOON.

'Cocksucker,' Sampson blurted out. 'He's in our face – all the time now.'

I figured the icon would bring up a new image or a video of some kind, but instead the computer opened a blank outgoing email. It was addressed to DCAK5569@hotmail.com, presumably as untraceable as everything else he'd done.

Bree came back into the room and stood behind me. She started to massage my neck and shoulders. 'I just let myself get overloaded. Won't happen again.'

'Yeah, it will. What do you think of this?' I asked her.

'Well, it's a direct communication, anyway. That's something we usually hope for, right? On the other hand, replying means we're still playing his game. But maybe we have to.'

'Sampson?'

'Seems like there's more to gain than lose at this point.'

My fingers hovered over the keyboard, and I typed the first thing that came to mind.

You're on your way down, you pathetic piece of shit.

'Um, Alex?' said Bree.

I was already deleting it, but at least I got a laugh from them. I tried something else.

I typed, *What do you want?*

Then I sat back and stared at the screen. 'Simple. To the point.'

'Go ahead,' Bree said. 'That's the right question.'

So I hit 'send.'

Chapter Ninety-Seven

The next order of business was pretty clear to all three of us: we got the Cyber Unit at the FBI involved with the new site. Our contact now was Anjali Patel, a tiny woman, no more than five feet, with steely gray eyes. Kitz's replacement. I wondered how much time Anjali had spent thinking about the fact that someone was killed doing the job she now had.

We met her in her second-floor cubicle at the Hoover Building. She had the new DCAK site up on two screens and was navigating from her laptop while she talked to us.

'Here's the situation, guys. There's no instance of *DCAK* anywhere in his code, including the metatags, which are what search engines look at. That probably explains why no one else has found it so far.'

'As long as it stays that way, we'd like to keep it up online,' Bree said. 'We've got a potential communication going, and we don't want to blow it unless we absolutely have to.'

That established, Patel moved on.

A few minutes later, she looked up from her work. 'Here's the other thing, guys. This site is something of a hybrid. Most of the content was posted using a normal file-transfer program, but two of the images, *here* and *here'* – she used her mouse to circle the photos of Kitz and his killer – 'were moblogged.'

Before we could ask, she explained, 'Posted to the Web using a mobile phone.'

'Is that easier to trace?' I asked, hoping that it would be but doubting it.

'In this particular case, *yes.*'

She slid a piece of paper around for us to see. It was a Verizon statement, with a billing address.

In Babb, Montana.

'Maybe he's finally made a mistake. Does the name Tyler Bell mean
anything to you?' Anjali asked.

'Should it?' said Bree.

'Not necessarily. Just thought I'd throw it out there. The phone
DCAK used was likely stolen.'

Patel started to turn back to her computer.

'Hold on a second,' I said.

I was looking at the Verizon statement. 'That last name – Bell. I had
a case a while ago when I was still with the Bureau. Happened out
in LA. It was coded "Mary Smith." Or "Mary, Mary."'

'Sure, I know it.' Patel nodded. 'The Hollywood murders. Actors,
producers, and such. That's when I first heard of you, actually.'

'The perp on that case was a Bell. Michael Bell.' He had killed several
innocent people – and then nearly killed me.

'How fast can you find out about known living relatives of Michael
Bell's?' I asked Anjali. 'I know that he has daughters.'

'Shouldn't be hard.'

'And we should get someone over to this Tyler Bell's house in
Montana. See if he's home,' Bree contributed.

'Why do I think he won't be?' Sampson said.

Bree was already dialing her cell phone. 'Maybe because Tyler Bell
is here in Washington.'

Anjali set us up at a few empty desks, and Sampson and I each
picked up a different thread. He quickly found five Tyler Bells listed in
the general DC area, three of them right in the city. It was a long shot
that he was listed here, but these leads would have to be checked out.

I did a run through the Uniform Crime Report. There was no record
of Tyler Bell, or Ty Bell, at least for the last five years.

That's as far as I got before Bree came back over, still holding her
phone against one ear.

'I've got Montana State Police on the line. Guess who disappeared
three months ago? Hint, hint. *Last name rhymes with* hell.'

PART FOUR

COLLISION COURSE

Chapter Ninety-Eight

N ow this was glorious. Truly.
    The last place Kyle Craig expected to be – ever again – was
on the Champs-Elysées, but here he was in Paris, probably his favorite
city in the world. Top three, for sure. With Rome and Amsterdam.
Maybe London. He supposed it was that intense yearning he had for
freedom that he was feeling now, the need to do the unexpected, to
follow his every whim, ultimately to kill again. To torture. To express
his rage in new ways.

Over the last few nights, he'd dined at some of the finest restaur-
ants in the world – Taillevent, Le Cinq inside the George V, right
next to the Prince de Galles, where he was staying. None of the
meals cost him less than four hundred Euros, about five bills
American, but he didn't care, not in the least. He had more than
enough money, and wasn't that what 'vacations' were about? Get
away from the job, the rat race, all the killing. Give himself time to
think, to plan.

The Prince de Galles was a good spot for him in all regards. It was
on the scenic Avenue George V, just a few blocks from the Champs-
Elysées. The hotel was gorgeous – Art Deco for the most part, gilded
– with the most beautiful chandeliers everywhere you looked. But he
particularly enjoyed the Regency Bar, which was English in style, lots
of leather, dark wood, and velvet. Elvis Presley had once stayed at the
Prince de Galles, and now so had Kyle Craig.

There had been museums to visit in the mornings – the Musée
d'Orsay and Musée de l'Orangerie were his two favorites – the
Impressionists. Maybe he'd go to the Louvre today as well, but just to

see the *Mona Lisa*. And he'd taken long walks along the Seine, where he'd done a lot of thinking – and some more planning.

There was one decision he'd made for sure: he wasn't going to let DCAK have Alex Cross as *his* trophy. No, Alex Cross belonged to him, and so did the Cross family – Nana, Janelle, Damon, and little Alex Jr. That had always been the plan. He'd obsessed on it for years.

And maybe, just maybe, he'd do a little wet work before he left Paris. That was his art, which was just as beautiful, and important, as anything created by the so-called old masters. *He was a* new *master, wasn't he?* Perfect for this barbaric age. Right for the times. No one had ever done it better, certainly not DCAK.

He spotted a pretty young woman in a tight gray blouse, black skirt, and high boots, with long hair that was almost auburn in color. She was sweeping the sidewalk in front of a small art gallery. Back and forth, back and forth – very efficient woman. And so attractive to be behind a broom.

So Kyle stopped at the gallery – went inside – and she left him to look around for the first few minutes. So independent – so very French. No wonder he adored them so.

Finally she appeared at his elbow. 'You wish some help?'

Kyle smiled, and his eyes went bright. He spoke to her in French. 'You are a detective? My clothes, my haircut – they gave me away.'

'No, it was your shoes, actually,' she said.

He laughed. 'You just say that to be perverse.'

Finally she laughed too. 'Or maybe humorous?'

'This isn't funny,' he told her then. It wasn't. He took over an hour to kill her. And then he used her broom – and not in the usual way, not to sweep, and handle first.

And then, a fabulous parting meal at L'Atelier de Joël Robuchon. *Ahhh, Paris.* A miracle city.

Chapter Ninety-Nine

This Montana connection was a big break in the case – with any luck, the one we needed. Information on Tyler Bell began to pile up quickly. He was in fact the brother of the late Michael Bell, and actually the more elusive character of the two. While Michael was becoming a minor player in Hollywood circles, Tyler made his living as a river guide and general handyman; he operated out of a Rocky Mountain cabin he had built himself. His reputation around Babb, Montana, population 560, was that of a quiet, nice-enough fellow who wasn't unsociable but mostly liked to be alone. There was no mention of a steady female companion.

More to the point, Tyler had inherited nearly a million dollars from his brother's estate, sat on it for six months, then closed the account and received several dozen cashier's checks in varying amounts on the last day anyone saw him out in Montana. *Now what was that all about? And where was Tyler Bell right now?*

Bree, Sampson, Anjali, and I had a conference call going with the sheriff's department in Glacier County, along with a senior agent named Christopher Forrest in the FBI's Salt Lake City field office. John Abate, a senior agent in charge of DCAK here in Washington, had joined us as well.

'What's the status of your missing-persons case?' Abate asked into the speakerphone.

'The file's certainly open but not what I'd call active. This bloke's either dead or doesn't want to be found.' The Montana deputy on the case, Steve Mills, had an unexpected English accent. *What was with that?*

'Forrest, what have you got?' asked Abate in a curt, take-charge voice. 'Tell us everything you can about Bell.'

'Far as we can tell, he was pretty much cut off from the world. His Verizon account was prepaid through December, including minutes he hasn't used, for whatever reason. And there's one credit card, a Visa, totally dormant.'

'Well, he did have a million or so at his disposal,' Sampson said.

'He took only a few things from his place,' Mills contributed. 'His phone, wallet, some clothes. Not that there was much to leave behind. He lived rather simply. Off the grid and all.'

'He doesn't sound like a cell-phone person to me,' I said.

'Except when the alternative is having wires strung out to your property,' Mills said. 'I doubt he ever used the cell much, though.'

'Well, someone used it.' Patel looked down at the phone report in front of her. 'Yesterday, two ten p.m.'

'*Someone?*' Christopher Forrest asked. 'Do you have reason to believe it wasn't him?'

'Not at all. We just don't have any hard evidence that it *was* him,' said Bree.

'Mighty big coincidence if it wasn't,' Mills said. 'Don't you think?'

'*Agreed.*' Patel sounded a little testy; they weren't keeping up with her. She'd also been working for more hours than she could count.

'What else about Bell?' Bree asked. 'How soon can we get a picture of him?'

'Here you go,' Forrest said. 'I just sent it your way.'

With a few keystrokes, Patel brought up an image of Tyler Bell's Montana driver's license. She flipped it over to the conference-room screen.

I remembered meeting his brother in California and how my first impression had been *lumberjack* but in a California rock-and-roll sort of way, like some lost member of the Eagles. Tyler looked like the real thing. His brown hair and full beard were shaggy but not unkempt. The license stats put him at six three, 220 pounds.

'What do you think, Bree? Recognize him? Could he be your AP reporter?'

She squinted at the license and took her time before answering.

'The way he can change his looks? Sure, it's possible. The reporter was a big man. Maybe six three.'

'What does your gut say?'

Here, she didn't pause. 'It tells me we just found the creep we've been looking for. And like I said before – he's going down.'

Chapter One Hundred

A s soon as word about a possible suspect named Tyler Bell reached the chief of police's office, a reply boomeranged back to us. We were told to 'go public' with the information immediately. Easy to say – a whole lot harder to do.

Certainly we had to tell the press *something*. If another murder came down and we hadn't shared what we knew, it wouldn't matter why we had made the decision to withhold. The damage control would become a huge time-suck, and the investigation would suffer badly.

On the other hand, our suspect was definitely part of the receiving public. Putting out too much information about what we knew, and didn't know, was a mistake that couldn't be undone.

So what should we do?

Our compromise was a quick, unscheduled press briefing out on the steps of the Daly Building. It was something none of us wanted to do, but there didn't seem to be an alternative that the chief was willing to agree to. He needed to communicate 'progress' on the case, no matter what the possible consequences for the investigation.

At eight that night, Sampson and I spoke with reporters, all right, but only long enough to name Tyler Bell as our primary suspect and to say that we weren't taking any questions at this time.

Bree stayed off camera. It was her decision all the way. She didn't want to make her recent attack any more of the story than it already was.

Afterward, the three of us went straight into an emergency session upstairs. It was hard to imagine that this case was heating up, but it was. DCAK seemed to want it that way.

Someone certainly did.

Chapter One Hundred and One

What a mess this was, and maybe getting worse. The extended team was waiting for us upstairs, along with just about every Major Case Squad detective and at least one representative from every district station house in the entire city.

Someone passed round an envelope for Officer Pearsall's family while I was up in the front getting ready to talk and answer any questions I could. I waited an extra couple of minutes for the sad, depressing collection to end, then I began.

'I'll make this as quick as I can. I know you want to get back out there on the street. So do I.' I held up Bell's photo. 'This is Tyler Bell. We'll circulate copies of the picture. There's a real good chance that he's DCAK.

'By the eleven o'clock news, this will be the most famous picture in Washington, probably in the entire country. The problem is, there's no way Bell's going to be seen looking like this. For what it's worth, we're working up simulations without all the hair. His height is the only given. Six two or six three. That's something he won't be able to change very much.'

One of the Second District guys raised a hand. 'Dr Cross, if this is about revenge for Bell's brother, why do you think he hasn't come directly after you?'

I nodded. It was a good question to get out of the way.

'First of all, I'd say that he *has* come after me, but not in the way you mean. The closer he can put himself to those of us who are looking for him, the bigger his emotional payoff. I'm guessing it's an extension of the kick he gets from killing in front of an audience.

But it's only an educated guess at this point. We just don't know for sure.

'Second, I'm not convinced yet that this is about revenge. We'll have to see. If anything, I'd say he might be trying to succeed against me where his brother failed, and he's using the brother to misdirect us. Maybe even to delude himself that this is serving something more than his own ego. But really it's all been about him from the beginning. Not revenge, not his brother – *his huge ego.*'

Lisa Johnson, one of our D-2s, looked up from her notes. 'How would Bell even know you'd be assigned to the case? You weren't back on the force when he started. That's right, isn't it?'

Bree took that one. 'Lisa, even if Alex wasn't involved at the beginning, the Michael Bell connection would have gotten him involved eventually. And remember, we were *led* right to this connection.'

'So you think he used the cell phone on purpose?' Johnson asked. 'Am I tracking this right?'

'Absolutely. I don't think he does anything without a reason,' I said. 'If we dropped the ball at some point, missed a clue, he would have lobbed another one our way. The more of this he can engineer, the more his needs will be met in the end.'

'Meaning the need to kill and get away with it?' somebody asked from way in the back.

'I was going to say, the need to *beat our brains in* at any cost, show us up. That's what he's done so far.'

Chapter One Hundred and Two

L ate that night, as if to underscore everything that had happened so far, I got a direct reply from DCAK that seemed to say, *ready or not, here I come – right in your face!*

I was home, doing online research. On account of the Michael and Tyler Bell connection, I was particularly curious about sibling relationships in serial-murder cases. I'd found out about Danny and Larry Ranes, who had gone on separate sprees in the '60s and '70s. And there was a case in Rochester, the identical-twin Spahalski brothers. One twin had confessed to two murders and was suspected in at least two others, while his brother was serving time for a single, much earlier, homicide.

Other than blood relation, neither instance showed any additional level of connection – no hookup to my role with the Bell brothers. And most of what I found involved two or more family members partnering for concurrent work.

There was also the ongoing mystery about the woman in Baltimore. *Who the hell was she? And what had happened to her after the car chase? Did DCAK have an accomplice? And possibly a mentor in Kyle Craig?*

I logged on to my department email to send around some of what I'd learned.

When it opened, I found a new message waiting for me. Not a nice one either.

What do I want, Detective Cross? That's it? Frankly. I'm surprised you have to ask. But let me spell it out for you as clearly as I can.

I WANT you to pay for what you did to my brother. That's reasonable, don't you think?

I WANT you to think about how you never really tried to under-stand him before you killed him. Just like you don't understand me, and never will.

I WANT to show you that you're not nearly as good at this game as you think you are. None of you forensic shrinks ever are. Or the profilers, who are such incredible frauds, as even you probably know.

And I WANT you to understand one more thing: this is never going to be on any terms but mine.

That's how it will end. The way I want it to, when I decide.

Any more questions?

— TB . . . or not TB?

The first thing I did was forward the message to Anjali Patel with a request for a fast turnaround, which she said wouldn't be a problem, despite the hour. She was working on nothing but DCAK.

Then I called Bree and read her the note twice.

'So, do you buy it?' she asked after I finished. 'The payback thing?'

'No, not really. You?'

'Why should we? Everything else he's done is a lie. And what about the way he signed it?'

That kept coming up, the way we didn't really know which parts of DCAK were Tyler Bell and which parts were some kind of theater. *Who was Tyler Bell? Specifically, who had he been before all this started, or at least before we got into the loop?*

'I'd sure like to see that cabin of his,' I said, my mind latching onto the idea as I said the words out loud. 'Snoop around.'

'I was thinking the same thing, but there's no way, is there? We've got this case slamming right now. But I agree with you – I'd like to look around that cabin.'

'We could leave Friday,' I said. 'Be back by Sunday.'

Bree didn't answer. I think she felt I might be joking at first. Then she laughed. 'Are you going to tell me this is how we get a weekend away together?'

Chapter One Hundred and Three

Kyle Craig was finally back in Washington. *Was this great, or what?* He was all rested and ready to go, too. Everything was on a collision course, and he couldn't wait for the final crash to happen. Or, rather, the *crashes.*

What would the Vegas odds have been against him when he was put away in that Colorado hellhole? Well, he'd beaten all the odds, all the predictions; he'd been doing it his entire life.

He had bought a used car in Maryland before he got to DC. The Buick was a surprisingly quick little whip, too. Plus, it had the advantage of not sticking out in a crowd. DC's car thieves wouldn't particularly covet it, which was worth something.

For a couple of hours in the early morning, four to six to be exact, he drove around the capital, played the sightseer, the tourist, remembered being an agent in this town. He went down First Street, past the Supreme Court Building, the House and Senate, the Capitol Building, even giving a salute to the *Statue of Freedom* on its dome. *Glorious city!* Still one of his favorites, though not quite up to the standards of Paris. At least, not in his opinion. He had always admired the French and their justifiable disdain for everything American.

Finally Kyle drove over to Pennsylvania Avenue and went right past the Hoover Building – FBI headquarters. Here was the scene of so many of his triumphs when he was an agent, then a director in charge – chasing down dastardly murderers, with an emphasis on pattern killers. Ironically, no one had a better closure record than him, not even Alex Cross.

And here he was again, ready to do some damage, feeling the old venom coursing through his body, ready to rip up the town again. Just like in the old days.

He had a small Sony VAIO computer, and he could get on the Internet right from his car. A lot of interesting things had happened in the tech world while he'd been wasting away in ADX Florence. He'd missed out on it, thanks to Cross and a few others from the Bureau who had helped betray him.

Kyle booted up the Sony.

Then he typed, *I'm in town. Kind of emotional for me. If you don't have a prior commitment, remember our meeting on Saturday night. I do believe we can be great together. X marks the spot.*

He didn't bother to add, *It's you versus me now.* Kyle thought that should be obvious to DCAK.

'We'll have to see, though. We'll just have to see.'

Chapter One Hundred and Four

The worst is yet to come! Kyle remembered the catchphrase from a long time ago, from before he was captured by Alex Cross. He had just murdered a most disrespectful crime reporter from the *Washington Post* and the arrogant fucker's wife as well. He had planned to outdo the great minds of his time – Gary Soneji; Geoffrey Shafer; Casanova, whom he had worked with as a coauthor, so to speak. Most of all, most important to him, Kyle planned to go one better – to grow, to evolve, to achieve greatness in his field, to follow his dream.

Suddenly, he remembered something else, something very painful from the time of his arrest. Alex Cross had knocked out his two front teeth! That's how he had *looked* when he was finally captured. In photographs that appeared in newspapers and magazines all over the world. On every single TV broadcast.

The Mastermind!

Toothless.

Like some kind of bloody fool.

Like a street person, a derelict.

And that woman! She had mocked him publicly too. Said to his face that he would never see the sun again. Boasted and bragged about it in front of all kinds of witnesses. She had even written a turgid book that the equally uninspired *Washington Post* had hailed as a 'masterpiece on criminal justice.'

So this dreary redbrick Colonial was where Judge Nina Wolff lived in the City of Fairfax. *The wages of sanctimony weren't worth so much, were they?*

Kyle began to walk toward the house – and as he did, he took out a small canister. He started to shake it furiously. He *was* furious, and he had every damn right to be. Judge Nina Wolff had taken four years of his life.

No doubt about it anymore – it was his time now.

DCAK was yesterday's news.

Starting.

Right.

Now.

He was the man again.

Just him.

He aimed the canister and wrote his message.

Chapter One Hundred and Five

Monnie Donnelley, a research analyst and a good friend out at Quantico, was the one who called me – probably because Monnie knew I was close to Judge Nina Wolff. The two of us had worked together at the time of Kyle Craig's trial. Then I had helped with her book. Nina was the doting mother of three teenage girls; her husband, George, was sweet-natured but also funny enough to do stand-up comedy. George was the perfect match for the sober-looking judge.

And now – this outrage, this abomination at their home. Of course, I knew who Nina Wolff's killer had to be, though I almost wanted to be wrong. I figured there was a slim possibility it could have been DCAK rather than Kyle Craig who had killed the judge, but that was a stretch of the imagination.

I arrived out in the City of Fairfax at two in the morning. I found dozens of cars and vans and trucks, most with garish lights revolving on the tops of their roofs. The suburban neighborhood was up too – every house I passed, just about every window was glowing brilliantly, like fearful, vigilant eyes.

So sad – a neighborhood like this. Peaceful and pretty. People just trying to live their lives with some kind of harmony and dignity. *Was that too much to ask?* Apparently it was.

I climbed out of the R350 at the end of a cul-de-sac, and I started to walk. Then I began to jog, probably because I *needed* to run. Maybe I even wanted to run away – in some saner part of my brain – but I was moving toward the Wolff house, just like I always did, drawn to danger, to chaos, to death and disaster.

Suddenly I stopped. A chill knifed through me. I hadn't even gotten to the house, but I had the first awful image. *It was right before my eyes.*

He'd known I would come here and see it myself, hadn't he?

A bright-red X was painted on top of the Wolffs' car, a black S-Class Mercedes.

A second red X was painted across the front door, almost top to bottom.

Except I knew they weren't Xs. *They were crosses! And they were meant just for me.*

The press was shouting questions from behind the police lines and also taking countless photographs of the house and car. It was all a blur for me right then.

'It's DCAK, isn't it?' I heard. 'What's he doing out here in Virginia? Is he going wide?'

No, I thought, but I kept it to myself. *Kyle Craig isn't going wide. Actually, he's homing in now. And he has his target all picked out.*

No – his targets. *Kyle always did think big.*

Chapter One Hundred and Six

Kyle had spared George Wolff and the three children, and I wondered why. Maybe because he was so focused now. He'd wanted Judge Nina Wolff . . . and only her. *So what would he do next? And how long would I have to wait before he appeared on my doorstep? Or maybe inside the house?*

My eight o'clock session that morning was with Sandy Quinlan. But she didn't show up. Which only helped to make me more uncomfortable about everything that was going on. Now my practice was blowing up too, going to hell before my eyes.

I was also concerned. Sandy had never missed before, so I waited in the office until past nine. Then, Anthony Demao didn't come to his session either. *What was going on with those two? Were they together now? What else could go wrong today?*

I waited as long as I could, then called Bree to tell her I was on my way to pick her up. We were heading off later that afternoon to Montana via Denver to check out Tyler Bell's cabin. It was something we felt we had to do. See his place firsthand, go through whatever he'd left there.

As I was leaving my building, I nearly bumped into Sandy Quinlan. She was standing outside the front door on the sidewalk. Sandy was dressed all in black, covered with sweat, and out of breath.

'Sandy, what's going on?' I asked, trying to keep my composure. 'Where were you today?'

'Oh, Dr Cross. I was afraid I'd miss you. I'm sorry I didn't call.' She squinted up at me and motioned me over to the curb. 'I had to come tell you . . . I'm leaving.'

'Leaving?' I asked.

'Going back to Michigan. I don't belong here in Washington, and frankly I came for the wrong reason. I mean, even if I did meet someone, what's the point if I hate the city, right?'

'Sandy, can we schedule one more appointment before you go? First thing on Monday?' I asked. 'I'm traveling, or I'd see you over the weekend.'

She smiled, looking as confident as I'd ever seen her. Then she shook her head. 'I just came to say good-bye, Dr Cross. My mind's all made up. I know what I have to do.'

'Well, all right, then,' I told her. I put out my hand, but she opened her arms and hugged me instead. Strange, forced, almost theatrical, it seemed to me.

'I'll tell you a secret,' she whispered against my shoulder. 'I wish I'd met you somewhere else. Not as my therapist.'

Then Sandy went up on her tiptoes and gave me a kiss on the lips. Her eyes flew wide; I think mine did too, and she blushed. 'I can't believe I just did that,' she gushed like a teenage girl.

'Well, I guess there's a first time for everything,' I said. I could have been angry, but what was the point? She was going back to Michigan, and maybe that was for the best.

After a short, awkward silence, Sandy pointed with her thumb over her shoulder. 'Walk me to my car?'

'I'm parked the other way,' I told her.

Her head tilted coyly. 'Walk you to your car, then?'

I laughed and took it as a compliment. 'Good-bye, Sandy. And good luck in Michigan.'

She finger-waved, then gave me a little wink. 'Good luck to you, Dr Cross.'

Chapter One Hundred and Seven

A t that moment, DCAK was playing another part, that of Detective
James Corning, who put down his surveillance camera and stared
out his car window, like, well, any dumb-ass cop would. He had just
snapped a pic of Alex Cross kissing his patient Sandy Quinlan, which,
of course, wasn't her real name. Sandy Quinlan was just another role
to play. Like Anthony Demao. And Detective James Corning.

Corning had made it his business to keep tabs on Cross and Bree
Stone all week. Getting too close wasn't wise, but their basic comings
and goings were easy enough to track.

Now he followed Cross to a parking lot near his officer and then
to Bree Stone's apartment building on Eighteenth.

The two of them left together about ten minutes later. Stone was
carrying an overnight bag, traveling light, something few women
seemed capable of doing. James Corning stayed on them until it was
obvious to him that they were headed for Reagan National. *Well, well.*
He wasn't all that surprised, actually.

At the entrance to the airport parking garage, he got in behind them
again. Cross found a space on level three, and Corning kept going up.
He parked on four and caught up with Cross and Stone again on the
skyway to the terminal.

James Corning stayed back in the pack to avoid any chance of being
spotted.

They checked in at American Airlines, so the departure board
narrowed things for him. *Denver was the logical choice.* He waited for
them to go down the escalator to security, then circled back to the
ticketing area.

He held up his badge for the next customer in line. 'Excuse me, just take a second here. Police business.'

Then he showed his creds to the American Airlines agent at the counter. 'I'm Detective Corning, MPD. I need a little information on two passengers you just checked in. Stone and Cross?'

After he got the information he needed, James Corning stopped and bought a doughnut, which he had no intention of eating. It was all part of his plan, though. An important prop. Fun one, too. He headed back to the parking garage.

On three, he stopped at Cross's car. He put a brand-new cell phone in with the doughnut, folded the bag over, and duct-taped it to the bottom of the driver's door seam. It was just out of sight for anyone passing by but surely wouldn't be missed when Cross and Stone came home.

On Sunday, four thirty, Flight 322 from Denver.

DCAK might just be back to meet the flight himself.

Chapter One Hundred and Eight

Bree and I flew to Denver on Friday afternoon, then up to Kalispell, Montana, the next morning. Our return flight was early on Sunday, so we had only a day or so to get everything done and find out as much as possible about Tyler Bell, about whatever had been going on up here in the North Woods, and about what he might be planning next.

The drive from Kalispell to Babb took us straight through Glacier National Park. I'd always wanted to see Glacier, and it didn't disappoint. The switchbacks on the Going-to-the-Sun Road had us alternately hugging a mountain wall, then looking straight down one. It was kind of humbling, actually, as well as beautiful, and would have been romantic – if Bree and I had any time for that on this trip. At one point, she did look over at me and say, 'Where there's a will!'

We got to Babb just after noon on Saturday. Deputy Steve Mills kindly agreed to drive up from the sheriff's office in Cut Bank, saving us about seventy-five miles on twisting country roads, more than an hour's trip.

Mills was loose and amiable, and answered our very first question without being asked.

'Met my wife while I was on holiday here from Manchester. Fishing trip, of all things. Twelve years ago, and never looked back,' he said in his proper English. 'Once this place grabs hold of you, it doesn't let go. You'll see, I'm quite sure. I used to call myself *Stephen*, not Steve.'

We followed Mills south on 89, past the Blackfeet reservation, to the tip of Lower St Mary Lake.

From there, he took an unmarked dirt road for another mile and a half, until we came to a mostly overgrown track on the right.

The side road was partitioned with two police sawhorses, one of them thrown over on its side. I wondered how effective these had been against the likes of CNN and God only knew who else had wanted to visit.

High wheatgrass brushed against the sides of the car as we drove back several hundred yards, then onto a cleared acre or more of land.

Tyler Bell's cabin certainly wasn't deluxe, but it was no Unabomber shack either. He had sided it with natural red cedar that blended nicely into the landscape. It was small and nestled in the crook of a west-flowing river, with a gorgeous view of the mountains in the distance.

I could certainly see why someone would choose this place to settle – so long as they had no need for human contact, and maybe murdered people for a living.

Chapter One Hundred and Nine

The front door to the cabin had no lock. Deputy Mills waited for us outside, and once we entered, we smelled why. Some combination of food and garbage had been rotting in here, possibly for months. It was beyond putrid.

'So much for this being a little slice of heaven on earth,' Bree said, putting a handkerchief over her nose as if this were a homicide scene. *Maybe it was.*

The main room was a kitchen/dining/living area – a picture window at the back looked onto the river. All along the sidewall, Bell had a workbench littered with tools and several dozen fishing flies in various stages of completion. A small collection of rods hung on the wall.

Other than two leather easy chairs, the furniture seemed to have been made by Tyler Bell himself, including a pair of pine bookcases.

'You can tell a lot about a man by his books,' Mills said, finally deciding to join us. He stood in front of them, scanning the lot. 'Biography, biography. Cosmology. All nonfiction. That say anything to you?'

'Whose biographies? That would be my first question,' I said, and came over to look for myself.

There were several volumes on American presidents – Truman, Lincoln, Clinton, Reagan, and both Bushes. Other world leaders too: Emperor Hirohito, Margaret Thatcher, bin Laden, Ho Chi Minh, Churchill.

'Delusions of grandeur, maybe?' I said. 'Fits the bill for DCAK. At least, what we think we know about him.'

'You don't sound too confident about your intel,' huffed Mills, who was a huffy sort.

'I'm not. He's been messing with us from the start. He's a game player.'

Bell's bedroom was smaller and darker – dank, actually. He had a toilet and sink right in the room, partitioned off with another bookcase. I didn't see a tub or shower, unless you counted the river. In fact it reminded me of a prison cell – and that made me think of Kyle Craig again. *What the hell did Kyle have to do with all this?*

The only decorations were three framed photos on the wall, in a vertical stack that reminded me of the new Web site. The top one was an old black-and-white wedding portrait, presumably Mom and Dad. The middle was a picture of two golden retrievers.

And then a shot of five adults standing in front of the same red pickup that now sat abandoned outside.

I recognized three of them right away, and that gave me a start: Tyler Bell, Michael Bell, and Marti Lowenstein-Bell, who would eventually be killed by her husband. The other two, a man and a woman, weren't familiar to me. One woman held two fingers up in a *V* behind Tyler's head. So, *she thought he was the devil?*

'It's strange, isn't it?' Bree said. 'They actually look happy. Don't you think so?'

'Maybe they were. Hell, maybe he still is.'

Finally, after hours of poring over every inch of the bedroom, we went back out to the main room to tackle the kitchen area, which we had saved for last. There was no sense opening that fridge any sooner than we had to. It was a propane appliance and had obviously run down a long time ago. The shelves were half stocked. Most of the food looked like bulk purchases – grains and beans in plastic bags alongside other unrecognizable produce mush.

'He sure likes mustard,' Bree said. There were several kinds in the door. 'And milk.' He had two half gallons, one of them unopened. I leaned in closer to look.

'Milk doesn't keep,' I said.

'Milk's not alone.' Bree had the handkerchief up over her mouth and nose again.

'No, I mean one of these is dated one day after anyone saw him around here.' I stood up and closed the refrigerator door. 'The other carton's dated nine days after that. Why would he buy more milk if he was getting ready to disappear?'

'And,' Bree said, 'why would he need to disappear so *suddenly*? He seemed pretty safe and secure here. Who would bother him?'

'Right. That's the other angle to figure out. So which one do we follow?'

But the question was almost immediately moot. As soon as I'd posed it, my phone rang, and everything changed all over again.

Chapter One Hundred and Ten

I looked at my caller ID. 'Probably the kids,' I told Bree, and picked up. 'Hello from Big Sky Country!' I said.

Instead, I heard, 'Alex, it's me. It's Nana.'

The tension in Nana's voice created waves of dread that traveled up and down my spine. 'What's going on? The kids okay?' I asked automatically. 'Damon?'

'The children are fine. It's—' She let out a quavering sigh. 'It's Sampson, Alex. John has gone missing. No one's heard from him all day.'

The words hit me like icy water. I'd been half expecting the kids' cheerful voices when I answered. *Hi, Daddy. When are you coming home? Will you bring me something?*

But instead, it was this.

'Alex, are you there?'

'I'm here.' The scene around me came back into focus. Bree was watching intently, wondering what was going on. Then her cell went off, and she took the call.

I had a feeling that we were hearing the same story, just from different sources.

'Davies,' Bree mouthed. The superintendent of detectives was on her line. 'Yes, Sir, I'm listening.'

'Nana, hold for a second,' I said.

'Sampson went to the gym around lunchtime.' Bree gave me a running commentary on her call from Davies. 'They just found his car. But not him. They found some blood in the car, Alex.'

'He's alive,' I told her. 'If he was dead, we'd have heard from DCAK already. *He's going to want an audience again.*'

Chapter One Hundred
and Eleven

He had controlled other killers before, in particular a brilliant boy who called himself Casanova and who had worked in the Research Triangle near the University of North Carolina and Duke. Of course, in those days, he had been with the FBI.

He'd even explained himself to Alex Cross once. 'What I do . . . it's what all men want to do. I live out their secret fantasies, their nasty little daydreams . . . I don't live by rules created by my so-called peers.' He claimed he attracted others who thought as he did.

Now Kyle Craig had his own ideas about how things should go. He knew it was time for him to take charge, maybe even past time. The man known as DCAK had contacted him through Wainwright, his lawyer, when he was in jail, as had other freaks of his kind. DCAK had claimed to be an admirer and a student – as had Wainwright himself – but now it was time for the teacher to step forward and take control of this game.

X *marks the spot. That should be easy enough to figure out,* he was thinking. *Especially for someone who considered himself so brilliant.*

Kyle was in position a few minutes before twelve on Saturday night. As promised. He was interested in what would happen next, from several perspectives. *First of all, was DCAK bright enough to get himself to the meeting place?* That was a legitimate question, but Kyle figured that the killer would be. DCAK was a clever enough fiend.

Then, would DCAK actually show his face to him? That proposition was a little trickier, and Kyle thought the odds were probably fifty-fifty.

I WANT you to think about how you never really tried to under-stand him before you killed him. Just like you don't understand me, and never will.

I WANT to show you that you're not nearly as good at this game as you think you are. None of you forensic shrinks ever are. Or the profilers, who are such incredible frauds, as even you probably know.

And I WANT you to understand one more thing: this is never going to be on any terms but mine.

That's how it will end. The way I want it to, when I decide.

Any more questions?

– TB . . . or not TB?

The first thing I did was forward the message to Anjali Patel with a request for a fast turnaround, which she said wouldn't be a problem, despite the hour. She was working on nothing but DCAK.

Then I called Bree and read her the note twice.

'So, do you buy it?' she asked after I finished. 'The payback thing?'

'No, not really. You?'

'Why should we? Everything else he's done is a lie. And what about the way he signed it?'

That kept coming up, the way we didn't really know which parts of DCAK were Tyler Bell and which parts were some kind of theater. *Who was Tyler Bell? Specifically, who had he been before all this started, or at least before we got into the loop?*

'I'd sure like to see that cabin of his,' I said, my mind latching onto the idea as I said the words out loud. 'Snoop around.'

'I was thinking the same thing, but there's no way, is there? We've got this case slamming right now. But I agree with you – I'd like to look around that cabin.'

'We could leave Friday,' I said. 'Be back by Sunday.'

Bree didn't answer. I think she felt I might be joking at first. Then she laughed. 'Are you going to tell me this is how we get a weekend away together?'

Chapter One Hundred and Three

Kyle Craig was finally back in Washington. *Was this great, or what?* He was all rested and ready to go, too. Everything was on a collision course, and he couldn't wait for the final crash to happen. Or, rather, the *crashes*.

What would the Vegas odds have been against him when he was put away in that Colorado hellhole? Well, he'd beaten all the odds, all the predictions; he'd been doing it his entire life.

He had bought a used car in Maryland before he got to DC. The Buick was a surprisingly quick little whip, too. Plus, it had the advantage of not sticking out in a crowd. DC's car thieves wouldn't particularly covet it, which was worth something.

For a couple of hours in the early morning, four to six to be exact, he drove around the capital, played the sightseer, the tourist, remembered being an agent in this town. He went down First Street, past the Supreme Court Building, the House and Senate, the Capitol Building, even giving a salute to the *Statue of Freedom* on its dome. *Glorious city!* Still one of his favorites, though not quite up to the standards of Paris. At least, not in his opinion. He had always admired the French and their justifiable disdain for everything American.

Finally Kyle drove over to Pennsylvania Avenue and went right past the Hoover Building – FBI headquarters. Here was the scene of so many of his triumphs when he was an agent, then a director in charge – chasing down dastardly murderers, with an emphasis on pattern killers. Ironically, no one had a better closure record than him, not even Alex Cross.

And here he was again, ready to do some damage, feeling the old

It all depended on what kind of a risk taker the killer turned out to be. *How truly confident was he?*

Or would he show up in one of his theatrical disguises? Maybe he'll come as me. Kyle smiled as he let the final thought drift across his mind. Then he moved on to other things. He continued to be intrigued with the concept of freedom to be out here in the world like this. He could feel his heart beating, steady but at an accelerated pace. He was getting better and better at controlling his body and mind.

Then he heard something. Someone was here. A voice coming from behind him.

'In your honor.'

DCAK had arrived, and now he stepped forward from a row of shadowy oak trees. No mask, no disguise. A tall, well-built man who looked to be in his thirties. Rather cocky.

Directly behind him loomed Alex Cross's house on Fifth Street.

X marks the spot. That would be Cross's house, of course.

'I'm honored as well,' said Kyle, knowing that they were both lying, wondering if this was as delicious for DCAK as it was for him.

Chapter One Hundred
and Twelve

'It's good to finally meet you in person,' DCAK said, but he seemed a little nervous and stiff. 'Everything you said has come true. All of it.'

'Yes. I told you I would get out of ADX, and here I am,' Kyle said. He too seemed a little shy, but it was only an act.

'Is he asleep in there? Does he sleep?' DCAK asked, gesturing toward the Cross house across Fifth. He knew the place well and already had dozens of photos from every angle.

'Top floor. That's where he usually works, figures out his puzzles,' Kyle said. 'He doesn't seem to be home, does he? No lights up there.'

'Actually, he isn't. He's in Montana, chasing me. You think he's figured this game of ours out. I don't,' said DCAK.

'There you have it, then. But you should be careful. I wouldn't ever underestimate Dr Cross. He has a sixth sense about these things, and he's obsessive, a very hard worker. He could surprise you.'

DCAK couldn't hold back a trace of a smile – cruel. 'Is that what happened to you? You mind me asking such a blunt question?'

'Not at all. What happened to me was that my worst enemy finally caught up with me – *my* pride, *my* ego, *my* hubris. Near the end, I made it too easy for Cross.'

'You hate him, don't you? You want to bring him down in a public way.'

Kyle smiled now. DCAK was projecting, revealing more than he should about himself. 'Well, I do want to humble Cross. I wouldn't mind destroying his reputation. But no, I don't hate Alex. Not at all. Actually, I consider him a dear friend.'

DCAK laughed out loud. 'I would hate to be one of your enemies.'

'Yes,' Kyle Craig said, and then he laughed too. 'You wouldn't want to get on my bad side.'

'So, am I? Have I gone too far?'

Kyle reached out and patted the killer's shoulder to let him know that everything was good between the two of them. 'Now tell me about yourself. I want to know it all. And then,' Kyle said, grinning again, 'you can tell me about your partner. I saw someone lurking back there in the shadows. I'd hate to have to shoot whoever it is. But, of course, I will.'

The woman who went by the name Sandy Quinlan stepped forward from the tree line.

'In your honor' were her first words to the great Kyle Craig. *Perhaps disingenuous, but maybe not?* Certainly fawning. Of course, she was an actress too.

Kyle nodded slowly, then said, 'So tell me about John Sampson. Where are you keeping him, and what do you have planned?'

Chapter One Hundred
and Thirteen

B ree and I rushed back to Kalispell late that evening – only to find that our original flights were still the fastest way home. There weren't any alternatives, at least not one that we could afford.

So we checked into a motel, where neither of us got much sleep. Not being able to help Sampson during those critical first hours was killing both of us, but especially me. John and I had been best friends since we were kids, and I had a bad feeling about this. Still, I was with Bree, and we slept in each other's arms.

We finally arrived in DC on Sunday – wired but totally focused. I called Billie Sampson from the gate and told her we'd be at their house in twenty minutes. I checked in with Superintendent Davies on our way to the car. He was overseeing this personally. Davies was a friend of John's too.

'New development while you were in the air,' Davies told me. 'The bastard's running a Webcast sometime today.'

'What do you mean? What kind of Webcast? What time?'

'We don't have all the details yet. There was an email around two – same distribution as the last one.' That meant a full media press. 'He gave the URL for his site and just said it'd be going live by tonight.'

'Bree and I will be there as soon as we can. We're going to see Billie Sampson first. It's more or less on the way. Don't take it off-line! Let it keep running. We need to see what he's up to.'

'Already with you on that. It may be our only way to track this.'

And by *this*, we both knew Davies meant Sampson's murder and the gross public spectacle it was meant to become.

I hung up with Davies just as we got to the car.

'What did he say?' Bree wanted to know.

I didn't answer right away. I was too busy staring at a package that was tape-mounted to the driver's door.

White paper, silver duct tape. I'd seen something very much like it before.

'Bree? Listen to me, now. Back away from the car. Come over here with me. Take it very slow, and keep back.'

She came around to look. 'Jesus. Is it an explosive?'

'I don't know what it is.' I took out my Mini Maglite and leaned in for a closer look. 'It could be anything.'

But when it *toned*, we both jumped back real fast.

Chapter One Hundred
and Fourteen

It took us a couple of seconds to realize that the sound we were hearing was a ringing phone and that it was *inside* the package.

I tore open the white paper and got a handful of doughnut crumbs, along with a black Motorola. The doughnut was some kind of lame cop joke, I figured.

Instead of caller ID, the phone showed a picture. It was of Sampson, and he was blindfolded. There was a wide gash and dried blood on the side of his face. I took a deep breath to keep the anger from overwhelming me before I answered the call.

'*Bell?*'

'*Cross?*' He mocked my inflection.

'Where is he?'

'I talk. You listen. Now, I want both of you to take out your own phones and hold them in the air. Hold them between two fingers, if you would.'

'No, you listen to me. I want to talk to Sampson before I do anything.'

There was a pause and a shuffle, then I heard a muted '*It's for you.*'

Then Sampson's voice, clear and unmistakable. 'Alex, don't do it!'

'John—' I called out.

But Bell was already back on the line. 'Your phones? In the air. *Both* of them.'

I swiveled around and scanned the garage. Someone was definitely watching us, relaying information, but I didn't see anyone anywhere.

'Now or never, Dr Cross. You don't want me hanging up on you. Trust me. You don't.'

'Bree, get out your phone. Hold it in the air.'

He had us put the cell phones behind the back wheels of my car and then get in.

'Now back up. Over the phones. Then leave the garage, and take a right turn.'

'Where are we going?'

'No questions. Just go. Hurry! Time's running out.' I heard the crunch of our cells as I backed out over them.

'Fuck,' Bree muttered. She wasn't angry about the phones, just that we were following his orders.

We had barely hit the street when Bree scribbled something and held it down low for me to see. *Black Highlander, DC plates. Female. Two cars behind.*

I saw the Highlander and the woman driver in my rearview mirror. Long, dark hair. Sunglasses. I couldn't tell much of anything else.

'Who's the tail, Bell? Is that my friend from Baltimore?'

There was a sickening thud on the line, and I heard Sampson moan loudly.

'That's what questions get you from here on out. Got any more?'

I didn't answer.

'Good thinking: Now take a left at the next light and keep your fucking mouths shut unless I ask for your opinion.'

Chapter One Hundred
and Fifteen

I would have probably suspended another officer for doing what we were doing, but with Sampson's life in jeopardy, I didn't see how there was any choice. For the next few minutes, Bree and I stuck to hand gestures and notes while DCAK barked out directions.

The black Highlander with the woman driver stayed right with us, never getting more than a couple of car lengths behind.

Bree scribbled, *Idea where we're going?*

I shook my head. Just enough for her to see.

How do we turn this thing around?

Another subtle head shake.

Weapons in the car?

I sighed, then shook my head again.

We had traveled to Montana without them. Maybe Tyler Bell guessed as much; there had been no mention of them when we ditched our phones.

He navigated us back into Washington. Eventually onto Massachusetts Avenue and then Seventh Street, moving away from Capitol Hill.

My mind raced in a dozen different directions during the stretches of silence. *Where the hell was he taking us? And what would happen when we got there?*

Seventh turned into Georgia; then we passed the Howard University campus and kept going. *Why this part of town? Why was any of this happening?*

Somewhere between Columbia Heights and Petworth, we came into a low-grade retail stretch with half a dozen fast-food and car-repair joints. Bell told me to slow down now and pay close attention.

'Trust me, I'm paying attention.'

I watched the numbers as we passed a Jamaican patty stand, a nail salon, a gas station, a pawnshop, and then one of several empty storefronts.

'*Number three three three seven,*' Bell said. 'See it?' I sure did. An orange RENTED banner was pasted over the original FOR RENT sign in the window.

'Take the next alleyway, and come into the building from the side,' Bell told me. 'No cheap tricks. I can't promise the same.'

Chapter One Hundred
and Sixteen

I pulled down a narrow single lane to a small parking area in back, with room for maybe three vehicles. When we got out, I saw the black Highlander blocking the alley entrance – or exit, depending on how you looked at it.

The driver watched us from behind the wheel, looking both mysterious and threatening. I was almost certain it was a woman, but so far not everything had been as it seemed.

Bree and I moved toward the building. We found a battered green steel door, propped open with half of a brick. Inside, there was an enclosed cement stairwell. It felt a little like a *Saw* movie set.

'Go down the stairs,' said Tyler Bell. 'Go ahead. Bite the bullet.'

An oddly brilliant strip of light showed under another door at the bottom of the stairs.

'Bell, what's down there?' I asked him. 'Where are we going?'

He answered, 'Close the door behind you when you come in. And *do* come in. Or else there will be a terrible accident momentarily – involving your friend.'

Bree and I looked at each other. This was the time to turn around, if any. And that wasn't going to happen, at least not for me.

'We don't have any choice,' Bree said. 'Let's go. We get any chance, we take it.'

I went down first.

The walls were rough cinder block, with no rail. There was a vague sulfuric smell that I could taste on the tip of my tongue. When we got to the door at the bottom of the stairs, I grabbed a rusted knob that wouldn't turn. So I pushed instead – and it swung open.

And then—

A spotlight hit my eyes! I focused as best I could and saw it was one of several on tripod stands, illuminating every corner of an otherwise dank basement.

'There's your boy!' said Bell.

Sampson sat tied to a chair with his hands behind his back. A band of silver tape was stretched over his eyes. When he turned toward the sound of the door, I saw the terrible gash on his face, still wet. What was worse, his blood had been used to smear the letters *DCAK* on the wall behind him. Lots of blood.

Two empty chairs stood to Sampson's right, each with a coil of rope on the floor next to it.

Somebody, presumably Tyler Bell, stood off to one side. He had a video camera in one hand and a gun in the other, both pointed our way. His face was still in shadows, always the mystery man to this point. *But that was going to end now, wasn't it?*

A cable snaked out of the camera, over to a sawhorse and a plank table full of equipment. I spotted a laptop, open to Bell's familiar home page, but with a difference. Where he'd once had an image of a static-filled television, now there was a live shot of Bree and me standing there, *looking at ourselves.*

Bell's head slowly moved from the camera viewfinder up to our faces. When he saw me watching him, he said, 'Welcome to my studio.'

Chapter One Hundred
and Seventeen

'Sampson, you okay?' I asked. 'John? *John?*'
Finally he gave a weak nod. 'Couldn't be better.' He didn't look it. He was hunched over severely, with dark stains down his gray T-shirt and sweats.

'Well said, Detective Sampson,' Bell cracked. 'It would appear that I'm not the only skilled thespian in the room.'

'Is that my Glock?' Bree was staring at the gun clenched in Bell's hand.

'Yes, it is. Very good. Don't you remember when Neil Stephens took it from you? Yes, yes, that was me. What can I say, I can act.'

'I remember everything, asshole. You're not as good as you think you are.'

'Perhaps. But apparently that still makes me good enough, doesn't it?'

'What is all this?' I asked, trying to slow things down, trying to slow Bell down, anyway, and maybe even get a few answers from him.

'Oh, I'm sure you've figured most of it out, Dr Cross. You're smart enough for that, aren't you?'

'So if I said *thirty-three thirty-seven Georgia Avenue*—' I tried.

'You'd be wasting your breath, of course. No one is watching – *yet.*'

Bell dipped his eyes toward the camera and back. '*Live* audio would have been nice, but then again, I'm not an idiot. Detective Stone, I want you facedown, hands out at your side. Cross' – he motioned toward the center chair – 'have a seat. Take a load off.'

'What about—'

He fired once into the wall just over Sampson's shoulder. 'I said *sit down.*'

I did as I was told, and then footsteps sounded overhead. They steadily crossed the floor and thumped down some nearby stairs. Not the ones Bree and I had used, though – another entrance.

Tyler Bell kept the camera aimed at me without actually looking around. I guessed that he wanted my reaction to this on film. A door at the far end of the room opened. I couldn't see who was there – not yet.

'What took you so long?' Bell said.

'Sorry. Had to lock up. Not the best of neighborhoods.'

Then I realized who it was. The woman I knew as Sandy Quinlan was just walking into the room. She'd taken off the dark wig and glasses she'd worn while she was driving the Highlander; now she looked the way I was used to seeing her. Except for her eyes. They played over me as though we'd never met.

And with the shock of seeing 'Sandy Quinlan' here came another rush of clarity, and of grudging respect for DCAK.

'Anthony,' I said. Not a question, *a statement of fact.*

I didn't fool myself into thinking that was his real name, but it was how I knew him. As I stared at DCAK, I could see the resemblance now. He was pretty good with makeup, and he was a talented actor. I had to give him that much.

He took a little bow. 'I am good, aren't I? Stage acting, for the most part. New York, San Francisco, New Haven, London. In many ways, I'm proudest of the way I played Anthony, and played you as well, Dr Cross. As they say – *in your face!*'

'So, are you Tyler Bell?' I asked next.

He seemed a little surprised by the question. *Or was he acting again?* 'Didn't you hear? The poor bastard went crazy. Came to DC and murdered a shitload of people. Including the detective who killed his brother. Then he just disappeared off the face of the earth. No one ever saw him again.'

Bree asked, 'Did you kill Bell in Montana?'

'Tell you what.' He wagged the Glock in little circles. 'Let's get you ready for the broadcast first. Then I'll *show* you what happened to Tyler Bell. How's that for cooperating fully with the police?'

'Sandy' was standing next to him now. He kissed her, making a show of it, and gave her the gun. Then he transferred the camera to her as well. *Now what?*

'Smile,' she said, 'or whatever. Just be natural. Be yourselves.'

She bent her knees for a steadier shot and zoomed out until the image on the laptop included Sampson, Bree, and me.

'Okay, I'm set here. Whenever you're ready, we can begin. We're going *live* now. We're rolling,' she said. 'And . . . *action.*'

Chapter One Hundred
and Eighteen

A nthony Demao – that was the only name I had for him – slowly walked around behind me, which was not exactly where I wanted him to be.

'Out of sight, out of mind?' he asked, and laughed. 'Or maybe not, Doc.'

Suddenly, the rope dug into my wrists as he tightened it, then knotted it off. Next he anchored it to an eye hook or grommet, something in the floor that I couldn't see. The contraption kept me from standing, though, or even sitting up straight. That's why Sampson's frame was so hunched over, I realized.

And it was all playing out *in real time* on the laptop across from me. I wondered how many people were watching this right now, and I hoped Nana and the kids weren't among them.

When he'd finished with me and then Bree, he retrieved his gun from Sandy and took his place at the center of the floor. He tucked the Glock in the rear of his waistband, then went into a half squat, hands clasped behind him like they were tied the same as ours. *What the hell was he doing now?*

His face screwed into a terrible grimace. Then he sobbed loudly. He continued to sob. *He was acting,* I realized with a start. *Playing another part. Who was he this time?*

He was definitely playing someone other than himself. Pretending to sob, to be sad. 'Why are you doing this to me? I don't understand.

Please, just let me get up. I won't run away, I promise. Please, man, I'm begging you. *I'm begging you!'*

Suddenly the gun came out from behind Anthony's back, and he pointed it *at his own head.* Now he spoke as DCAK: 'You want to stay alive, Mr Bell, you just keep on talking for me. Let me hear you say "A, E, I, O, U."'

'A, E, I, O, U,' he blubbered, in what I assumed was a pretty good imitation of Tyler Bell.

'You closed Bell's bank account yourself, right?' Bree asked before I got the chance.

'And played Tyler Bell at the grocery store before that,' I added. That explained the milk and other duplicate food we'd found in the refrigerator back at the cabin.

Anthony stood up straight again and turned side to side, showing off the beard, the nose, the heavy brow. 'Pretty good makeup job, right? Took the molds right off Tyler Bell's face.'

'Jesus Christ.' Bree sounded more disgusted than anything. 'You almost make me ashamed to be human.'

'Wait, I've got another one for you. This is good shit. Check it out, Detectives.'

He grew still for a moment. His face morphed into anguish, but *someone else's,* not Bell's.

The posture turned crooked, the energy was less frenetic, and the voice – the one he'd used in our sessions – was deeper, southern, with a different timbre than the others.

'Oh, Jesus, I killed my best friend. Matthew, man, I'm so sorry. I'm so, so sorry. What am I gonna do now?' His speech slowed as he went on, and the accent broadened until it had become a caricature of itself. 'I ain't nothin' but a poor sumbitch of a vet with a shrink that don't know Gulf War syndrome from German fuckin' measles.'

His eyes fell coldly on me.

'I got it all on tape, Dr Cross. Every one of our sessions on audio, with me right there under your nose. I took some pictures too.' He looked over at Sandy. 'You and her. When Sandy tongue kissed you in front of your office and said she wished you'd met under different circumstances.'

'I'll tell you a secret.' Sandy replayed the moment between her and me from outside my office. 'I wish I'd met you somewhere else.'

I remembered the kiss and how Sandy had motioned me over to the curb, apparently setting up a photo op for Anthony.

'Okay,' I said. 'Now how about *why*?'

'How about because no one else can do what we can do? No one! Or how about because we worked almost ten years in the *thea*ter and barely made enough money to pay the rent. Or 'cause we saw the shine you have, or used to have, and wanted some for ourselves.'

He stopped and stared at me for several beats. 'Is that what you want to hear, Dr Cross? Does that help you put us into some little box that you can understand a little better?'

I stared back. 'It all depends. Is any of it the truth?'

He laughed, and so did Sandy. 'Nah. Not a word. How could someone like me not do well in life? I have money, and now I have fame. Even Kyle Craig is a fan, and we're fans of Kyle's. Talk about a small world.

'Kyle Craig is a hero of ours, just like Bundy and Gacy. And Gary Soneji. When Kyle got slammed into ADX Florence, we figured out how to make contact. He wanted to hear all about what we were up to; we felt the same way about him. There are a lot of us out there, Doctor. The ones who kill, and the ones who only wish they could. Kyle's lawyer was a fan too. A devoted fan, you'd have to say. And now Kyle Craig is following our story the way we used to follow his. He's right here in Washington. That's exciting, don't you think?'

Chapter One Hundred and Nineteen

I watched DCAK's live performance, because that's what it was – a calculated act – but something else was happening here, something much more interesting to me right now. It all went back to that camping trip at Catoctin Mountain Park.

Bree's hands worked steadily behind her back, mostly indiscernibly, from what I could tell. She was trying to undo the ropes around her wrists – my view of the laptop let me know that much. It also told me I needed to keep Anthony and Sandy face-to-face – focused on me, not on what Bree was trying to do.

'But Tyler Bell gets the credit for all this? Not the two of you? Especially not Sandy?' I asked, as if I cared.

'You're not paying attention. *All this*' – he swept his arm around the room – 'is just today's mindfuck. Once we're gone, once everyone sees the story, *then it happens all over again.* Maybe with a new cop stooge. Or maybe a news reporter. A news anchor? A big shot at the *Washington Post* or *USA Today.*'

'You know you're not the first to run something like this, right? Colin Johns? Miami, 1995?'

And here, Anthony's veneer cracked just a little bit. 'Never heard of him.'

'That's my point exactly. Colin Johns was famous for about, oh, five minutes. And he was a lot better at this than you are – either of you.'

Anthony stood there with his arms folded, shaking his head back and forth. I could tell he was angry at me now. 'You're really pretty bad as a shrink, you know that? This is supposed to – what? Make me not kill you?'

'No, but it might take some of the enjoyment out of it.' Confidence was the game here, not facts, not the techniques of therapy. I was making it up as fast as I could.

I asked, 'How about Ronny Jessup? Three homicides, all of them on live TV. He even used his real name. You ever hear of Ronny Jessup? You, Sandy?'

'No, but a dirty little birdie told me that *you're* about to die,' she said, and grinned. 'I can't wait.'

In two strides, Anthony crossed the floor and smashed me in the face with the butt of his gun. 'Keep it up, Dr Cross!' He loomed there, ready to swing again, but I figured he wouldn't want me unconscious now.

I was here to watch!

I spit a mouthful of blood on the floor. 'Madeline Purvis. Boston, 1958.' I threw out another psychopathic killer's name for him.

'All right, that's it. I'm invoking the gag rule.' He stormed over to the 'props' table, tucked the gun in his waistband again, and picked up a roll of duct tape. It crackled loudly as he tore off a length, then started back to me.

I turned my head away, not to stop him but to get him into a better position. One way or the other, this was it. Either Bree was ready or she wasn't.

As Anthony stepped in close with the strip of tape, Bree's hands flew up from behind her back.

Sandy saw it too. 'Bro, look out!'

Bro? The two of them were brother and sister? That was a twist that I hadn't seen coming. Maybe because of the sex scene on the couch in my office. *But possibly they were lovers too?*

Chapter One Hundred
and Twenty

Whoever Anthony was, he wheeled on Bree as she managed to pull away his gun. He caught her face with a fast, hard backhand. The Glock fired – missed Anthony – but Bree went spinning to one side. She hit the wall behind her overturned chair.

Suddenly Sandy had a gun in her hand, and it was aimed at me.

Bree managed to level the Glock at her and fire. Twice! She wasn't fooling around. Both shots struck Sandy Quinlan in the chest. Her mouth opened wide in shock, and I think she was dead as she stood there with the gun in her hand. Then Sandy crumpled like a marionette, and that didn't make me feel very good. I'd spent too much time with her; I thought I knew her, even if I hadn't. She'd been a patient.

I was struggling to my feet now, pulling with all my might on the spike in the floor, which started to give. It *had* to give.

Bree fired again!

One of the spotlights exploded as Anthony passed under it. He was getting away – running in a low crouch. He was also laughing. *Playing another part? Or just being himself?*

I heaved, legs straining, and the rope finally pulled free. It slackened on my wrists, enough for me to wrench my hands out, anyway.

Then I ran after Anthony.

'Call for backup!' I shouted to Bree. The black Motorola was still on the ground. So was Sandy Quinlan, wide-eyed and bleeding from two wounds so tightly bunched that they almost looked like one.

I hit the stairs and immediately heard glass smashing above me.

Anthony – DCAK – was getting out of there, wasn't he? Seconds later, I stumbled up into an empty storefront.

The door to the street was closed and still had a padlock. But the display window was no more than glass shards and air. I spotted an old wooden chair lying out on the sidewalk.

I ran up and climbed through the opening in the window. People hovered outside, watching me like I was the boogeyman. A kid pointed up the block. 'White guy,' he said.

I saw Anthony then, running at a full clip on the other side of the street. He looked back and spotted me too. Then he ducked into a store on his right.

'Call the police!' I shouted for anyone who would listen and maybe help. *'That's DCAK!'* I added. Then I tore up the sidewalk after him.

Chapter One Hundred and Twenty-One

The place DCAK had entered was a hole-in-the-wall restaurant for Mexican take-out. There were no tables in the front, just one very shaken old woman splayed on the floor and a skinny cashier still pressed to the wall like he was his own shadow.

I ran around the counter, pushing through a swinging door back into the kitchen.

The temperature instantly went up about twenty degrees. Two cooks shouted at me in Spanish.

Too late – I saw Anthony come at me from the right. *What the hell?* A cast-iron pan burned through my shirt and sent searing pain up my arm and right into my brain.

I countered reflexively with my other hand, an uppercut to his temple, a second punch to his throat.

He let go of the frying pan, and I grabbed it myself. I pushed it into Anthony's face, then let it go before it fried the skin off my hand. He howled and stumbled back, blackened prosthetic skin sagging around one ear. Both of the cooks screamed as if they were the ones who'd just gotten burned.

Anthony steadied himself on the edge of an industrial range. He grabbed another cooking pan and hurled sizzling oil and vegetables in my direction. I avoided the flying grease, but Anthony was headed toward the back door.

He pulled down a set of baker's shelves as he went. Dishes and equipment crashed everywhere. Lots of noise and chaos and shattering pottery.

'*My sister's dead!*' he screamed back at me. *Meaning what – that now he was really mad?*

I grabbed a kitchen knife and went after him.

Chapter One Hundred
and Twenty-Two

As I jumped out into a long, wide alleyway – the delivery entrance – I heard sirens wailing from somewhere in the neighborhood. I hoped to hell they were for us and that somebody would figure out real fast that I was back here with DCAK.

The alley ran behind several buildings, with a dead end to my right and a busy street to my left, about fifty yards off – farther than he could have run by now, anyway.

So where was he hiding? He had to be close. But where?

I threw open the nearest Dumpster, and a repulsive wave of garbage smell came up at me, but no Anthony. No DCAK. I turned my back on the alley just long enough to lean into the trash and make sure he wasn't there.

Another three Dumpsters lined the wall. Dusty, rusting cars were stacked on the other side. I checked down low. *He wasn't hiding under any of them. Where was he?*

I saw him out of the corner of my eye – and just in time. I narrowly missed getting sliced across the face. He'd been behind one of the Dumpsters, and he had a knife. He seemed confident and scarily under control considering the circumstances, almost like he was playing another role.

I sure wasn't; knives weren't my thing. But the kitchen blade was the only weapon I had right now.

He came for me again. The blade whiffed past my face, barely missing flesh. He sliced the blade at me again, and again, and again.

I feinted a short thrust back at him, and he laughed. 'I think I'm going to like this,' he said. 'I know I am. I trained in hand-to-hand. How about you, Dr Cross?'

He didn't bother to taunt or test, just stabbed the knife at me again. I jumped away, and he missed. But not by much. An inch or so.

Anthony's face was intense, the veins pulsed, but his eyes remained playful. He was toying with me. *Was he missing on purpose? Stretching this out?*

'The once great Alex Cross,' he said. 'Too bad we don't have an audience.'

'Oh, but you do. I'm your audience this time, DCAK,' said a voice. We both turned – *and there was Kyle Craig.*

Chapter One Hundred
and Twenty-Three

K yle spoke, and he sounded exuberant, almost joyful. *To see us? To be seen?* 'What a sight for sore eyes! The *great* DCAK – the *great* Alex Cross. Together at last in a duel to the death. With kitchen knives? I'd pay to see that one. But hey, I don't have to pay. I'm right here, aren't I?'

DCAK held his knife up and poised, but he kept sneaking glances at Kyle. 'What are you doing here?' he asked.

'Admiring your work, of course,' Kyle said, and he seemed sincere enough. 'Just like any of your other fans would if they could. They'd be lined up twenty-deep on the street to see this. I've been following you. Ever since we met at the Cross house.'

'You think I don't get your sarcasm,' DCAK snarled.

'Be a waste of breath if you didn't. Be careful with Dr Cross, now. Watch him. He'll slice you up if he can. He's a cagey one.'

'He can't,' DCAK stated flatly, 'hurt me. He's out of his league. And so are you.'

'Oh my,' said Kyle. 'Now you've gone and cut *me,* so to speak.'

I said nothing to either of them. I was still looking for some kind of an opening. I wasn't very good with knives, but I was quick on my feet. Maybe that would help me, save me somehow. But now I had Kyle to worry about too. *How had he gotten here, and what was his current connection to DCAK? Had it just* changed?

'He's focused on the fight. You're not,' Kyle coached DCAK from the sidelines. 'That's all I'm trying to point out. Take it for what it's worth.'

DCAK looked back at me. 'All right, then. Let me put Cross down. In your honor.'

In your honor? What was that supposed to mean? Then he thrust his knife again and missed, but this time he meant business. Another fast swipe, and he sliced my arm. Blood streamed onto my shirt and dripped onto the pavement.

'That's better, DCAK,' Kyle cheered him on, his voice suddenly guttural. 'Now go for it! *Put him down! Kill the bastard!*'

DCAK was starting to breathe harder, through his mouth. *Maybe that could be an advantage for me?* I circled to the left, then I changed direction. No logic to it, just instinct.

I was moving the other way when he swiped his knife at me again. He missed! I stabbed at him and nicked his arm. Blood spurted from the wound. Nasty game, knives.

Kyle applauded. He slowly, slowly clapped his hands, but he didn't speak any more encouragement.

I moved in a circle again, but I went faster this time. Abruptly I reversed directions. Then I came back the other way.

Suddenly DCAK roared in a deep voice and charged at me. I pivoted to the left, and for a second my back was exposed. He was still leaning the other way. *Which meant . . . what?* I continued to pivot – all the way around. Then I set my right leg and drove my knife up and under his arm. The knife found flesh, muscle. It finally sank into his chest.

He moaned almost as loudly as he had roared a second before. 'You stupid sonofabitch!' Then he went down and lay there on his back, wide eyes staring at nothing. I spun away from DCAK and looked at Kyle.

I had a knife.

He had a gun.

'He wasn't much, was he?' Kyle said, and grinned.

Chapter One Hundred
and Twenty-Four

He kept on talking, almost as if he were excited to see me. Maybe *I* was the one he'd been following. 'I was so hurt that you didn't come out to Florence to visit me more, Alex. You have no idea. They put you in a tiny cell and keep you there twenty-three hours every day. It's inhuman and does no good at all. I'm serious about that.

'Maybe I'll make a *deeply disturbing* film, like *An Inconvenient Truth*, or *The Road to Guantánamo*. Call it *Never See the Sun Again*. Play it in all the art houses here in the East. Get the bleeding hearts on my side.'

'You killed a lot of people, Kyle. You've committed murders since you've been out. How many this time?'

Kyle shrugged, and then he mugged for me. He wasn't as good an actor as Anthony, just a more subtle killer. 'Honestly, I didn't bother to keep count. There was Mom, of course. Or was that a hallucination that I had?'

'No, you slaughtered your mother.'

'*Slaughtered* her, did I? That seems extreme. I don't actually recall that much about it. Perhaps I was in a rage state. Can you give me some gory details? I want to hear it from you, Dr Cross.'

'Is that part of this, Kyle? The psychologist connection?'

'Could be. I never thought about it quite like that.'

I stared at Kyle for a moment and didn't speak. He was so incredibly evil, with no conscience. I wondered how his reflexes were these days. He seemed confident enough with the gun in his hand. *And why shouldn't he be? Why would he have any trouble shooting me now?*

'Kneel on the ground, Alex. Just to be on the safe side. All that training at Quantico is kicking in.'

I stood there, refused to obey him.

Kyle held his gun arm out, perfectly straight and still. 'I said – *kneel on the ground*. There's still a chance that I won't kill you. I might want an audience for what I'm going to do *next*.'

That got my attention. *An audience?* 'What are you going to do now, Kyle? And what part did you play for DCAK and his partner?'

He smiled and seemed to be formulating an answer. 'Interesting questions. If I tell you, is it because you won't be around to see it or because I want you to be able to anticipate the *slaughter*, as you call it? Kneel! This is your last warning, Alex.'

I bent my knees slightly, and then I went down on them. I didn't see that I had a choice. Kyle didn't like to be disobeyed. That much I knew for sure.

'Ah, that's good. This is how I like seeing you. As a supplicant. You know, I almost wish DCAK was alive to witness this.'

'You could have saved him.'

'Maybe. Probably not. I really think the boy wanted to die. I studied his early murders while I was still an agent. He made contact with me at Florence. I think . . . I might have been a father figure to him. You'd know better than me. I can't live in the past, though. I'm not much for regrets either. You can understand that, can't you?'

'What did he mean when he said, *"In your honor"*?'

'Oh, that. He was a fan, of course. Who isn't? So was the girl. His sister? Who knows? They got the messages to me at ADX through my lawyer. Another fan. They're all just freaks, Alex. Although . . . he did give *you* a good run.

'I helped him with a few ideas. The football stadium – that was me. And I suggested Tess Olsen, of course. That one was *in my honor*.'

Kyle walked forward, and he put the gun to my temple. There wasn't any unsteadiness in his hand.

'I, Kyle Craig, being of sound mind and body,' he said, and smiled broadly, wickedly, insanely, 'choose to *spare* the life of Alex Cross. At this time, anyway.'

He took a step away. 'I told you, twenty-three hours a day. Four years in there. I can't let you off this easy. A couple of minutes of abject fear – that's *nothing* in comparison to what I went through. It's not enough payback. Not even close! You'll see.'

Kyle continued to back away. 'I have bigger and better plans for you, Alex. One thing is for sure, I'm going to torture you and your family to death. Don't bother to try to hide them. I'm really good at finding people. That was my specialty at the Bureau. I have skills, Alex. The Mastermind. Remember?'

'Put the gun down, Craig. Do it slowly, you piece of shit. Or you really will understand *payback*.'

It was Bree. I couldn't see her yet, but I wanted to warn her.

About Kyle Craig, and why you should never, ever warn him.

My mouth opened—

Chapter One Hundred and Twenty-Five

'**B**ree!'

Kyle had been an FBI field agent, and before that he was with Special Forces in the army. He was an expert with knives, guns, even explosives, and I knew that from past experience. He was no one to fool with – no one to *warn*.

He heard Bree's voice, and before she finished her threat, he was twisting his body around toward her and diving at the ground. I watched – unable to do anything to stop it from happening.

'Bree!'

His Beretta came up level and was aimed at the center of her chest – he wouldn't take a chance of missing what would be a difficult shot, especially while he was still moving. He had her in his sights, and I had one thought: *Take me instead.*

I'm not sure if Bree waited until she had finished the words 'you really will understand *payback.*' I doubt it.

She fired – and Kyle Craig jerked in midair. His mouth flew open in surprise. His eyes went wide.

He never got a shot off. He landed with a dull thud on the ground and lay there with one leg twitching. Finally he let go of the Beretta. Then, nothing at all.

Nothing.

Blessedly, *nothing.*

I hurried forward, kicked away his gun. I crouched beside Kyle, who I'd once thought was a friend and who had turned into my worst enemy. His eyes were open, and he looked at me, right into my eyes, maybe my soul. He stared, and I wondered if he was dying at that instant, and if he knew it.

Then Kyle spoke, and he said something so very strange, something I didn't understand, not to this day. 'In your honor,' he said.

Then a horrible rattle began to stir somewhere back in his throat.

And I liked it. Sad to say, horrifying to me, I was relieved and exult-ant. I'd liked being in *the audience*, so much so that I clapped my hands together and applauded Bree.

And then, suddenly, Kyle was on all fours, then up on his feet. He pulled another gun from a holster behind his back.

Bree had lowered her gun, and now he had us.

'Put down the gun, Detective,' he said in the calmest voice I'd ever heard. 'I don't want to kill you right now. Not just yet. *Tell her, Alex.*'

'She won't listen,' I said.

'Then she's a dead girl. *Put the gun down.* For Christ's sake, if I wanted to kill you, I would have pulled the trigger already.'

Bree bent at the knees and lowered her gun to the ground.

Kyle pulled the trigger.

But he missed her on purpose.

'You know, Bree,' he said in the same deadly calm voice, 'the advice about chest shots versus head shots is good as far as it goes, but' – he patted his own chest – 'it doesn't allow for the possibility of vests, which I always wear to parties like this one. You should too. Especially with that exemplary chest of yours.'

Kyle started to back away from us. Then he smiled and said, 'Oh, what the hell! Sorry, Alex!'

He fired in Bree's direction – twice – and purposely missed again. Then he laughed and ran down the alley, disappearing around the first corner, still laughing.

The Mastermind.

Chapter One Hundred
and Twenty-Six

*D*CAK *was still alive.* Bree and I met up with Nana and the kids at Washington Hospital Center, where Sampson and 'Anthony' were being treated. 'Sandy Quinlan' hadn't made it; she died before the ambulance came.

Sampson was going to be fine, according to his doctors. He needed stitches and fluids, but I had no doubt he'd be driving the staff crazy by checkout time tomorrow. Eventually, we retreated to a waiting area so that Billie and Djakata could have some alone time with the Big Man. Billie didn't seem too happy with him, though, or with me.

The kids were full of questions, and Bree and I answered as many as we could. Though – as always – we didn't have all the answers ourselves. Not yet, and maybe not ever. Especially where Kyle Craig was concerned.

'So, who were those people really? DCAK?' Jannie wanted to know. I've always loved her curiosity, but I wasn't sure what to make of this budding interest in things forensic. The last thing we needed was another Dragon Slayer in our house on Fifth Street.

'We should know more soon,' I told her. Both Anthony and Sandy – her body, anyway – had been fingerprinted. I thought they'd probably show up somewhere, in somebody's files, maybe even in Kyle Craig's old notes from his FBI days.

I finally sent the family home, and Bree and I went to look in on our captive. We watched 'Anthony' through a window while a post-op medical team got him stabilized for transfer. He was handcuffed to a hospital bed and lay there the whole time, staring at the ceiling. I'd seen this stillness in him earlier that day. It was impossible to read. *Was it defeat? Calculation? Boredom?* The answers would help us know whether he was headed for a penitentiary or a psych ward.

'The names are Aaron and Sarah Dennison.'

I turned to see Ramon Davies standing behind us. 'IAFIS turned Aaron up. He's wanted in two states that we know of so far. California and Nevada. Aaron was a suspect in two murder cases, one in each state. His sister Sarah's record was clean. They did some acting in Vegas, Tahoe, Sacramento – mostly regional theater.'

'Where were they right before DC? Do we know that?' I asked the superintendent.

'In and out of LA. Why?'

I shook my head and looked back through the window at him – *Aaron,* not Anthony. 'Just curious if any of it was the truth, the things he told me. LA would be where he followed the case with Michael Bell. The Mary, Mary case. He must have been in touch with Kyle Craig from there too.'

'What about the Webcast?' Bree asked. 'We have any idea how many people saw it?'

Davies looked from her face to mine. 'Let's just say if you ever wanted to sell your story, now would be a good time.' We laughed but only because there was nothing we could do about the reach and popularity of the Webcast.

'He basically got what he wanted, didn't he?' Bree said. 'He got famous, anyway. She'll be famous now too. As disciples of Kyle Craig, at the least.'

I turned away from the window, suddenly done looking at him, and done with this case. 'Hope it was worth it, *Anthony.*'

I heard a shout that was muffled by the observation window. I looked back.

'Dead man walking!' Aaron yelled. 'That's what you are, Cross.'

EPILOGUE

LAST DAYS

I didn't hear anything from Kyle Craig, which didn't completely surprise me. He'd made terrible threats, but if he had wanted me dead, he would have done it. He had his chance in the alleyway. So the next few days passed quickly for me, but probably slowly for Damon. My boy was leaving home.

By the time we were packing the car to send him off to his first semester at Cushing Academy, he was showing his emotions on a fairly regular basis. Cool just didn't cut it for him anymore.

He and I spent the final couple of days driving up to Massachusetts together. We stopped to see our cousin Jimmy at the Red Hat in Irvington, and had a fine meal and listened to some jazz, then continued on our way. I noticed that *I* was showing my emotions on a regular basis now too. I figured that was a good thing, growth maybe. I was troubled by my life, though. I wondered if I had a soul anymore. All these killings, understanding the killers . . .

'So you know when Family Weekend is?' Damon asked me as we got close to Sturbridge, Massachusetts.

'Don't worry, it's already on my calendar. I'll be there with bells on.'

'Well, if you have a case or whatever, I understand.'

'Damon.' I waited for him to look at me. 'I'll be there. No matter what.'

'Dad.' He gave me a grown-up stare and a little frown he'd inherited from Nana Mama. 'It's okay. I know you'll come if you can.' It wasn't quite like looking at myself across the front seat, but there was no closer copy in the world.

'You're going to have a great year, Day. In school and on the basketball court. I'm really proud of you. One hundred percent.'

'Thanks. I think you're going to have a great year too. Keep an eye on Bree. She's good for you. Everybody thinks so. Your decision, though. Of course.'

Just then, my cell phone rang. *What now?* I had a crazy thought – to throw the damn thing right out the car window.

And that's what I did.

And Damon clapped, and we laughed as if it were the funniest thing I'd ever done. Maybe it was, too.

We arrived at the school in Ashburnham, Massachusetts, and it was so gorgeous, such an eyeful, that I wished I could spend the next four years there myself, relive my youth, or something like that.

A message was waiting for me at the admin building. It was from Superintendent Davies. *Alex, I have bad news. There have been some murders in Georgetown.*

But that's another story, for another time.